KOKO TAKES A HOLIDAY

Coming soon from Kieran Shea and Titan Books

KOKO THE MIGHTY

(June 2015)

KIERAN SHEA
KOKO TAKES A HOLIDAY

TITANBOOKS.COM

Koko Takes a Holiday
Print edition ISBN: 9781781168608
E-book edition ISBN: 9781781168615

Published by Titan Books
A division of Titan Publishing Group Ltd
144 Southwark Street, London SE1 0UP

First edition: June 2014
1 3 5 7 9 10 8 6 4 2

A CIP catalogue record for this title is available from the British Library.

Printed and bound in the United States.

Did you enjoy this book? We love to hear from our readers.
Please email us at readerfeedback@titanemail.com or write to us at
Reader Feedback at the above address.

To receive advance information, news, competitions, and exclusive
offers online, please sign up for the Titan newsletter on our website:
WWW.TITANBOOKS.COM

TO ALL THE INSPIRED FLAMETHROWERS
I HAVE KNOWN—BURN, BABY, BURN.

"ICARUS FELL. BUT, OH, WHAT A TAN."

FUN IS KING

THE SIXTY ISLANDS PROMO—1:00

CLIENT: Custom Pleasure Bureau—The Sixty Islands

PRODUCTION ENGAGEMENT: 2516 All-Seasonal Hemispheric Cycles

VISUAL FEED 1: CAMERA DRAWS IN FROM SATELLITE VIEW, FLIES OVER THE RENOWNED TROPICAL ISLAND RESORT—*THE SIXTY ISLANDS*. SMOOTH PAN CONTINUES UNTIL CAMERA DIVES TOWARD A FLAWLESS BEACH LAGOON WHERE A LOIN-CLOTHED MAN POSES PROVOCATIVELY. EXTREME CLOSE UP. HE PURSES HIS LIPS WHILE LOOKING DEEPLY INTO CAMERA LENS AND THEN SAVAGELY RIPS INTO A HUNK OF BUTCHERED MEAT. CHEWS.

[CUT TO] VISUAL FEED 2: FOOTAGE OF ISLAND EXPLOSIONS. ISLAND ORGY MASSACRES. PULSE-GUN FIRE. CRUMBLING BUILDINGS. GENERAL MAYHEM ON *THE SIXTY ISLANDS*.

[CUT TO] VISUAL FEED 3: KOMODO DRAGON SPRINGS ON A CRYING BABY.

[CUT TO] VISUAL FEED 1 (CONT.): MAN UNFASTENS HIS LOIN CLOTH REVEALING A MASSIVE ERECTION.
AUDIO: UPBEAT MUSIC

[FADE IN] VISUAL FEED 4: VARYING ATTRACTIONS ON *THE SIXTY ISLANDS*.

VOICEOVER: If there is true adventure in what's left of your soul, *THE SIXTY ISLANDS* is the one place to indulge your holiday junket passions! A manufactured archipelago engineered on reinforced tectonic plates, *THE SIXTY ISLANDS* teems with attractions and luxuries found nowhere else on the planet. Whether you seek romance, prefrontal cortex obliteration, simulated death consumption, or the ultimate eco-destruction escapade for your family, you will find what you are looking for on *THE SIXTY ISLANDS*. Yes-yes, here-here!

[CUT TO] VISUAL FEED 5: AERIAL SHOT ROTATING ABOVE *THE SIXTY ISLANDS*. [NOTE: No maintenance, power-plant turbines, or SI waste scuppers visible.]

VOICEOVER: A nature-lover's delight, *THE SIXTY ISLANDS* has taken great pains to hyper-grow protected, unspoiled environments of extreme beauty and abject hostility. And you can destroy it all! Experience firsthand the primal delights of corporatism's progressive power and Earth's blessed rush to rebirth.

[SIDEBAR, RIGHT] VISUAL FEED 6: RATE FEES SLIDE BY IN MULTIPLE LANGUAGES WITH REGIONAL CREDIT FLUCTUATIONS,

PENALTIES, AND RESTRICTIONS. AS RATE FEES REACH CONCLUSION, SIDEBAR WIPES RIGHT.

VOICEOVER (CONT.): Riot with dangerous synthetic beasts, relax with indiscriminate slaughter, indulge in sexual lawlessness and pestilent disease fantasies. Yes-yes, you can have it all! Vigorous regenerating schedules and cyborg augmentations are designed to accommodate your maximum pleasure and release.

[CUT TO] VISUAL FEED 1 (CONT.): HEAVILY ARMED WOMAN LASHES A CHAIN COLLAR AND LEASH ON THE NOW NAKED MAN. THE WOMAN WINKS AT THE CAMERA. COUPLE WALKS OFF DOWN THE BEACH AS THE WOMAN CUPS THE MAN'S BARE BUTTOCKS.

[CUT TO] VISUAL FEED 7: SUNSET. WHOLE JUNGLE FORESTS DETONATE.

VISUAL FEED 8 [LOGO ZOOM]: *THE SIXTY ISLANDS!*

KEY OF SMALL, UNREADABLE DISCLAIMER TEXT. [READ AND SCROLLED RAPIDLY]: This message is from the Custom Pleasure Bureau. To travel to The Sixty Islands you must be over sixteen or have signed guardian's or warden's consent. Not accessible from de-civ hot zones, the resettled South African Colonies, or quarantined resource regions. All re-access laws apply from the Second Free Zone. Member Earth Syndicate Alliance-TC 34-AOP.

LET'S HEAR IT FROM THE BOYWHORE...

So the dead Kongercat raiders who were in the bar? The ones who called themselves Ying Fong and Chuòhào? You bet them nasty dakini re-civs, but them foolish. Them no expect my Koko-sama. Be on The Sixty for carnival and all wasted on big liquor and high-happy with shift and shake, thinking them be better than her, but those two be dead wrong. Koko-sama upright alphamama. Koko-sama see many-much fighting and swing the big guns long time before her working on The Sixty proper. Koko-sama shoot them dakini re-civs straight up so now there be red scrambled eggs everywhere. Blood all over floor. All over damn bar.

Koko-sama say to me, she say, "See, Archimedes? Stashing that big pulse gun upstairs was a smart move. I mean, phew, did you see how those two Kongercats' heads burst apart?"

Oh, Archimedes see that plenty all right. Like a couple of wax gourds that. When Koko-sama hear me shout there be big trouble in the bar downstairs, she zip out of her room all angry-like and waste no time, no way. Take that big gun from the trunk on the landing and warn them two troublemakers to behave and be peace-like, but them no listen. Draw nasty on my Koko-sama. Big mistake that, you bet. Koko-sama cut them two baddies down.

Me sop up some squishy red goo with a sponge and carry the bucket outside. Koko-sama say she want me to splash the bloody water in the street 'cause Komodos like the dirty water. Them dragons hiss and crackle and slurp up that water, you bet. Funny buggers. Like all huff and scruff on The Sixty—the bats, the itty-bitty boars, the frogs and birds—them dragons half animal, half machine.

Me go back inside.

"When you're done cleaning, make sure you scrub out the mop bucket with a squirt of bleach, okay, Arch? Just don't go overboard like last time. Maybe half a shot glass's worth. The flies are on that muck already, and we sure as hell don't need no more mosquitoes laying eggs and spreading disease."

"Yes, Koko-sama. Bleach in bucket."

"And cage up the good liquor when you're through."

"Got it. Cage up the good liquor, right-right."

"And take a shower."

"Yes-yes. All good scrubby."

"Atta boy…"

Koko-sama blow me a kiss then and throw back her hair. Me like that. How her long hair fall in a beautiful dark wave.

Supersexy, my Koko-sama.

Koko Martstellar watches Archimedes sleep beside her in bed and blows out a plume of crinkle-flake smoke straight at the room's ceiling fan.

Yeah, so things got a little out of hand tonight, she thinks. *Big deal.* Koko knew an incident like this was bound to happen sooner or later. All of The Sixty's pleasure vendors have been hurting of late, what with the instability in the lower trade markets tamping down discretionary income and all, but honestly, what was the CPB HQ thinking? Opening up The Sixty Islands to the Kongercat re-civ ilk—what, just because they're flush with credits and can afford it? Not to besmirch the heavily promoted ceasefires and the internationals kowtowing to re-civ play niceties, but those freaks are just plumb crazy.

After crushing out her smoke in a halved husk of a coconut on the nightstand, Koko leaves Archimedes in bed and slips on a pink silk kimono. She leaves her bedroom and tramps downstairs to check the incoming messages on the bar's central register. The news on the projection prompts is as bad as she expected. The Custom Pleasure Bureau is sending a security detail around in a few hours. The communication indicates it was their intention to be there sooner, but Koko's brothel operation is built on one of the few SI islands without a connecting bridge system. ETA 9:00 AM, sharp. Huh. For a fleeting moment, Koko rues not letting those two re-civ Kongercats just have their way.

Koko had been going over the books in bed upstairs when Archimedes cried out for her that there was a problem in the main bar. Archimedes has always been a bit of a fusspot, so Koko figured the boy was merely out of fresh ice or grenadine or something. Not the case at all. Koko stalked right out of her bedroom and instantly knew the score. As her fellow mercenaries used to say back on deployment, the two Kongercats had jacked up a total BSGD situation.

Bad shit, going down.

Kongercat re-civs are pretty easy to distinguish from the run-of-the-mill SI patrons, what with their hereditary facial lesions, papery skin, and Chinese heritage. Generations of excessive radiation exposure from smartwars and general malnutrition have a way of muddying up the breeding, and those two were no exception. Loud, too. Eight drinks into a mean-drunk loud. The women held knives to two of Koko's best boywhores' throats, and from the look of things, they were raising their elbows and getting ready to saw.

Koko didn't hesitate. On the landing outside her room, she kicked open the bamboo trunk braced against the railing and snatched up the Belgian sub-cutter. A hell of a weapon—favored for street-sweeping action. Of course, when those two re-civs saw the huge gun in her arms they drew sidearms concealed beneath their vests. Expected, of course, and a quick finger-squeeze and a wipe left to right was all it took.

Oh, well. No matter. Portia Delacompte will have her back on something like this. A self-defense infraction with a couple of former hostiles on The Sixty for carnival? Are you kidding? Portia Delacompte has seen plenty of bad craziness with the likes of such savages herself, and Delacompte knows how these BSGD scenarios go.

Ten years Koko's senior, Portia Delacompte hung up her own mercenary spurs years before Koko. Traded in her weapons for spreadsheets, went corporate, and sharked her way up through multiple leisure-syndicate postings until Delacompte landed the cherry gig of all cherry gigs—Executive Vice President of The Sixty Islands Operations. It wasn't long after this wild success that Delacompte reached out to her old comrade, and at the time it was an offer that was, as they say, hard for Koko to refuse.

Run her own brothel and saloon on The Sixty? The most expensive and violent pleasure resort on the planet? Color Koko grateful. She took that opportunity with both hands and feet. Koko figured she was more than a tad overdue, actually. After all, she'd yanked Delacompte's fat out of the fire on more than one occasion, and after that one terrible night back in Finland, Koko just assumed things had finally found their way of working themselves out.

It isn't such a bad life running a brothel. Keep the customers well-oiled with the hooch, manage the games of chance, and pair up guests with whomever they desire from her roster of sexual pleasers. Nearly an equal split between haimish work and a snoozing hammock routine. It beats making planetary regions stable for long-term capital concerns, that's for sure. Most evenings Koko even kicks off early and finds herself joining the party.

Standing at the bar, Koko reflects upon an earlier time when she and Delacompte were out fighting for the multinational conglomerates. They had been on a re-stabilization mission for ElektroCorp and were pinned down beneath marginally radioactive debris near the obliterated ancient seaport of Sanya. A former noodle-manufacturing facility. Jejune, Koko had been a few years into her service, but one bombed-apart industrial landscape looked pretty much like any other to her. Initially, things had gone well on the mission. But then, in a blink of an eye, everything went straight to hell. With two operatives from their brick killed, she and Delacompte ended up cut off from the rest of their unit.

"Hey, Delacompte," Koko said, "has ElektroCorp even looked at the recon saves we uploaded? Their pre-op barrages scorched out everything, and this whole sector is toast. What's the big deal with this place anyway?"

Delacompte was using her tactical knife to cut a chunk of amphetamine chew from a block she had removed from the flak rack on her compression suit. Delacompte handed a wedge of the sticky black chew to Koko and then slabbed off a chunk for herself. With her thumb, Koko crammed the chew into the feeding gate below the chin on her helmet. After a short disinfectant spray, the inner seal on the helmet's feeding gate opened and Koko fished out the potent gunk with her tongue. Like gnawing on a burnt hunk of rubber. Amphetamine chew was vile-tasting stuff, but it sure as hell kept you focused when you were in the shit.

"Real estate," Delacompte answered, waving the barrel of her KRISS F9 pulse rifle slightly. "All this? This area is a prime shipping quarter. Grind it out and dump the scrap offshore, bring in the prefab hardware, and ElektroCorp can be online for immediate manufacturing and distribution in a year flat. This is all about emerging markets, Martstellar. These de-civ Kongercat gang lords know the investment value, and the short of it is they think they deserve a piece of the action."

"Friggin' bottomfeeders."

"That they are. That they surely are."

Koko shifted her legs. "I hate to break it to you, D," Koko said, "but we're kind of on the worse side of screwed here."

A sneer slithered across Delacompte's lips. "No, we're not."

Delacompte's blasé contradiction floored Koko. "What? What do you mean, 'no, we're not'?"

"Just that," she answered. "We are not screwed. Not entirely."

Koko looked left and then right. "How do you figure? One, we're outnumbered. Two, our unit is fragged and down multiple heads. And, three, we're at least an hour from any sort of evac from ElektroCorp."

Delacompte sheathed her tactical knife on her belt. Chewed thoughtfully.

"You're not framing the big picture, kid," Delacompte said. "Look, Davidson's and Kamiński's bricks are holed up right over there near the waste tanks on either side of the gap framing the Kongercats' position, right? You and me, we're going to lay down a diversion and draw them out. That's how we're going to play this."

Koko uneasily ventured a peek over the pile of rubble in front of them and then hunkered back down.

"Um, I know you're point on this mission, D, so no disrespect here, okay? Those are some long freakin' odds."

"Have a little faith," Delacompte said.

A little faith? Screw faith, Koko thought. The data streaming into her ocular implant told Koko both Corporal Davidson's and Corporal Kamiński's bricks were down two mercs each. That meant, including their own two casualties, the insertion team was short six heads in total. Davidson had their entire unit's medic under her wing, for crying out loud, and the medic's beacon indicated that the medic's body was now in four, count them, four separate pieces. Additional bio sweeps also indicated the Kongercat de-civs were in a spiraled thatch formation of at least three hundred, dug in at fifty-seven meters in front of their position. True, the Kongercats' weapons were antiques and they couldn't hit water falling out of a boat, but this was their ground. All they had to do was let fly, toss a few IEDs, and the whole ElektroCorp mission in Sanya was cooked.

Koko stared at her boots.

Man, she didn't want to die here. Not here. Not in some smoking wasteland surrounded and outnumbered by a bunch of tumor-faced de-civs. Koko expected some kind of fry-out at any second and secretly hoped if an assault did come it would be mercifully quick.

Once again, Koko admired Delacompte's absolute calm under fire, her unflappable leadership. Whenever they happened to be paired up on a mission, Delacompte never let even the most lethal of situations appear out of her stalwart control. Her tenacity and élan was something Koko had been trying to emulate ever since she had the good fortune to meet Delacompte. And the ElektroCorp assignment in Sanya was, what? Their tenth syndicate mission in the field together?

At first Koko thought their crossing paths on so many aggressive actions was merely coincidence, but eventually Koko learned there was no such thing as coincidence on reconstruction and industrialization ops. Too much at stake. And rudimentary examination of such operations showed success was in the statistics, right? So the corporations and syndicates took great pains to build complete, efficient teams. After all, when world conglomerates and their surviving puppet governments are trying to jumpstart commerce after a couple of centuries' worth of false-start Armageddons, all the deadly ducks needed to be in a row.

Koko took a quick look at the webbed-out carcasses of the two mercenaries who were with them up until about five minutes prior. The dead faces of the two fallen were so serene inside their helmets, if it weren't for the blood and pulverized bone you'd swear they were catching a few Zs. Poor bastards never knew what hit them. One minute you're dittybopping around, collecting operational data and sucking down your morning's paste rations, the next you're lit up and deep-fried.

Delacompte saw Koko looking at the bodies and slapped Koko's arm.

"You see that tower structure there?"

Koko turned her head and peeked over the mound of broken debris in front of them.

"You mean the one leaning just to the right of the enemy's position?"

Delacompte nodded. The condensation in her helmet's screen made her look almost faceless, like a ghost. "Yeah, that's the one. Totally weakened base on that sucker. We're going to discharge everything we got at the foot of that tower and hope she'll topple right over in front of the Kongercats."

"Everything we've got?"

"Yup."

"But we'll be defenseless."

"That's the idea," Delacompte said confidently. "These de-civs have to believe we're desperate. Unloading on them full bore like that will convey a sense of panic. If they think we've unloaded everything, then maybe they'll take the opportunity to launch an all-out counter-offensive. If they do, the plan is to have Davidson's and Kamiński's crews out-flank them. If we're lucky and we lure the Kongercats out, only a few of them will be left standing when the smoke clears."

Koko motioned to the dead bodies behind them.

"And what? We just hope they don't cut us to pieces like these two?"

Delacompte didn't waste a look on the dead mercs. Instead she squatted down closer to Koko to make her point clear.

"Look, Martstellar," Delacompte said. "I'm real sorry about these two. Hell, when ElektroCorp does our wash-up, I'll even take the heat, let them dock my credits for their expense. The truth is we can't wait this out. No way, no how. Those Kongercats are going to make their move, and they're going to make it soon."

Koko dipped her helmet. The rush from the amphetamine chew

kicked in just then, and Koko felt the chemical heat burning up her blood.

"God, I hate this," she griped. "Why can't these obstructionist de-civs roll over for initiatives like everybody else?"

Delacompte laughed. "Hundreds of years of tested living, that's why. Global contagions, a few centuries of smartwars, all the environmental and geopolitical ruin... like anyone, these pains in the butt are just trying to make their way in the world. Not to mention this is your job, soldier, so quit complaining. This works out and we go one-on-one with these de-civs? You're going to impress the hell out of them with your moves."

Koko grinned. "Didn't know flattery was part of my compensation package, Big D."

"Martstellar, you're a shit-hot hand-to-hand fighter, and you know it."

Koko couldn't help but feel a small flash of pride.

Screw it, Koko thought. She cranked the levels on her weapon and armed every last pulse grenade on her rack. Koko then attached a grenade launcher to her own KRISS F9 pulse rifle and fed the grenades into the weapon's breech. Meanwhile, Delacompte patched the orders to Davidson and Kamiński's bricks via her own ocular. After some confirmation static, a synchronized countdown began on Delacompte's mark.

"You ready?" Delacompte asked.

Koko sucked in a deep breath. Exhaled.

"Born and bred, boss."

"Then let's do this."

Turns out, Delacompte's plan that day worked out just as she described it. It was as though Delacompte had foreseen every single one of the Kongercats' useless tactics. Their group didn't lose another specialist, and none of the Kongercat de-civ militants were left alive. Gutsy-as-hell move was what ElektroCorp called it.

Gutsy-as-hell and bonus credits were awarded all around.

So, yeah, Koko thinks. Portia Delacompte has had her mettle tested with fringe clingers like this before. All in all, she'll probably finagle Koko a slap on the wrist or perhaps a small fine. Plus, Koko tells herself, be realistic. It's not the first time somebody stepped over the line on The Sixty Islands and got themselves popped for their troubles.

Koko picks up a glass and pours herself two fingers' worth of rail beauty. She hasn't spoken with Delacompte in almost a year, and when Koko did it was to see about financing a second brothel operation out near The Sixty's landing fields. Something catering strictly to the merchant contractors and overworked SI staff. When Koko presented her pitch to Delacompte, Delacompte was excessively cool to the proposal and even chillier to Koko. Sure, she and Delacompte move in different circles now, with Delacompte being an executive and everything, but deep down Koko feels that something had somehow changed between them. Of course Koko realizes that even the best of friendships fade, so she attributed Delacompte's quiet distance to Delacompte's polishing her image above her bloody past, wrapping the façades of establishment and pretentiousness around her rough edges. Hell, could she blame the woman? Delacompte has been through a lot, and, like Koko herself, everybody reinvents herself some time.

Koko shuts down the prompts on the register and kills the last of the bar lights except for some piping blue neon looped above the projection piano. Tucking in at the projection piano's hover bench for a spell, she fiddles on the holographic keys with an ancient tune she used to know and before Koko knows it, it's a mere three hours before sunrise.

After taking a final throat-clearing splash of rail beauty on some shaved ice, she yawns and wanders back upstairs to bed. She slides beneath the damp sheets next to Archimedes, and reflexively the young man reaches down between her warm, smooth thighs. Coaxing.

"Koko-sama…"

Koko pushes Archimedes' hand away. Phew, don't get her wrong. She adores the boy's panther-like athleticism in the sack and how he spends hours tripping her bells and whistles, but it's well past late, and Koko is bushed.

With a sigh, Koko rolls over and quickly falls asleep.

DISMAL NEWS COMES A-KNOCKING

A few hours later, Archimedes rouses Koko with a triple-shot cup of hydroponic espresso on a saucer.

Archimedes is dressed in a red cotton macramé thong and black rubber sandals and gushes a non-stop stream of indecipherable burbles and clicks, the gist of which suggests that a group of six CPB security personnel are downstairs in the main bar and very, very angry.

Koko rubs the heels of her hands into her eyes and sits up on sweat-soaked pillows. She takes the offered coffee from Archimedes' trembling hands and downs the scalding liquid in a string of sharp, wincing slurps.

"What time is it?" she asks, stretching.

Archimedes takes the empty espresso cup and sets it on the saucer.

"Six-fifteen, Koko-sama."

Koko's eyes pop. "Six-fif-what? Goddamn it! Since when do CPB security clowns get their collective acts together before eight? The message on the prompts said they wouldn't be here until nine. What the—"

Koko pushes Archimedes aside. Planting her bare feet on the broad planks of the bedroom floor, she searches for her discarded clothes and finds them draped over the arm of a nearby chair. Quickly, Koko yanks on a pair of khaki shorts and pulls a plain white tank top over the top of her head. She jabs her bare feet into a heavy pair of tan utility boots and jerks open her suite's door.

On the upstairs landing, Koko finds a group of boywhores huddled and gazing down at the morning visitors in the bar below with awe and fascination. Koko stamps an impatient foot, and the young men quickly flutter back inside their respective rooms.

A voice calls up.

"Koko Martstellar?"

Koko edges forward and peers over the railing. Sure enough, six Custom Pleasure Bureau security personnel are fanned out in an inverted U pattern in the bar's main dance area. Three men and three women. All are heavily side-armed and grim-faced to beat the proverbial band.

"Speaking."

A tall blonde woman, apparently the group's senior officer, breaks off from the formation and assesses her with humorless gray eyes.

"SI Security. Can we have a moment with you, please?"

Koko sighs, turns, and takes the stairs, making her way down the steps two at a time. When Koko reaches the bottom, she draws back her hair and cinches it off with a rubber band pulled from her front pocket.

"What can I do for you this morning, officer?" Koko asks.

The tall blonde officer takes a few steps and speaks as though from a memorized script. "Koko P. Martstellar, you are hereby charged with the following violations of Vendor Operator Decree Measures of the Custom Pleasure Bureau: Article One, Chapter One; Article Six, Chapter Two; and Article Twenty-One, Chapter Three. Are you familiar with revised VDOMs for The Sixty Islands?"

Koko scratches her chin. Besides not getting enough sleep she's a touch hung over, and it takes her a few foggy seconds to process the woman's officious-sounding drivel.

"The VDOMs?" Koko brews her best pondering look. "Hmm, let's see. Gee, to be honest, not really."

The blonde officer glares disapprovingly.

"As a pleasure vendor on The Sixty Islands, you should be familiar with any and all CPB updates. In fact, if I'm not mistaken, you should have a complete list of VDOMs displayed for public view." The blonde officer looks around the room as she clucks her tongue. "Where are yours, may I ask?"

Koko folds her arms. Koko is a pretty good judge of character and has gone toe to toe with plenty of uppity, by-the-letter authority figures in her past, but rather than push back on the blonde officer's posturing she tries for an air of nonchalance and moves behind the bar. Picking out a key hidden beneath the register, she unlocks the cage on the good liquor bottles arranged on a tiered shelf behind the bar and grabs a bottle of good twelve-year-old beauty. Koko flips a clean glass from the stacks and pours herself a generous eye-opener.

"I guess I must've misplaced them," Koko says. "But hey, I'm sure they're around here someplace."

"Are you being facetious with me this morning, Martstellar?"

"Facetious? Oh, no, not at all. I wouldn't dream of it."

"Because this is not a laughing matter, I assure you."

"This time of morning, I'm sure it's not."

"Good," the officer replies. "Very well, let's get right to the specifics of the matter, shall we? It is our understanding that you cut down, by last count, two SI patrons several hours ago in a direct violation of CPB policy, is this correct?"

Koko nods. "That's affirmative."

"So, you're not denying killing these tourists?"

"No, ma'am."

"Fine. I appreciate your being so forthright with me. Now, then, if you did in fact shoot and kill these two patrons, where have you stored their bodies?"

Koko picks up her glass and a bit of the twelve-year-old beauty slops over onto her thumb. She licks the back of her hand and then motions outside.

"Well, after the Komodos had their fill, I just sort of went ahead and torched what was left out by the waste bins."

The blonde officer's head jerks back as though stung.

"You *burned* their bodies?"

"Yeah."

"But why? Why would you even think of doing something like that?"

Koko bunches her shoulders. "Seemed sanitary."

"But that's not SI crisis protocol."

Koko shakes her head and downs the rest of her drink. "No offense, officer," she says, "but SI crisis protocol can kiss my ass. I greased those two troublemakers fair and square and in self-defense. Anyway, re-civ Kongercat truce agreements or not, CPB and SI HQ should have their heads examined, letting trash like that onto The Sixty."

"Well, if you'd bothered to read the VDOM amendments relating to emergency management issues, you would have seen that engaging in any and all lethal means against paying customers, including re-civ Kongercats, is now strictly forbidden on The Sixty. And tampering with evidence on top of a violation like this? I'm afraid your actions are completely unacceptable. Have you any idea of how behavior like this can tarnish The Sixty Islands' overall brand?"

Koko throws back her head and laughs. "Oh c'mon! Tarnish The Sixty Islands' overall brand? Seriously, isn't that blowing the public-relations slant on this a bit out of proportion?"

"CPB HQ doesn't seem to see it that way."

"Yeah, well," Koko chuffs, "those two freakshows were threatening my staff. There were other customers present last night too. Paying customers too, mind you. Has CPB HQ even given a thought about their safety and vacation experience? Or to my own employees' welfare, for that matter? Honey, I did CPB a favor." Koko spins her now empty glass on the bar. "Look, I know you're out here this morning just doing your job and all, so why don't we cut the bullshit, all right? Contact Portia Delacompte over at HQ. Vice President Delacompte is an old friend of mine, and I'm sure she'll find some way to take care of all this."

The blonde officer throws a glance to the other members of the security team.

"You know, I've taken a good look at your file, Martstellar."

"Oh, yeah?"

"Yes. A fairly impressive career on the mercenary circuits for the multinationals before you downshifted to," the officer looks around the room until she ogles Archimedes standing by the stairs in his red macramé thong, "the leisure industry."

"I take it from your tone you don't approve of what I do here."

"No, I know such lustful pursuits are part of the SI's overall appeal. However, I also know there are more refined ways to make one's living on The Sixty."

Koko scoffs. "Like what? Setting up massacre simulations so Dick and Jane Deep-Pockets and their spoiled, elitist brats can get their rocks off? Give me a break. You puckered types are all the same. Vacation extravagance in the realm of replicated hyper-violence is fine and dandy, but if someone wants to release her pent-up tensions with a little shift and shake you guys turn into a bunch of right-angled prudes. Anyway, if you say you've seen my file, you no doubt noted my employment recommendation. Like I said, Delacompte and I are old friends. I'd be careful where I was treading with that attitude of yours if I were you."

"Really, now?"

"Yeah, really."

"Well, I hate to be the one to break it to you, but we are here this morning on Portia Delacompte's direct orders."

The words sandbag her. Koko does a double take. "Wait. Come again?"

The blonde officer unfastens a pouch on her belt. She withdraws a data plug and wings it directly at Koko's head. Koko snatches it from the air just before the data plug tags her on the nose.

Without taking her eyes off the officer, Koko jacks the plug into the bar register and opens the plug's file on the projection prompts. She reads the file's content twice just to be sure she's not imagining things. It's unreal. Totally indefensible corporate bullshit of the most bureaucratic order. In essence the file says Koko is finished as an SI pleasure vendor and is to be incarcerated immediately until a penalty hearing can be arranged. In addition, if she is not compliant, Koko is to be terminated—effective immediately.

A chill spreads out from the pit of Koko's stomach. When she confirms the indictment's authorization code she sees that the orders have indeed been encoded by Portia Delacompte herself.

What the—

Terminated?

Terminated?

Another one of the CPB security detail—a chesty, moon-faced female on the end of the formation—pipes up.

"It'd be better if you go quietly, Martstellar."

Koko shoots the moon-faced woman a black look and then notices with some alarm that the other security team members' hands have drifted to their holsters.

The peevish glint in the blonde officer's eyes grows lean.

"Your whores will be reassigned, naturally…"

Koko's eyes drift left. Archimedes is retreating backward up the staircase, and she can hear his sandals snapping at his heels like small, barely audible kisses. When Archimedes reaches the landing upstairs, he sidesteps over to the large wooden trunk set against the landing's railing. No one in the group seems to notice his movements or even care. After all, Archimedes is just another boywhore. What threat could he possibly be?

Archimedes quietly slides the Belgian sub-cutter from the trunk.

A surge of warmth flushes through Koko's heart. She can't believe her young stud has read the deteriorating situation like a pro. *Go,* Koko thinks.

Go, boy, go...

A collective snigger passes among the security detail as they inch closer, and Koko, as casually as she can, slides her hands under the bar. Half a second later she finds what she is looking for: the stock of an MG-88-Ventilator. Koko installed the weapon almost a year ago because she was bored one rainy afternoon. Just like with the sub-cutter in the bamboo trunk upstairs, she never thought there would be a circumstance in which she'd actually have to use it. But like all long-shot wagers, sooner or later there you fucking are.

Like so many times before, the cold edge of hyperawareness narrows Koko's world. The pulmonic tempo in her chest increases, and the details of her surroundings sharpen. Koko sees everything. The mist of perspiration on the senior officer's forehead. The long golden shaft of morning sunlight pouring through the open window, a lone fly lazily sputtering in its beam. Koko can even hear each distinct, curling whoop of a troop of Gibbon monkeys clutched in the nearby Banyan trees. Archimedes raises the sub-cutter to his shoulder, and Koko sees the indicator lights winking that the weapon is now hot and ready to rock.

As Koko releases the Ventilator's safety, a charge prickles beneath her hand.

The senior officer barks, "Hands where we can see them, Martstellar!"

Koko drops right, and the room explodes with pulse-gun fire.

Archimedes is a lousy shot with the sub-cutter. The first cerulean-colored blasts from the wide mouth of the weapon smash the floorboards and allow the CPB squad members to scatter for cover. Subsequent blue blasts fly clean, and Archimedes finally gets some. Two searing orbs of light catch the moon-faced officer just beneath the heft of her breasts and slam her backward into the far wall.

Meanwhile, on the rubber runner mats behind the bar, Koko

pushes up, tightens her grip on the Ventilator, and starts blasting straight through the bar's wooden skin. The majority of the bar's siding is reinforced with steel except for a narrow slotted track that allows Koko to unload the weapon in a wide arc, and the arc covers the room.

Squeezing the trigger at will, Koko hopes she'll hit someone, and she does—the blonde officer attempting a go-for-broke hurdle over the bar. The Ventilator round tears through the woman's stomach and pitches her sideways into a table, smashing it to pieces.

Archimedes screams wildly from the landing.

"You mess with my Koko-sama, you die-die! You die-die!"

Archimedes returns fire at the remaining security personnel, but his aim is just plain awful. The heavy recoil of the sub-cutter is too unwieldy for his slight arms and black acrid smoke blinds him. The remaining security detail remember their training. They triangulate their aims and eviscerate Archimedes in a grotesque gyration of sizzling flesh.

Koko peeks over the lip of the bar just as Archimedes' jawbone flies across the room like a ragged, bloody bird.

"NO!"

Koko snaps the Ventilator off its mount beneath the bar and brings the weapon up. She targets those remaining and lets fly without pause.

FU-CHEW! FU-CHEW! FU-CHEW! Heads liquefying.

Dandelions of bone and bloody discharge patterning out.

Four shots are four kills, and the whole room is swallowed in flame.

Koko's eyes sweep the burning area for signs of life before she charges up the stairs. Not looking at Archimedes' crumpled body on the landing, she yanks open all the doors to the rooms, shouting at the boywhores to move, move, move. She hustles the crying and hysterical young men down the stairs, through the slaughter, and out the bar's batwing doors.

In the sandy street outside, Koko uses the Ventilator to blast a perimeter to keep the Komodos away. In complimentary SI robes, curious onlookers from thatch-roofed cabanas and modular bungalows across the way have gathered outside to watch. They eat bananas and sip coffee, thinking the morning's bedlam is just one more simulated part of their vacation experience. A few even pose for pictures, mugging and gesticulating to the burning building behind them.

Koko storms back inside the growling inferno. With no time, she knows what she has to do. The safe is in the pantry behind the building's small galley kitchen in the rear. It takes a couple of wipes of her watering eyes to get a clean retinal scan, but once the safe pops open Koko grabs all the credits she can carry, a small stash of crinkle-flake, plus an extra bottle of aged forty-five-year-old beauty she's been saving for a special occasion. *What the hell*, Koko thinks. She may not live through this, and now is as good a time as any. She cracks the seal on the bottle and chugs a huge gulp.

Fuckin'-a.

Smoke singeing her lungs, Koko scrambles to her feet and punches out the back door. Outside, she whips a camouflaged tarp off an escape pod half-buried beside the storage shed next to the waste bins.

Koko knows if she moves fast enough and gets enough altitude she can sail on through to the atmospheric orbital barges of the Second Free Zone before the SI security batteries can knock her from the sky. The sky barges and arks of the Second Free Zone are not the greatest places to lay low as a fugitive, but her life on The Sixty is all but a memory for her now.

Saddled inside the pod, Koko clips in and hauls the hatch shut on top of her. Four thrown switches later and the craft is online. Koko hits the primary ignition and a single fusion engine beneath her growls.

The pod shakes and shakes and shakes, but soon it's free from the shallow rut in the ground. Hovering at fifteen meters, Koko engages the secondary engine and her organs practically flatten out as the liftoff booms her skyward.

As the escape pod climbs, G-forces wobble the skin back across Koko's skull. Her teeth chatter, and she strains to take one last look to port. The burning building and the lush, tropical smear of The Sixty Islands recedes beneath her like a coiled, emerald serpent fixed in an impossible expanse of oceanic blue. A single thought creases Koko's mind.

Archimedes.

Man, she's sure going to miss that boy.

FIFTEEN MINUTES LATER, AT SI HQ...

Vice President Portia Delacompte slumps in her desk chair and visibly fumes.

Across the gleaming, sterile expanse of her dojo-esque office chamber her assistant, Vincent Lee, braces on his feet. Lee is twenty-three, groomed and polished to CPB junior executive standards, and quite unaccustomed to delivering such bad news so early in the day.

"Please tell me you're joking," Delacompte begins.

As he clears some gummy residue from his throat, Lee is unsure as to where he should clasp his hands. At first Lee laces them in front of his pressed trousers, but quickly he decides the submissive gesture might intensify his boss's irritation. Lee decides to adopt a full at-ease posture and wrings his hands behind his back.

"I'm afraid not, Madam Vice President," he replies. "Six security personnel were assigned to the Martstellar detail. All six are dead apparently, and the firefight razed the building."

Delacompte kneads the space above her eyebrows with four fingers. "And where is Martstellar now?"

"She's heading for the Second Free Zone."

"The Second Free Zone! *What?* How is that even possible?"

Lee shuffles nervously. "It seems she had a suborbital escape pod. I'm not sure how she concealed the craft from The Sixty Islands' trace sensors and routine inspections, but Martstellar was out of range before anything could be done to stop her in mid-flight. Best guess is she smuggled the pod onto The Sixty in pieces and cobbled it together over time with modified electronics. Her training, naturally." Lee clears his throat again. "I've already dispatched a confidential memorandum to our enforcement office. Robust penalty assessments for not discovering this are attached, of course."

Delacompte scowls. "Idiots…"

"Yes," Lee agrees. "I should have added myself to the detail as oversight, so I accept full responsibility for the mix-up. I've prepared my file for downgrade penalties across the roster as well."

Delacompte snaps, "Not you, you slimy little twerp. That security detail! Incompetents the lot. Bunch of good-for-nothings living the high life on a cushy CPB assignment. Tell me, they were briefed on Martstellar's background, were they not?"

"Most definitely. A complete history."

"And still they screwed this up?"

Lee nods.

Delacompte bangs a fist on the arm of her chair. "Order a full staff recycle immediately. Flush all the corpulent deadwood. I mean, it's not like we can't find fresh militarized personnel salivating for SI duty. Now, then, as long as my day has turned into a giant flume of shit, how's media? As bad as I expect?"

Lee swallows. "Unfortunately the feeds picked the incident up right away and containment on our end was impossible. As you know, Martstellar's brothel operation was in a dense area, well-traveled and quite popular with SI guests given the nature of the sector's… uh… um," Lee searches for the precise words, "offerings."

"So you're telling me the witness distortions went viral almost immediately?"

"I'm afraid so, but all witnesses have been quarantined pending debrief assessments and fact cleansing. I'm confident we'll be able to correct narrative fundamentals shortly. Public-relations containment is on full alert and working on distraction insertions as we speak. I expect an update in a few minutes."

Delacompte fidgets. Working her shoulders and tightly cropped silver hair against her chair's backing, she steers her eyes downward and fishes out a lime-colored plastic bottle from her bolero-style jacket. Refusing to meet Lee's gaze, she snaps open the bottle's lid and shakes out a small yellow capsule—a dose of the anti-anxiety drug Quelizan, commonly known as Q. Delacompte swallows the capsule dry and then pinches the bridge of her nose.

"What a mess…"

"Again, I'm so sorry, Vice President Delacompte."

"So sorry does not unfuck this situation, Lee. Are you familiar with the sinister physics of a PR disaster such as this? The CPB and The Sixty may be all about licentious gratifications but our customers—moreover, our shareholders—demand rigid professionalism and oversight. Administrative decrees have to be respected. Even the slightest blowback from an incident like this and we could incur significant commercial losses. Minor at first, of course. A mere point tick here and there before adjustment corrections. But those annoying ticks can pick up steam, and if not redressed…" Delacompte lets the air completely leave her chest. "Not on my watch and not ever, do you understand me?"

"Yes, Madam Vice President."

"Good. So, what else?"

"Excuse me?"

"What. *Else*?"

"Well," Lee says, "like I said, we've tracked Martstellar to the Second Free Zone, so anticipating your anger I've taken the liberty of assigning a freelance bounty operative, one Cleo Heinz, for pursuit."

Delacompte's flinty eyes slit. "You do realize that hiring a bounty agent for pursuit into the orbital confederacies of the Second Free Zone is illegal, don't you?"

"I do," Lee quickly answers. "But given the extenuating circumstances and anticipating your displeasure I thought you'd approve of the measure. I mean, this Heinz… she's good."

"How good?"

Lee puckers his lips and whistles. "Really good."

"Good, really good, I don't want to hear either. I want—no, I demand—perfection. We wouldn't even be in such a position if that team of assembled screwheads you sent had their acts together."

"Again, I can't possibly express how sorry I am."

"So, if you've already engaged this operative, I trust you're being discreet?"

"Yes, of course."

"You'd damn well better be."

Delacompte stomps her boots on the floor and stands. The sound of her boots' thunderclap jolts Lee in his stance. Sweat is running heavy for him now, and he watches helplessly as Delacompte retrieves a gun from inside the desk's top drawer. Delacompte sets the weapon down on the right side of her desk.

Good lord, he thinks. Dealing with his boss's narcissistic mood fluctuations has always been difficult, but Portia Delacompte brandishing a weapon? Well, that certainly is a new one. Would she actually use the gun, though? No, that seems unlikely. But then again, you never really know with Portia Delacompte. The woman has unrealistic standards and is, as they say, six jars past crazy.

Lee half-heartedly assures himself that the move is merely one more of his boss's aberrant and malicious efforts at dehumanizing him. Yet, despite his telling himself this, a slow worm of dread twists inside. Corporal punishments on The Sixty are covered by executive immunity. Perhaps she would just wound him. Perhaps.

Lee looks out at the surrounding CPB HQ campus. The clean angles of glass and steel, and the mossy jungles, thick and vast, beyond. Five kilometers away he sees the rigged explosions in the Trauma Quadrant scorch the sky, wealthy vacationers burning whole manufactured villages to the ground. To the right and further out beyond the barrier reefs, an ad hoc regatta appears to be under way and the pristine blades of so many silver trimarans heel over on reach. Lee drinks in the whole panoramic view from Delacompte's window with yearning and a twinge of despair. As if the next second might hold his last breath, he finds himself thinking on the last time he and his lover, a merchant seaman, engaged in affection—just that morning. Will his sailor truly mourn his loss? Lee has his doubts.

Delacompte smacks her hands down on either side of the weapon on her desk.

"Get me this freelancer Heinz's file. I don't care if she's won a small war all by herself, I want to see it. And secure me a patch for the board of directors. Now. No doubt with the virals on the feeds they know about this disaster and already have their hackles up."

Lee straightens with relief. "Yes, Madam Vice President! Right away." He turns to go but freezes when he hears Delacompte snap her fingers.

"One more thing," Delacompte says.

Lee turns. "Yes?"

Like the patient paw of an animal preparing to strike, Delacompte's hand raises with a single finger upheld for Lee to take in. He nods and quickly scuttles out of the room.

Two and a half years on the job, a nearly perfect CPB junior executive record, and he can't believe it.

Vincent Lee's CPB penalty count has finally begun.

HEAVY IS THE MANTLE

After Lee leaves, Delacompte drops into her chair with a huff.

Quite desperately she wishes she could recall why the need to eliminate her former friend Koko Martstellar still plagues her, but for the life of her she can't. Selective memory treatment; my goodness, that therapy took care of everything, didn't it?

Years back, when Delacompte was recruited and offered her oversight position on The Sixty, one of her first measures was to sign up for the neurological erasure therapy. At the time, the elective brain scrubbing seemed prudent given her aspirations. Delacompte saw herself one day rising to a board-level position with the Custom Pleasure Bureau, and absolute memory downloads were required for final board-level clearance. True, making her way to such impressive heights was probably a long way off, but Delacompte realized both then and now that corporate advancement is a long-haul game, like chess. It's imperative to strategize ahead and play things shrewd.

But why? Why does she want Martstellar dead? Didn't she once serve alongside the woman? Weren't they once friends? Martstellar's file seems to confirm this, yet every time Delacompte even attempts to evoke a shred of insight as to why she wants Koko dead, the electrical impulses of her brain fail and betray her. Truly a frustrating and strange sensation. Sort of like casting lines out into a soft black abyss or as though a stack of warm, dark blankets has been drawn over the caged, fluttering canaries of her mind.

Mapped to brain cells' degenerative DNA parameters, SMT therapy allowed Delacompte to privately and consciously select her memory erasures. The procedure required several visits to the clinic, and while she can't remember exactly what took place, back then Delacompte likened the experience to watching short bursts of a montage. Glimpses of her past slid by like the soundless tags on the market feeds: assaults for syndicates like Klover International (WG INDEX SYMBOL—KLI Credit PPS/49) where she and Martstellar were part of a commando team sent to seize a rival corporation's carbon mine. Or that long, brutal offensive for Tien Shan Initiatives (WG INDEX SYMBOL—TSI Credit PPS/12½) sanctioned by the Selvas Latin American Fund (WG INDEX SLAF: Total Return—17.9%). Private improvised militias clearing the way for international profit, whittling away all those who dared to stand in the way of Earth's progressive reconstruction. Good times on Happy Street for sure, but life for Delacompte is all so different now.

Since the Custom Pleasure Board knew and respected Delacompte's military background, it wasn't all the wholesale bloodshed and mayhem Delacompte took part in that she fretted over. She has her suspicions the now-purged actions were something much worse. A transgression so abhorrent it would have chopped off her ambitions at the knees.

But what was it?

Damned if she knows now.

Delacompte rolls her chair forward and pulls up Martstellar's file on her projection prompts. She stares fiercely at a three-dimensional image of Koko's head in 360-degree rotation—a portrait, atop a translucent rectangle, gazing blankly into space. The emptiness of Martstellar's eyes evokes nothing for Delacompte.

There must have been a good reason for all of this, but what? All Delacompte knows now is that before undergoing the SMT therapy she predated an irrevocable *aide memoire* to herself, and the memo's reminder has been palpitating on her private-prompt retrievals for far too long. When word came several hours ago that Martstellar had killed those two Kongercat guests, she decided to get this tiresome chore off her desk once and for all.

With a few passes of her fingers, Delacompte pulls up and lays the contents of the memorandum over Martstellar's spinning head. The greenish, veiling text of the memo is cryptic and short:

- Hire Koko P. Martstellar.
- Make Martstellar welcome.
- Kill Martstellar at the earliest possible convenience.

So strange.

Delacompte shuts down all the open prompt screens, closes her eyes, and leans back in her chair. Once more she attempts to will her mind over the selcouth chasms in her brain. She's almost convinced that if she just relaxes and breathes, if just she concentrates long enough and bears down, she'll be able to force her memory to refresh like a programming reboot. But it's useless.

Sorry, Martstellar.

I must have had a damn good reason at the time and, well, you're a former professional soldier. You should know how this sort of thing goes better than anyone. Like it or not, business is business.

Business is business.

CAN A GIRL GET A BREAK?

As Koko's pod approaches the lower Second Free Zone orbits, the clearance message streaming into the helm tells her that her luck is still hard lapping the drain.

"To all approaching vessels, welcome to the Second Free Zone. Your craft is on an immediate heading for the docking bays of the Lawrence Class barge and commerce vessel *Hesperus 6*. Please have your customs data ready for official upload on arrival. Due to unexpected delays, there may be a waiting period for officials to clear your craft and your passengers. For your safety and the safety of your fellow travelers today, please take a moment to familiarize yourself with the listed contraband and health restrictions for *Hesperus 6*, which are streaming on band twelve. Failure to comply with the defined access restrictions, to disclose contraband, or to declare any and all cargo will mean immediate denial of access to *Hesperus 6* and possible hostile actions. The senior command crew and populace of *Hesperus 6* apologize in advance for any inconvenience this may cause you regarding your travel intentions today and your stay in the Second Free Zone. Again, welcome to the Second Free Zone and welcome aboard."

Koko doesn't have much choice. Her escape pod is a deadhead craft with only enough fuel to get her to the first Second Free Zone vessel intersecting her immediate ascent trajectory. If the pod's limited fuel cells bottom out and she declines to continue on into *Hesperus 6*'s docking bays, there will be only two outcomes: One, she'll be adrift and at the mercy of lower-orbit salvage hunters—pretty bad odds on those cruising foragers (see nefarious whim and indiscriminate brutality)—or two, if she risks a low-tanked re-entry run, she'll more than likely run out of power and end up pancaking in some empty stretch of boiling ocean. Unfortunately, Koko's hasty exit from The Sixty has resulted in a situation not unlike playing roulette—the worst odds in the house.

The fact that the *Hesperus 6* message even mentions contraband makes Koko's shoulder muscles constrict. Some barges in the Second Free Zone orbits don't care what you have stowed, but others are vigilant to the point of being despotic. She isn't familiar with *Hesperus 6* at all, and she prays for a line of magnanimous prattle as she brings up band twelve on the com's central navigational screen.

Koko selects her primary tongues and dialects and scrolls through the data. At first, it's the usual fare (diseases and exposures, volatile chemicals, restricted vegetation and life forms), but when the ominous yellow and black bar blinks Koko can't help but groan out loud.

All personal weapons, stimulants, and/or narcotics are strictly forbidden.

Shit.

Fading adrenaline has her nerves crashing and shaky. Sure, Koko knows that sometimes overworked attachés at customs can turn a blind eye to contraband in exchange for a bribe or even a crude, lusty wink, but her choice right now is clear. Jettison the Ventilator she ripped from under the bar back on The Sixty, the bottle of aged forty-five-year-old beauty she's been saving, and her stash of crinkle-flake, or face the consequences.

Koko unscrews the cap on the beauty and takes a few hungry

pulls. The brown liquor tastes too good, but she has the presence of mind not to swallow too much. She slips her stash of crinkle-flake into the disposal tube on starboard side and then slides the Ventilator and the bottle of beauty after. A sharp clank and hiss answer the discharge switch as the contraband is razed in a short sizzle of precious fuel. A pungent metallic fog leaks through the interior vents and quickly fades.

The hulking curved outline of *Hesperus 6* dwarfs Koko's escape pod. The ship is a drab, foil-skinned, lower-atmospheric orbital with dual-keels drooping on either end of the fuselage like a gigantic funnel-capped ear of corn. Other, slicker craft are lined up in *Hesperus 6*'s arrival queue and their sleek, aerodynamic designs vaguely niggle at Koko's vanity. All in all, Koko would be a bit surprised if anyone on *Hesperus 6* noticed her rinky-dink homemade craft at all.

Through the tinted angle of the pod's single curved window she sees that the weather is somewhat stable. Not at all squally and blustery, as is typical for the Second Free Zone, but still the surrounding sky is an ominous bruised valley of swift-moving stratocumulus. In washing curtains, rain ticks against the bow window, abates some, and splutters again briefly. Far off, she can hear a soft rumble of thunder.

Looking to starboard, Koko catches glimpses through the clouds of numerous and enormous Second Free Zone residential arks and barges lumbering through their selective tracks like a slow-motion game of hide and seek played by listless, blunt whales. The massive ships slip through their rising and descending glides, and swarms of smaller aircraft slice to and fro in their wakes. Strat-sleds, service transports, cargo freighters, interplanetaries, and the like. Given the heavy air traffic, Koko has always been astounded that air-to-air collisions aren't more frequent aloft. Two hundred fifty thousand years since we chimps stood upright and our arrogance hasn't bucked an inch. Like so many technological innovations that have come and gone before, the miracles of magnetic micro-fusion and anti-gravity propulsion have led to wretched extremes.

Koko types in "nothing to declare" and forwards her intent to flight control. A minute later an audio response from *Hesperus 6* pours through the helm.

"Pod 288?"

Koko responds. "This is Pod 288 on arrival."

"Pod 288, you are cleared for initial influx processing. Power down all onboard systems and initiate docking sequences. Bay five. Over."

Koko does as instructed. She kills the pod's main fuel switches, and the ship yaws forward with the cancelled propulsion wash. Koko bumps about in her seat a bit as the *Hesperus 6* docking claws grip fore and aft. Landing aboard vessels in the Second Free Zone is always a little rough, but it seems rougher than normal, as Koko never budgeted for stabilizers. Like a tightly drawn curtain of snapping white lace, the protective pressure membranes of *Hesperus 6* landing bays radiate five hundred meters ahead as the docking claws draw her inward.

"Pod 288, we have you. Prepare for debarkation, de-cam inspection, and customs. Over."

"Roger."

Koko unclasps her safety harness and tilts her head back. She shuts her eyes. She tries not to think about poor Archimedes or her livelihood down below on The Sixty up in flames, and instead broods about Portia Delacompte and why Delacompte would send a bunch of flunkies to take her out.

Because of a small lapse with some stupid updated CPB Decree Measures? Pretty rash even given the CPB's hardhearted administrative standards.

No, that doesn't seem likely at all.

Koko's bafflement consumes her.

WELCOME TO THE SECOND FREE ZONE

And Koko's bafflement doesn't subside once she is aboard.

The customs and naturalization envoy on *Hesperus 6* is a hairless, pudgy twit with breath so vile it reminds Koko of the splashing, gelatinous waste scuppers out near The Sixty Islands' landing strips. The man's pale eyes roam, lizard-like, as he sways back and forth in front of her and preens over his gadgets and wares.

"Koko P. Martstellar," the envoy intones unctuously in a quivering voice. "Ooooh. Oh my, my, my, eh? My, my, my, my, my. Saloon keeper and madam of the finest tastes and fornicating fancy on The Sixty, yes-yes? Shame-shame, eh? There was a small newsflash over the feeds just earlier. Quicky-quick, but all over."

Koko frowns. The media feeds picked up what went down on The Sixty already? She admits she isn't surprised and figures it was probably those tourists gawking at her burning place from across the street, polluting the feed streams with gleeful, self-absorbed takes on the whole mess. Bad news always travels fast, even up to the Second Free Zone.

Fancying himself a bit of a wag, Sewage Breath chirps on. "Quite the scene down there, yes-yes? Updates I think say you vaporized two dozen CPB security personnel and slaughtered your own staff, as well as several innocent bystanders."

Koko shakes her head.

"Exaggeration and lies, as usual," she says.

"Is that so?"

"Eyewitnesses… you can't trust them messing up the feeds."

"Well, a proper misunderstanding then, yes-yes?"

Koko looks away. "Buddy, you don't know the half of it."

The envoy titters. "Of course, you're up here now. Within generous confederate clemency of the Second Free Zone orbits, yes-yes? I'm sure you are aware that judgment is not what we do here. For all intents and purposes, you're a free citizen up here now, with amnesty and liberty within the limits of commercial law. That is, if you elect to stay up." The envoy bobs about on his feet. "Our scans noted your contraband dump on arrival. I must say, a smart move, that. But tell me… why would someone such as yourself choose a boring old barge like *Hesperus 6*? Of all the orbitals, life here is far duller than the hospitality someone like you must be accustomed to. Truer than true, our work is a simple and necessary function for the greater planetary trades, but why sky here?"

Koko studies the man. It's obvious the envoy knows how bad his breath is, so she pegs him as the type of small-minded jerk who relishes making people squirm because he thinks his position affords him some petty level of clout.

Koko speaks into her shoulder to cover her nose. "My pod is a dead-header, and you know it," she answers. "I didn't have enough fuel and didn't have much of a choice. Kind of blasted off and just hoped for the best. By the way, what is *Hesperus 6* anyway?"

The envoy's mouth audibly pops open. He is amused by her query. "You don't know? Oh. *Hesperus 6* is an atmospheric recycling vessel."

An atmospheric recycling vessel? That explained the giant funnels on the ship's droopy, foiled fuselage. *Great*, Koko thinks. Her luck is no longer waning. It's in screaming free fall.

The envoy gestures for Koko to stretch her neck back, and then with the heartless motions of a man who has done such mundane tasks forever, he takes a small wand and injects a nano probe into Koko's carotidal artery. There is a tingling sensation as the probe dose spreads out. It warms to a fluey ache in Koko's limbs, and shortly thereafter an intense pain takes hold as Koko's organs, bones, and muscles are combed and searched.

"You may feel some discomfort as the probes search for imbedded contraband."

Koko draws in a quick breath through clenched teeth. "I've been through de-cam before."

She gasps a little as the probes loop through the chambers of her heart and buzz outward again toward skin level. When the nano probes hit the tender flesh around Koko's piercings she instantly regrets all seven of them, each and every one.

After waiting around to void the probes in a rank-smelling steam toilet, Koko declares no intention of keeping her escape craft and takes the offered measly salvage credits along with her updated authorizations for SFZ travel. As she leaves the debarkation area, the envoy wiggles his fingers at her like a happy clown and wishes her Godspeed with her travels. Koko flips the envoy the bird and swaggers out of the gates.

Checking the departure schedules, Koko purchases a ticket at a free-standing kiosk for a direct shuttle to a larger residential barge called *Alaungpaya*. *Alaungpaya* is a residential behemoth nearly 2.5 million square meters in size and rotates on the inner atmospheric orbits like a giant, inverted mushroom cap. The fact that *Alaungpaya* is listed third on the departure schedule makes Koko think that maybe her luck is changing. She's pretty sure an old contact, Juke Ramirez, once mentioned a while back that he now lives aboard *Alaungpaya*. If Juke has moved on or if Koko is mistaken, well, *Alaungpaya* or any place else is better than hanging around some floating sky sponge like *Hesperus 6*.

Taking her ticket, Koko heads for a kebab bodega just off the arrival and departure area. Naturally there isn't any liquor or beauty for sale at the drone-operated bodega, as alcohol is forbidden on *Hesperus 6* (hydro-atmospheric recycle vessel and completely dry— slay her with the irony), but the food stand has plenty of water in a vast array of artificial flavors and chemical boosts. *Achy-Boom. Fault Line Quake. Orange-Za.* Koko chooses a triple slosh of Fault Line Quake in a tall cup and the rush of fortified caffeine sears off what's left of her post-adrenaline fatigue. She orders a fried-protein kebab off the menu to go with the drink and decides to wait around in front of the bodega until the shuttle departs for *Alaungpaya*.

From the look of things *Hesperus 6* is a lonely, damp suck. Even with the thinner and much chillier air up top in the Second Free Zone, the humidity aboard cloys and slicks her skin and clothes like a gooey, cold tongue. When her protein kebab is ready, Koko takes it over and stands at a chest-high hover table with a view of the arrival and departure areas. One bite of the kebab and Koko spits out the food. The reheated blocks of translucent soy are rancid and mealy.

A small, plastic vermin trap is wedged against a nearby partition, and Koko tosses the remains of the kebab at the device. It has always amazed Koko that they even have rodents up here in the orbits. Despite routine vacuum exterminations, those little bastards just endure. She has to respect that.

A huge sucking *whoosh* rushes through a warren of dripping conduits overhead, and Koko flinches a bit. Centuries of the ratcheting up of worldwide conflict and the obliteration of ever-dwindling planetary resources have required such innovations as atmospheric distillation for human survival. Koko clocks the corporate logos. Apparently *Hesperus 6* is owned by Energia-ASA—a big-boned South American syndicate. A few years back, another one of Energia-ASA's sky-distillation arks ruptured like a rotten piñata due to a catastrophic ballast malfunction and the ensuing mega-tsunami killed hundreds of thousands below on Earth. Wrecked the ungovernable, shantytown economy of what used to be France's Silver Coast, if Koko remembers correctly.

Koko pictures *Hesperus 6* falling from the sky into the sea and remembers her time down in Hossegor for the briefest of moments. *Man*, she thinks, *I'm sure glad I spent that week down there when I had the chance.*

Koko checks the digitized countdown readout on her ticket again. The next shuttle to *Alaungpaya* leaves in fifteen minutes. *Good God*, she thinks. *Get me out of this floating humidor.*

She takes another sip of her drink to swish some of the lingering foul kebab taste from her mouth and then dumps the rest of it in a nearby waste receptacle. As Koko wipes her hands on her shorts, she looks across the arrival and departure area and freezes.

In a glass-boxed office just beyond the debarkation and customs section, the naturalization envoy, Mister Dire Oral Hygiene, is talking with a long-locked redheaded woman with neck extension bands. The woman is a tall, severe-looking creature stylishly glossed in midnight black—trench coat, bodysuit, and calf-high buckled boots. The discussion appears fairly heated, but it's the ocular implant affixed to the redhead's right temple that gives Koko pause.

The envoy gestures in Koko's general vicinity and quickly Koko takes cover behind a support column. Beneath her breastbone her heart is a jackrabbit, and a moment later Koko forces herself to peer around the column's edge. She sees the redhead forfeit a vest of state-of-the-art body armor and then several vicious-looking guns.

Well, Koko thinks, *that sure as hell didn't take long.*

Ocular implants.

Pretty much standard communication issue for militarized personnel.

And bounty hunters.

THE LAWMAN COMETH

A little over an hour later on the residential barge known as *Alaungpaya*, Security Deputy Jedidiah Flynn draws a weary hand down and over his trim, brown beard and rechecks the save patterns on the witness's statement.

"Let's go over it one more time," Flynn says.

The kid in front of Flynn is an overfed adolescent doing his best to keep up with the trends popular with kids his age, and to Flynn it appears the kid is failing miserably on all the cool fronts. Reverse-braille digital tats percolating beneath the skin, the knockoff torture boots with the inward blades for discreet on-the-go masturbatory flagellation, canary-striped Caesar hairdo plastered down with scented gel—one more plagued by juvenile desire and unease.

The kid asks nervously, "Am I in hook and claw?"

Flynn shakes his head. "No, son."

The kid jiggles a bit in his gold-colored slicker.

"I mean, you know, I can't have me no hook and claw points, officer. No-no. Not even one. Not even baby hook and claw points. My mother will've me all up and lockdown domestic and you bet me hate that some."

Flynn holds the neural statement recorder against the kid's forehead and sighs. The kid's pimply flesh looks like diseased chicken skin, and Flynn immediately wishes he'd put on protective rubber gloves.

"You're underage," Flynn assures him. "This type of minor incident reportage is strictly an anonymous procedure. Seriously now, just tell me what you remember and this will all be over in a minute. But hold still, okay? The neural recorder here is low on juice."

The kid relaxes a mere fraction beneath Flynn's hands. "Right-right," he says, "'kay-o. So, um, like, me? I'm on errand for my mother for the chem-macy 'cause my mother be sick and need her pressure pins, right-right? So I come out, out of that chem-macy right over there, and this danger smoke? This totally hot, danger smoke—me can't help myself but heavy goon."

"The first woman."

"Right-right. The first woman. Like I say, total danger smoke. Got her this long black hair, shorty-shorts, and boots. Can't miss me a high sexy danger smoke dressed like that, for sure." The kid gives Flynn a conspiratorial roll of his hips. "Don't know about you, officer, but for heavy credit maybe she be the type tug me jam-spout for clear, right-right? Knock a little shift and shake?"

Flynn needs to flatten the kid's raging hormones but quick.

"Let's just keep use of slanguage to a minimum, all right? First woman, second woman. And don't say danger smoke, okay? It's derogatory."

"Derogatory?"

Flynn sighs. "Offensive."

"Oh. Right-right. Sorry."

"Really. We'll be through in a minute and you can be on your way. Just cooperate and speak clearly, okay?"

A tremble sends a rolling creak through the boy's plastic slicker. "Right-right. So, I'm doing my errand thing and the first one, the danger, err, the first woman? She go lefty, yeah? She go all lefty and down that access tunnel right over there. Then this second danger smo—I mean, this second woman? Big redhead with the neck chokers. That one follow the first quicky-quick right after. And I'm, like, minding my own, but then when I pass by the tunnel? Me gets a goon all proper. Yeah, that it's all going off speedy-like. Like mega boom."

"The altercation."

"Yeah-yeah," the kid says. "The altercation. Full-on tiger fighting, that. I mean, I've seen plenty of full-on tiger combat before on the media feeds and on my hobby games and such, but never for real and never for real up close like that for sure. My mother, she won't let me go all spectator at real tiger fights 'cause of my old man forbid. Both front and say going to the real tiger fights rot my bean. And my old man? My old man, he be down below in India for re-civ rebuildin' and just me and my mom living on *Alaungpaya*. My mom, she's a dealer in the casino so you'd think she'd be all kinds of stretchy since she works the floor as a table skipper, but no way. Those tiger fights, my mom say, those tiger fights are real sin. Kind of crazy religious she. New One Roman Church of the Most Holy Liberator and all that. Not me, though. If you ask me, full-on tiger fighting is hot. You ever watch the tiger fights, officer?"

Flynn grinds his teeth. *God*, he thinks wearily, *this incident reporting is for the freaking birds.* Why this statistical garbage couldn't be handled by some rookie is beyond him. For the love of God, here he is… his last couple of hours left as a security officer, hell, his last few hours alive at all, and he's acting like some kind of glorified meter ward.

For nearly ten years Flynn has been rising through the security ranks aboard *Alaungpaya*, and life as a lawman has been pretty much a fair deal. Steady advancement. Plenty of respect, if not tepid admiration, from most of his fellow officers. Flynn was even nominated for sergeant-at-arms at a local security fraternity chapter a couple of years back. But of course that was before his diagnosis—a full-blown case of Depressus—and Flynn's fall from favor and grace since has been utterly degrading.

When he was first diagnosed with the dreaded affliction, Flynn debated whether to use his knowledge of *Alaungpaya*'s access codes and take matters into his own hands. In the past, at least, that's what a real man would do. Pitch himself right off some restricted staging deck and be done with it. But as a security officer Flynn knows and respects Second Free Zone law. Private Depressus suicides are now prohibited in the confederate orbits with personal estate forfeit penalties assessed at one hundred percent. Even though he has little to his name, Flynn still likes to think he has some semblance of a soul and has a few charities in mind.

His lieutenant, on the other hand, was hardly sympathetic when Flynn leveled the bad news.

"Oh, you've got to be shitting me, Flynn. Really? Depressus?"

"I'm afraid so, sir."

"Perfect. That's just perfect. Damn it to hell, are you sure?"

"The ship doctors seem fairly convinced, sir."

The lieutenant looked away and then back at Flynn. "So, how far along are you?"

Flynn rolled one shoulder and then the other. He stood as tall and courageously as he could. "A few weeks," Flynn replied. "Barge docs told me they patched a notice advising divisional personnel and they were, in turn, supposed to inform you of my situation and medications. The docs also said if I keep on the meds I might be able to cycle out the quarter. I've already locked in an open reservation for Embrace, but I'd really like to keep working as long as I can, if that's all right with you."

His lieutenant threw a stack of folders down on his desk.

"Give me a number."

"I'm sorry, sir? A number?"

"Yeah, give me a number. A timeline. Like, how long do you got? Two months? Five weeks? What's your prognosis?"

"I'd like to keep working as long as I am able, sir."

"That's not an answer. Look, Flynn, I know this has to suck for you and all, but I need to be honest with you here. I've seen plenty of Depressus cases in my time, and believe me, you sad sacks of uselessness just go from worse to pathetic to the point I want to shoot you in the head myself. I'm running a division here, deputy, and if you haven't noticed it's a division on one of the largest residential barges orbiting in the Second Free Zone. The last thing I need is one of my own flaking out and losing his marbles on some *Alaungpaya* civilian or breaking down in tears. So, hey, do me a favor here. Give me a number I can work with."

After a few seconds of mulling it over, Flynn said, "Does a month sound okay?"

His lieutenant scowled. "Pull your file and encode your resignation today. You've got two weeks. Officially I'm putting you on statistics for the remainder of your tenure until termination."

"I don't watch the tiger fights," Flynn says, instantly regretting engaging with the kid's passions.

The kid gasps and rocks back on his heels. "Don't watch the tiger fights?"

"No," Flynn answers. "I don't watch the tiger fights."

"Not even a little?"

"No."

"How come?"

"I don't know, I just don't."

The kid slouches, still unable to contain his disbelief. "But why? Me, I can't help myself but heavy goon at those tiger fights. Grrrrr, they the bestest."

Flynn has had enough. Quickly he slips his left hand around the kid's head and presses the recorder hard into the side of the boy's skull. The intensity of his grip and the edged pressure from the small device hurts like hell and Flynn knows it. It feels good to Flynn to inflict a little pain, and once more he feels dark waves of misplaced, Depressus-fueled rage bubbling up inside. The kid gets his focus swift.

"Hey, man—take it easy!"

"I don't have time for this, son. What happened?"

The boy winces. "Right-right—ow! So, that big redhead? Sh-she goes after the first woman at speed and attacks. And that first one? She like knows that redhead be coming at her so she drops sideways with a kick and bounces that redhead right off the walls. The redhead hits the ground and next the first woman drops, like, a zillion elbows rapid, like, all over on her. Never seen such speed. I can't be sure, but I think she might've broken that redhead's leg."

"Did the redhead scream?"

"Nah, but she be done for sure, you bet. Hallelujah chorus and done. Then—drong! The other woman start to mark her."

"Mark her?"

"C'mon, man. See, that's what I'm talking about. If you ever bothered to goon the tiger fights, now, you'd know."

Flynn recalls hearing something about the fighters' sadistic traditions.

"Did the first woman bite out the redhead's eye?"

"Didn't look like it to me," the kid answers, squirming. "But that other one? She looked up and saw me gooning straight at her. Freaked me all out. Kind of thought for a second there she was going to attack me, but then she turned and dropped down one of those plummet chutes back there. The second one, I think."

Flynn skeptically eyeballs the access tunnel and the plummet chute mouths along the walls. On *Alaungpaya*, plummet chutes are used to provide convenient deck-to-deck transitions. But no one really uses the chutes that much anymore because the twisting, one-way tubes are dank, poorly lit, and sticky with trash. For the nine-billionth time in his wretched life, Flynn wonders why visual verifiers aren't on *Alaungpaya*'s commercial decks. Screw the whining about freedoms and personal liberties, not having visuals in sectors like this is just plain stupid.

"What happened next?" Flynn asks.

"I run and report it straight up. Then, like, ten minutes later you come."

"What about the redhead? A messed-up leg like you say, I don't think she could have gotten far. Did you see where she took off to?"

"No," the kid answers. "When I run and report it and wait for you, she was, like, gone. Maybe she took a plummet chute too."

Flynn releases the kid's neck and steps back. Grumbling, the kid makes a big show of rubbing the indentations on the side of his head.

"Is that it?" the kid asks.

"Yeah," Flynn answers. "That's it."

Flynn puts a header of MISCELLANEOUS on the incident record file and presses the save icon. So a couple of hard cases go at it, what does he care? The two women are not around now and only this goofy-looking kid here is the wiser. Without visual documentation to confirm the boy's story, who can honestly prove this incident even happened?

But Flynn knows the kid is telling the truth. Emotional fluctuations on the recording device don't lie. An assault was committed, and following up on it is still his duty. But as he chews it over some more, he decides to let the whole misadventure pass and erases the file.

Statistical beat, his ass.

Flynn holsters the recording device on his duty belt and then droops his uniform's hood over his head.

"Thank you for your cooperation," Flynn says. He shoos the boy away. "Now, do me a favor, kid, and get lost. Your mother needs her pressure pins."

GOONING ON THE FEEDS

TIGER FIGHT "SEA RAGE BONANZA XVI" PROMO FEED—0:30

CLIENT: Tiger Fight Federation International, TFFI
PRODUCTION ENGAGEMENT: 2516 Spring/Autumn Cycles N/S
Hemispheres

VISUAL FEED 1: (OPENING GRAPHICS) IN HAMMERED, RUSTY
STEEL—EACH LETTER OF THE TFFI LOGO DROPPING INTO
PLACE LIKE A HEAVY ANVIL. TFFI LOGO BLOWN AWAY IN A
BLINDING FIREBALL. ZOOM FROM THE LINGERING SMOKE, THE
WORD—*PRESENTS*—AGAIN, BLOWN AWAY IN A SECOND, MORE
EXPLOSIVE, FIREBALL.

AUDIO: LOUD EXPLOSIONS

[CUT TO] (LOGO): *SEA RAGE BONANZA XVI*

VOICEOVER: (WOMAN—HUSKY-VOICED, SEDUCTIVE) Your wait
(*pause*) is over!

AUDIO: POUNDING DRUM BEATS, HYPER-PACED MUSIC, THE
DEAFENING ROAR OF CHEERING TIGER FIGHT FANS.

VOICEOVER (CONT.): TFFI's Sea Rage Bonanza XVI! Friday,
June 6th! Live! Credit broadcast feeds 88-138. Goon it!

[CUT TO] VISUAL FEED 2: RAPID MONTAGE SHOTS OF VARIOUS
TIGER FIGHT MATCH ACTION. MAN-ON-WOMAN. WOMAN-ON-
WOMAN. MAN-ON-MAN. BODY BLOWS. COMPOUND FRACTURES.
TEETH SPLASHED WITH BLOOD.

AUDIO: SOUNDS OF FLESH-ON-FLESH FIGHTING, AGONIZED
SCREAMS, DEFIANT WARRIOR ROARS.

VOICEOVER (CONT.): On the deck of European Alliance
Carrier *Forseti*... the most anticipated, multi-match tiger-
fighting spectacle ever assembled. An all-star lineup
including twelve-time Golden Band welterweight champion
Jinx Belskaia and South American Central Jujitsu
Institute takedown champ Carlos "Soul Killer" Marta.
Their last match was a draw, this time it's to the death!

AUDIO: MORE HYPER-PACED MUSIC. HEAVY DRUMS CLIMBING TO
CRESCENDO.

[CUT TO] VISUAL FEED 3: HIGHLIGHTS OF SOME OF BELSKAIA
AND MARTA'S MORE VIOLENT FINISHES. (Note: TFFI
Authorized Visuals only.)

VOICEOVER (CONT.): Watch as former warriors from across
the world take their grudge matches to a whole new level.
Twenty sponsored tiger fights on the Sea Rage card in
all! With weaponized zip rounds! All live! All action!

[CUT TO] VISUAL FEED 4: SIDEBAR OF FEED CHANNELS SCROLL RIGHT AS ADDITIONAL MONTAGE OF FIGHT ACTION AND KILLS ROLLS. INCLUDE AERIAL SHOT OF PREVIOUS SEA RAGE EVENTS ON THE EUROPEAN ALLIANCE CARRIER *FORSETI.*

VOICEOVER (CONT.) One hundred percent certified combat and murderous mêlées! Goon your heart out as up-and-coming fighters fresh from the syndicate enlistment obligations clash and claw their way to glory on the open seas! Friday, June 6th! *Be there!*

[DISSOLVE] VISUAL FEED 5: THIRD GARGANTUAN FIREBALL FILLS THE ENTIRE SCREEN.

AUDIO: MASSIVE, ROLLING EXPLOSION.

[Note: *Translation budget covers all remaining languages and surviving Chinese dialects (Mandarin, Wu, Min Nan, etcetera.)*]

FLYNN, THE EXIT INTERVIEW

ALAUNGPAYA SECURITY EMPLOYEE—FLYNN, JEDIDIAH—C-CLASS.
BADGE NUMBER: 2294; SFZ Citizen Identification 821612403;
Mandatory Exit Assessment: Case #363-737-E/Recorded for
Archive Retrieval/Date: 7.1.2521 Current Cycle

PERSONNEL ASSESSMENT AGENT: What is your primary reason for leaving
Alaungpaya Security Services, Deputy Flynn?

JEDIDIAH FLYNN: [Inaudible]

PAA: Deputy Flynn?

JF: You're not really asking me that, are you?

PAA: Just answer the stated questions, please.

JF: I mean, wouldn't something like that be in my file already?
God, you know damn well why I put in my notice. My lieutenant
practically held my hand when I encoded my resignation.

PAA: This may be true. However, the archive needs linear cohesion, deputy. Please, just state the reason for your resignation for the audio record.

JF: Fine. I have Depressus. Linear cohesion happy now?

PAA: Yes. And for what it's worth, let me offer you my condolences. I know how this must be difficult for you. Now, then, first things first. Are you lucid this afternoon, Deputy Flynn?

JF: What do you mean?

PAA: Are you clear-headed? Are you on any heavier-than-normal medication or substances unknown that might affect your answers today?

JF: I'm still on duty.

PAA: Yes-yes.

JF: I'm still a security officer for the next twenty-four hours.

PAA: Yes, but your file indicates you have been reprimanded twice for overindulging your medication levels in recent weeks. It's not that I don't believe you, but I also know it's not uncommon for personnel to throw caution to the wind so close to termination.

JF: Look, I'm fine. Basic even dosage and barge-medical-approved. I know the rules. All that stuff? I was going through a rough couple of days and made a mistake. What, you want to give me a blood test right now, is that it? Wipe my tongue and take a saliva sample?

PAA: We just want perfect linear cohesion for the archive.

JF: Yeah, right.

PAA: Please calm down.

JF: I'm calmed down.

PAA: Deputy Flynn, let me be frank. While I sympathize with your distress, yours is not the first Depressus security case I've interviewed. I fully understand how normal discourse can cause aggravation and induce radical temperament fluxes in those with Depressus. I repeat, I mean to cause you no grief this afternoon. So if you simply answer the questions succinctly and with proper composure, we'll be done with this in no time.

JF: [Inaudible]

PAA: What?

JF: Just how many questions are you going to ask me anyway?

PAA: Mmm. Fifty, give or take.

JF: [Inaudible]

PAA: How's that?

JF: Nothing. Just forget it.

PAA: Good. Now, then, let's move on with some basics. In your own words, what was most satisfying about your position as a deputy for *Alaungpaya* Security Services?

JF: Nothing.

PAA: Nothing? Come, come. All those years of service, there must be something you found satisfying.

JF: Well, maybe some of the respect, I suppose.

PAA: Excellent answer. Good, good.

JF: Some of the camaraderie. Helping people out of bad situations, you know, stuff like that.

PAA: I see. And what during your tenure did you find the least gratifying?

JF: Besides the fact that you guys should seriously consider changing the name of *Alaungpaya*'s security force? I'd say the least satisfying would be the compensation.

PAA: Of course you do realize *Alaungpaya* Security Service personnel are some of the highest-compensated law-enforcement officers in the Second Free Zone.

JF: Oh, come off it. Some of the highest paid? We both know for a fact the compensation assessment for *Alaungpaya* security bites the big one. It's laughable even with last year's benefit upgrades. And I should know—I'm in the union.

PAA: Again, I must caution you about your tone of voice.

JF: My tone of voice? My tone of voice? You know what? Get bent.

PAA: See, the direction you seem so insistent on taking this—

JF: What? Can't I even express myself openly anymore outside of a doctor's office? Or is speaking my mind forbidden now too?

I just don't like the fact that you jerks have to do some kind of post mortem on me and I haven't even killed myself yet. Damn it... [Inaudible] See? This is what I'm talking about. Shit, I knew I should have just opted for uploading this crap instead of doing an exit interview in person.

PAA: That was your choice.

JF: My choice. None of us have a choice.

PAA: Is something wrong, deputy?

JF: [Inaudible]

PAA: Deputy? Are you all right?

JF: No, wait. I'm okay. I'm sorry. I just need to breathe for a second or two. Hold on.

PAA: Do you want a glass of water?

JF: [Inaudible] Just get on with whatever you're going to ask.

PAA: Maybe we should arrange for another time.

JF: Do I look like I have time to spare? I've signed up for the next Embrace ceremony, you officious putz. Just finish the interview. Please, just ask whatever it is you're supposed to ask.

PAA: Okay, then. Let's see. Above average arrest records, substantial and noted commendations, etcetera, etcetera... Well, if it weren't for several of your recent outbursts and the aforementioned medication indulgences, I'd say your career record is quite admirable and worthy of full termination benefits.

JF: [Inaudible] Nope—not fine. Not fine at all. Here it comes...

PAA: Excuse me?

JF: I said, do you have any tissues?

WHY SO BLUE?

In the diagnostic silos of Fogarty's Medical Conditions and Diseases Index, the following brief synopsis is provided for Second Free Zone cases of the affliction known as Depressus:

Depressus (VAST D.), *n.*—a severe, stage-classified psychosis. VAST D. is a mental disorder affiliated with the liberalized citizens of the Second Free Zone confederacies (suborbital tracking orbits) characterized by abject downward mood swings, sudden bouts of misplaced rage, anhedonia, sleep disturbances, and feelings of worthlessness and hopelessness. The diagnostic criteria for VAST D. include the following: a depressed form, a marked reduction of interest or pleasure in virtually all normal behaviors, as well as occasional flare-ups of intense anger [*see* substratum Endogenous D., Exogenous D., bipolar disorder, also 2-79A Syn. Clinical depressive disorders.] According to the FG & SFZHO Depressus affects 5.5% of the liberalized citizens of the Second Free Zone, and the negative bearing on commercial interests is estimated at 16 trillion credits annually. The disorder is theorized to result from a genetic electrochemical malfunction of the limbic system aggravated by continued variance in high-altitude exposure in the Second Free Zone. Recent research has shown the number of glial cells in the subgenual prefrontal cortexes of people with familial VAST D. to be significantly dwarfed by those of otherwise mentally healthy citizens. Treatment with psychopharmaceutical agents (including tenth-generation tricyclic antidepressants, nano-selective serotonin reuptake inhibitors [NSSRIs], ancient monoamine oxidase [A-MAO] inhibitors) is ineffective for sustained control in most cases. To date, long-term stabilization of the disease is impossible, with affected persons opting for now-sanctioned mass-suicide events.

Ah, Depressus.

Quite the bitch, but it sure does thin the herd.

GOING DOWN

Koko rockets down the plummet chute.

It is greasy in the chute's core. The inner funneling dimensions wind her around and around as though she's being flushed through an industrialized carnival ride, and the tangy pong of runny garbage and dried urine is so intense it makes her eyes water. Knowing she needs distance, she tucks in her limbs for speed. How many decks has she passed? Thirty? Maybe fifty? How big is *Alaungpaya* anyway?

Soon a graffiti-streaked sign whips by overhead, indicating Koko is nearing the plummet chute's bottom and approaching *Alaungpaya*'s main entertainment decks. Easing her rate of speed with friction points on her boot heels and chafed elbows, she readies herself and three seconds later is ejected out a set of rubberized doors with all the fanfare of a mechanical fart.

Koko lands on her back and loses her wind. She sucks and sucks and finally finds her air. Whipping her head around, she discovers she's in another access tunnel and quickly gets to her feet. She straightens her soiled tank top, dislodges her shorts from the crack of her butt, and prepares herself for the bounty agent. After a full minute of her being cocked in a ready stance and waiting for the redhead's imminent arrival, it dawns on Koko she must have lost the bounty agent, at least for now.

Relaxing some and adopting the stride of just another SFZ citizen, Koko struts out of the access tunnel. In some buffed chrome near the tunnel's exit, she catches her reflection and notices a splotch of blood still on her chin from when she started to mark the woman. Koko licks her thumb and wipes the blood clear.

Emerging from the tunnel, Koko enters a colossal skylighted atrium that stretches upward through the rigid circularized core of *Alaungpaya*. A set of elevated and dual-directional causeways encircles the hive-like core and apparently serves as the main thoroughfare around a huge centralized casino. The perimeter of the concourse is lined with narrow storefronts, seedy discotheques, and the standard hot-holes of the vice trades. Not overly crowded, but not exactly starved for business either; it's pretty easy for Koko to blend into the multi-pigmented ebb humping its way around. She trucks left on the inner loop, the cacophony of a thousand whistles and thrums amplifying into an oceanic roar in her ears.

She needs a place to hole up and get her head together, and there are a lot of tall time-break bins and hospitality grottos to choose from. Even if she's still being tracked by that redhead, it would take the agent more than a little while to search all the endless crannies towering around her. Koko's blood buzzes. Gunfights on the fly with a cluster of cocky CPB security stiffs are one thing. Getting all personal with someone trained to kill you in hundreds of brutal ways is another matter entirely. Regretfully Koko knows she should have just finished that bounty agent off and taken her eye, but that dopey kid with the weird yellow hair was watching her.

No matter, Koko. Keep moving.

Keep moving.

In her past, when booking a place to stay, Koko has always opted for ponying up the extra credits to be around a better stratum of people. But seeing that things have gone all tiger-fight with Delacompte siccing a freelance asset after her, Koko realizes she needs to ratchet down her usual modus operandi. She looks for a cheesier tower unit, and after three thousand meters slaloming through the crowds, she settles on one called, of all things, Wonderwall. Wall, yes, but calling the low-rent tower facility a wonder is more than a bit of a stretch. Twenty stories, set back on a furcated spur, with daily and extended occupancy rates, it'll have to do. Koko pushes through the frosted lobby doors.

Inside it takes Koko more than a little while to manage one of Wonderwall's unstaffed hospitality displays. The interface is a convoluted mess, the Byzantine navigation resets no doubt programmed by fumble-headed curve draggers. Finally, she manages to steer through the registration silos, and selects an available smoking room on quick exits with a decent view of the concourses and *Alaungpaya*'s central casino. Koko could have opted for an exterior unit but her hunch is, if Delacompte sent that bounty agent after her, she'll stand a better chance of catching the woman by making a fuss down on the concourse than by taking in a pressurized view of the weather-strewn sky. When she confirms her reservation, a bright blue balloon squeaks—a message from Wonderwall management congratulating her on her reservation. A second balloon fades in on the display, boasting that her room includes a state-of-the-art flash shower and complimentary mini bar. La-dee-fucking-dah.

Koko crosses the lobby and one set of two lift doors yawns wide, sensing her presence. As she enters the lift, it takes her all of a half-second to make an anemic-looking dealer painted in the corner like a pale stain. The dealer wears a checkered polyester cowl, and the give and take between them assures them both that they are not enemies. Using some universally accepted sign language, Koko signals for a quarter pouch of crinkle-flake and the dealer's sleepy eyes drift clear for the transaction. He holds up three fingers as the price. Koko nods and takes out her credits. The dealer takes the credits, and with a smile he hands over a black plastic baggie bundled with a red pig-tail ribbon.

Once upstairs and in her room, Koko is nearly bowled over by the sharp, acrid stink of chlorine disinfectant masked pathetically with a crisp haze of lime. As described on the registration display in the lobby, the view from the room's smudged window does tunnel down onto the barge's casino, and, parting the thin blinds, Koko stands still for a moment.

A few hours ago she'd been asleep with Archimedes without a care, and now this. This. On the run and on her own, her confidence shaken. For a moment Koko recalls all her recruitment trips to Melbourne and Perth, when she found Archimedes and the rest of his giddy mates bopping around the discotheques. Those hot nights when she worked him through his boywhore tryouts and found Arch knew how to please a woman in all the right ways.

The stress of her predicament finally starts to catch up with her. She shivers in the chilly recycled air and thinks about The Sixty. Pines for it, actually. All the space, light, and pore-drenching warmth. Images of Archimedes' blown-apart corpse and her bar aflame rush back, and Koko has to steady herself.

She pushes back the bitterness.

No time to feel sorry for yourself, Koko. No time for thinking like that at all.

Koko inspects the room's touted mini-bar basket and discovers some rolling skins along with some arousal lubricants, an assortment of tiny bottles of cut-rate alcohol, and a Jacob's ladder of antibiotic condoms. The package of rolling skins is Second Free Zone micro, cherry-flavored and emblazoned with scrolling advertisements for oxygenized supplements. Koko flips the package and snaps out a couple of papers. Crushing some of her newly purchased crinkle-flake into the skin's fold, she rolls a tight, sedative smoke to even out her nerves.

She pats her pockets and looks around. Keeping with the lowbrow nature of Wonderwall, no free laser sticks are about to spark her spliff to life, and she hangs her head. Great, more of her crappy luck on the wane.

She rolls a few more smokes for later and drops the unlit spliffs on the night table next to the bed. Then she snatches a couple of bottles of generic beauty from the mini-bar basket and—*crack-crack*—pours the two vials of knockoff booze straight down her throat to avoid the cheap taste. Her esophagus protests the liquor's burn, but the sudden warmth in her belly helps a bit. Koko kicks off her heavy boots and strips out of the rest of her clothes.

Entering the bathroom, she takes a thin white towel from the rack and takes a good look at her body in the wall mirror behind the sink. Her piercings, the slight cellulite dimples just off the curve of her snugged panties, the tattoo of scrolled flames slashed up and down her inner right arm. Just past a slight sheen of alcohol fat, she still has some of the hammered definition left to her stomach, and she's grateful her small breasts aren't losing their youthful lift just yet.

After removing the rings and studs from all her piercings and placing them on the edge of the sink, Koko considers the two major scars on her body: a mottled star on the right side where a rib poked through and a sash of pink tissue on her upper left shoulder. The second scar was her first major wound from action. Caught the full, brunt force of a rebounding mortar pulse on deployment in some godforsaken North African ghetto, back when she was all gung-ho and keen to bring the hammer down on de-civ militants. She can't recall how or where the rib wound happened or even when. 2510? Or was it 2513? The later year sounds right, but where was it? So much proxy-nation and de-civ craziness the years blur. The rib wound might have happened during a building collapse in Luxembourg, she can't be sure.

Koko braces herself against the sink.

Delacompte.

Sending an SI security team and now some bounty agent to take her out? What, over some vendor infraction with a couple of vacationing Kongercat re-civs? This has to be some kind of a mistake. It doesn't make sense.

KIERAN SHEA

Standing there, Koko recollects a time when she accidentally met up with Delacompte at an airbase near the last played-out wells of the Samotlor oil fields. At the time, Koko hadn't shared any duty assignments with Delacompte for a few cycles, and she remembers they were both powering on toward separate syndicate actions: Koko heading to a six-week deployment on lignite resource operations in Aduun Chuluu, and Delacompte locked in on an unclassified government assassination. It was, as they say, just one of those things. A chance crossing of paths on a layover, duly forgettable.

Delacompte claimed her assignment was to be one of her last stints in the field and the hefty payday was more than going to cover her tuition at the Institut d'Etudes Politiques in Paris. What was it Delacompte said she was going to specialize in? Oh yeah, that's right: restorative consumption patterns. Whatever that meant. Strapped up tight in their BDUs, they were throwing back drinks at the airbase bar when Delacompte shared the news she was planning to pull the plug on her military career.

"Wow, so Portia Delacompte is giving up the life? Well, I can't say that I'm totally shocked. Always knew you were headed for something better than the rest of us, Big D. Someplace special."

"Can't fight forever," Delacompte said. "And you and I both know there's no real future in all this. Think about it. Over the long haul, doing the dirty work on planet restructuring for the corporate masters and their sock-puppet governments? You've seen the life-expectancy charts for humps like us. Sooner or later, we all go down. And when we do, we go down ugly."

"Says the Miss Officer Class here buying the drinks."

Delacompte frowned. "Don't give me that shit. Yeah, I'm raking in the officer credits these days, but so fucking what? I've earned it. Don't forget, I'm a lot older than you, Martstellar, and I've been lucky too. Sure, you stay with it and quit bucking the systems, maybe you too can get promoted someday, but then what, huh? Answer me that. Trust me, girl, being an officer ain't all it's cracked up to be. Just penury of a different color, and me, I want more out of the time I got left."

"You're not that old."

"Cresting thirty-four, babe."

"Oh, boo-hoo-hoo. You look great."

"Thanks." Delacompte stabbed her finger on the top of the bar. "But what about you, huh? Don't you want something better than this?"

Delacompte's question made Koko uncomfortable. What was she talking about? More than being a soldier for hire? Honestly, Koko didn't know. Commercial mercenary work was what Koko had trained for. It'd been her life, her entire world, and she felt she was good at it. Even in her rare free moments of reflection, Koko never truly considered anything other than the next mission that came down the pike or her mind-numbing times off on leave. Yeah, the grind sometimes got her down, but Koko assumed that was just part of being a warrior on call. After all, she was engineered in the third reconstruction collectives. At fifteen she tested average intelligence, but received high marks for stamina and physicality. What else was she supposed to do? Work in some goddamn re-civ manufacturing plant? Be a passive service worker and click off time in an underpaid, trenched existence like an ordinary schmo? No way.

Koko tried to change the subject.

"Well, my hat's off to you anyway, D," Koko said. "I mean, if I had a hat. Hey, do tactical helmets count as hats?"

"You didn't answer my question."

Koko swallowed an inch of poison from her glass and coughed. "Which one?"

"Don't you want more than this?"

"And what? Go to some fancy business school like you?"

"Maybe. Or something else. You've got options."

"Options? Yeah, right. Face facts, D. I'm not as smart as you. Never have been, but I sure as hell wish I was. Like you said before, you've been really lucky and you're older, cranking in that officer-class pay. I've always admired you, and maybe someday when I make a decent rank and don't screw it up I'll think of something else to do. But for now? Like it or not, this is the life I lead."

Delacompte picked up her drink. She took a reflective sip and then motioned to a feed monitor above the bar, squinting.

"You know, if you cycled out of your current obligations you could always try your hand at some cage raging."

Koko looked fuzzily up at the feed screen. The monitor was showing some old highlight footage of TFFI tiger fights with the sound turned down low. Koko grimaced and then spluttered.

"Oh, come off it. Don't make me laugh…"

"I'm not kidding around," Delacompte persisted. "You can make some decent credits in those matches, and you're a natural. Don't forget, I've seen you in close-quarter situations. When those tiger fighters hit it big, some of them make good money."

Koko drank some more poison. "I'll pass."

"Hey, if you want, I know somebody over at TFFI. Guy is a former syndicate merc, just like us. I could patch him and see if he can get you a slot in one of their training programs."

"Oh, yeah? What guy is this?"

"Former demolition specialist I fucked back in Panjshir."

"Oh, in Panjshir. When the hell were you in Panjshir?"

"Year back."

"So this guy? Any good?"

"I think so."

"You think so?"

Delacompte looks off with mock wistfulness. "Ah, there are so many. I get confused."

They both broke down laughing.

"Yeah, well," Koko said, getting control of herself, "thanks for the suggestion, but seriously. No way in hell am I doing some media slut's version of staged combat just so some loser on credit-view can get off, thank you very much. Besides, that stuff, D? Full-on tiger fighting at the professional level? From what I hear I'd last a day in those fighting pits, tops. Even with their so-called training program, don't you know those pros love taking out fresh meat like me? I hear they even handicap the matches to weed out the up-and-comers. Probably drop me in a four-on-one bout for my first go-around. Oh, yeah, some big payday that would be. Eye-gouge and body-bag central."

Delacompte shook her head and set down her drink.

"You know," Koko said, "now that you're going all hotshot professional, you're going to have to play nice on a whole other bunch of fronts."

"I know..."

"All buttoned up and grounded. No social wilding. Definitely no more sportfucking whoever happens your way in Panjshir. I hate to bring it up, but have you selected your creed yet?"

Delacompte flung back the rest of her drink and winced. "Working on it. Been studying the executive hiring trends, and the monistic approach might be the call. Non-exclusivity leveraging the most job opportunities."

Koko paused. "Wait. You don't mean?"

Delacompte nodded. "The New One Roman Church of the Most Holy Liberator."

"Wow. That's, uh, that's—"

An announcement in rolling languages began to bleat overhead, and Delacompte realized her transport was boarding. They both stiffened a bit and said their goodbyes, finishing the rest of their "good running into you" banter with a couple of fist pounds.

After lifting her pack, Delacompte shoved off and was almost to her gate when Koko shouted at her from the bar.

"Hey!"

Delacompte turned.

"I bet I could run a place better than this!"

Delacompte looked around, puzzled.

"Not an airbase, D! A bar! I bet I could run a really great bar!"

Delacompte gave Koko a thumbs up and hit the ramp.

* * *

Yeah, I guess I planted the seed then, didn't I? Koko thinks wretchedly. Man, maybe if they hadn't crossed paths that day Koko wouldn't be in such a jam now.

But why? Why would Delacompte want to do this to her? Is Koko some sort of liability? She has nothing but veneration and respect for the woman and for what she's accomplished. After all their time campaigning for the syndicates and multinationals together, after all she has done for Delacompte and—good God—if you consider that night back in—

A light snaps on in Koko's head.

"Oh, no…" she whispers.

Finland.

No. It can't be.

No way. It can't possibly be that simple. Suddenly, a dark, violent tide of memories starts to seize Koko and her knees weaken. She has to force her mind to go blank lest the recollections overwhelm her.

Why that little… Now? Now? After hiring me on The Sixty? Wasn't it understood? Delacompte is coming after me after all this time has passed? Good God, I saved her from—damn it. Get a hold of yourself, Koko. Even if this is all about what went down back in Finland, no way does whatever happened have any bearing on your present situation. What matters right now is survival. Like it or not, an order has been given and there is a price on your head and you're in unfamiliar territory. Focus.

Her mind sufficiently seared with the most likely reason for Delacompte's vendetta, Koko twists the towel and grips both ends of it just above her breasts. Elbows tucked inward and chin down, she steams back into the bedroom and breaks into a series of long-neglected kick drills. Motor patterns riding on drilled but not forgotten reflexes, she teeters a bit as she centers her core and it takes more than a few missed kicks to find her rhythm. Echoes from fight instructors resonate in her memory.

Protect on attack and keep your head clear.

Be alert. Be ready.

Be *balanced*.

Fully limbered up, Koko whips the towel onto the bed. Along the wall she sees a power cord trailing from a set of two floor sockets. The cord doesn't seem critical to the room's functionality, so Koko yanks it free from its housing and whips the cord over her head for ten minutes of footwork until the balls of her bare feet grow hot. A belch percolates from her lips, and she charges back into the bathroom. Koko retches up the cheap mini-bar beauty along with the last remnants of the drink she bought back on *Hesperus 6*.

She stares at her sweaty reflection in the mirror and smears the dripping bile from her lips. Her eyes are green, hard flames.

Goddamn you, Delacompte.

Cranking the flash shower settings to just above freezing, Koko tugs off her dingy panties, steps into the stall, and lets the surrounding jets of misted, cold water lash away the pungent film seeping from her flesh. She rinses the last of the vomit from her gums with repeated jabs of her index finger and lathers herself all over with a heavy squeeze of cinnamon-scented disinfectant. Soon her aches are numb and her head clears. After stepping out of the shower, Koko buffs the remaining cold moisture from her nakedness with a second thin towel hanging by the sink. She feels cleaner than she's felt for days.

If he's still on *Alaungpaya*, it's high time to track down her old contact, Juke Ramirez. Get strapped and work on getting good and gone. Ditch her look. Definitely a new hairstyle for cover too. Something different, but cut short for if and when things get ugly again.

Koko picks up and jams her clothes into the room's courtesy cleaner mounted on the wall and sets the device for quick clean. As the clothes run through the ionizing cycles, she crosses the room to the window and looks down on the red pulsating lights in

Alaungpaya's central casino. Thirty seconds later, a soft ping tells her the clothes are sterilized and dry.

Pocketing her piercing jewelry and her rolled crinkle-flake smokes for later, Koko dresses quickly and heads out.

JUKE'S

"What is this stuff?" Koko asks.

At nearly twenty-two stone in his ratty red bathrobe and yellow dhoti, Juke Ramirez sways in his paraplegic swing like a shaved ape.

"Mock tequila," Juke answers with a slight chuckle that is as fleshy as it is deep. "Do you like it, my dear? Made this zippy little batch myself."

Koko frowns at the greenish liquor in her glass. "When you offered me a drink before, I thought I specifically asked for some beauty."

Juke smiles. "Ah, beauty. Your drink of choice. Beauty is always good, but this will get you there, only faster. I made it as an indulgent nod to my late ancestors, the long-ago great kings of the vast American narco-haciendas. You wouldn't think it from the look of me, but I come from a long bloodline of drug-cartel royalty. Back when there still was a semblance of the drug-cartel royalty or an America."

Koko finishes the venom with a shiver and drops the glass on the table between them. She glances back behind her and sees the blackened windows and locked doorway to Juke's small storefront as she runs her tongue over her upper front teeth. Juke's shop is located in *Alaungpaya*'s commercial sector, Deck 7.

"Tastes like moss clippings," Koko says, turning back around.

Juke's bushy eyebrows pump. "Familiar with that, are we?"

"Yeah," Koko shoots back. "Maybe my unknown ancient ancestors were part Malinois attack dog."

"Mmm. Bellyaches. Could be from all your fun-in-the-sun, crotch-lapping introspection, no?"

"Are you always this agitating with your customers?"

"Only the ones I'm fond of, dearest."

"Yeah, right."

"Forgive me," Juke adds languidly, "but what's with the chaste get-up? The last time I saw you I believe you were sashaying around in a string bikini. I like the blue hair, though. A nice touch. Quite sassy."

Koko surveys her new threads and runs her fingers through the spiky fronds of her new hairstyle. It's true, back on The Sixty she did favor clothes that showed a little more skin. The manufactured islands are a jungle after all, but the ultraviolet exposure and high-altitude nippiness of the Second Free Zone demands a full-coverage, sartorial upgrade. Now none of Koko's skin is bare other than her head, the rest cloaked in an acrylic black bodysuit complete with gloves. Over the bodysuit she wears a faux leather jacket with plenty of pockets. The jacket hangs beyond her hips and is also black.

God, it practically killed her to cut off and color her hair, but it was necessary. At the salon during the coloring process the attendant suggested a nail treatment, and Koko played along. She then asked the attendant if they did fingernail strengthening and sharpening. The salon attendant gave Koko a measured look and said yes, in fact, they did. Now Koko's fingernails are scalpel-sharp and ready for combat, the pale tips peeking through slits slashed into the bodysuit's gloves.

In any other circumstance, having to see a craven bowel-scrounge like Juke Ramirez would be about as high on Koko's to-do list as jamming a rusty tack in her own eye. A slobbering troll with a perilous lack of loyalty, Juke is a former full-time arms dealer who used to indiscriminately sell weaponry to all sides during minor commercial conflicts. A real go-to guy if your syndicate handlers pinched the budget, an enabler with no moral stakes whatsoever. For a long time Juke was quite successful at plying his dark wares from the fringes, but then came his paralysis (the result of a truly unsatisfied customer feeling gypped on an ordnance transaction), and Juke decided he'd tried his dissolute fortunes for far too long. Now, sporting a quiet air of respectability as a game-maintenance vendor on *Alaungpaya*, Juke still manages to peddle a deadly sideline. When Koko learned he was still aboard, she knew he'd have the hardware she needs.

Beneath his bathrobe Juke scratches a hairy pectoral and powers forward on his sling. "This lovely piece right here has all the capabilities I think you're looking for," he says. "Four settings, radial stun coverage, collapsible housing, and the improved seventy-two-hour power grid for pulse optimization. What do you think? Shall I wrap it up for you or do you have fresh errands you need to run on *Alaungpaya* today?"

Koko takes the gun from Juke's outstretched hand and drops into a few firing stances. She swings the weapon around for weight and switches grips. She has to hand it to the doughy blackguard, the big pervert knows her tastes. Inserting the power chip into the gun, she inspects the digitized readout on the weapon's housing. The number indicates three thousand rounds.

Wow... Koko *likey*.

Sig Sauer.

Five hundred years of worldwide collapse and chaos—bet those lederhosen-sporting artifacts had no idea their little wagon factory would still be around, kicking so much ass. Chocolate and guns, those Swiss sons of bitches truly knew their way to a girl's heart.

"How long before—"

"Before the Sig is too hot to handle?" Juke ponders this question. "If I'm not mistaken, I believe the Sig 1-9Z can nudge up against the pulse round limits and barely feel warmer than a kitten soaking up some sun."

"Cool."

"Improved aeration technology," Juke adds and then switches the subject. "I assume, given your being here and inquiring about a gun, that you're in a wee spot of trouble."

Koko fills Juke in on her woeful tale so far, leaving out her suspicions about Delacompte and their experience back in Finland.

"My word, that is peculiar," he replies. "But Portia Delacompte? Why would Delacompte want to get rid of you? I thought you two were old war chums. I mean, wasn't she the one who set you up with your operation down on The Sixty in the first place?"

"She did."

"And now she wants you dead? It's just so odd. So, is Delacompte up here on *Alaungpaya* as well?"

"No. Little Miss Gutless Corporate Hotshot sent a freelancer. Some big-boned redhead. Had those freaky neck-extension chokers—you know, the ones those jintoes from New South Africa favor? Came over with me on a shuttle from *Hesperus 6*. Once aboard, she followed me down an access tunnel. Guess she thought she had the drop on me. Reflexes kicked in."

Juke rubs his chin. "Ah, but a bounty hunter in the Second Free Zone? If I'm not mistaken, isn't that illegal? Then again, Portia Delacompte never struck me as one who played by the rules."

"Rules are out the window."

"So, tell me, Koko. Do you know this redhead?"

Koko shakes her head. "Been out of the game for a while now, Juke," she says. "No, I've never seen her before."

"Any good?"

"Let's just say I was faster."

Juke bobs his head knowingly. "Ah… taking care of business. Just like the good old days, eh, my dear?"

Koko works her jaw. "Yeah, the good old days that I thought were well behind me. Back in the good old days I would have killed her and taken her eye. But like I said, there was this goofy-looking kid staring right at me." Koko pauses. "By the way, Juke, just so you know and all? Archimedes? He died in the firefight down on The Sixty."

Juke's mouth forms a perfect stunned zero for a few seconds before he shakes his head sadly. "Oh, no. Not Archimedes. Oh, that is a tough break, my dear. I'm so sorry. I know how fond you were of that young man."

"Yeah, well. A lot of people were fond of him."

"Of course he did have one of the most perfect asses I've ever caressed."

"Watch it, Juke."

Juke brushes some dandruff from his shoulders. "So, are there any operatives other than this incapacitated redhead looking for you?"

"I don't know yet," Koko says. "Let's just say that your mentioning it reminds me to ask if you have any blades for sale. Based on my recent tangle, I'm probably headed for more one-on-one intensity. Serrated lift point would be great. Something with a clean edge on the opposite side too. Galvanized ceramic is okay, but I definitely want something that's not going to fail on me when I decide to break bones."

"How about something with a little more oomph? I have a batch of the Krier-Tech detonator series. Excellent pitch knives and all the bang you need for when you want to level the playing field. Not even on the market until next quarter."

"A regular knife will be fine."

"Right, then. I believe I have just the item you're looking for. Iberian curved stiletto. Don't even make them anymore. Conceals perfectly and light as a dream. So, will there be anything else beside the knife and gun, then?"

"Nope. That'll do."

Juke powers away on his sling and returns a half-minute later with the blade. As described, the knife is incredibly slim and has a stiletto mechanism with the curved blade secreted away in a textured hilt of webbed rubber. Koko checks the lightweight action on the stiletto and then slides the knife into a pocket on the lower back of her new jacket.

"You know," Juke says, "if I was a man of, say, lesser scruples? I bet I could fire up a quick patch to Delacompte myself in exchange for a nice vacation down there on The Sixty. I'm sure she would be oh so grateful for the assistance, and I must confess, I so do like to swim in the filtered sea."

Koko laughs to herself. Displace the filtered sea is more like it.

"Yeah," Koko says, "but I know you, Juke. You won't rat me out to Delacompte. It's bad for business. Besides, you and me? We have a history. And you damn well know if I survive I'll have to come all the way back here and rip out your throat. Hey, about this Sig. Where's the what-do-you-call-it?"

Juke tugs on an earlobe. He crooks a stubby finger into a packet of chocolate-coated biscuits, hauls out a wafer, and munches. "Can you be a tad more specific?" he asks.

"Does the Sig have a holster?"

"Oh. I'm afraid a holster is not part of the price."

Koko waves the gun at Juke. "Really? Here I stand with a loaded weapon and new attack blade in my back jacket pocket, and now you decide it's time to haggle?"

Juke's chuckles—the sound of bubbles popping in molten cheese.

"Loaded?" Juke caws. "Ha! The Sig 1-9Z doesn't fully arm itself until you leave my quarters. Jamming the hardware in stock and trade is only prudent given my corporal limitations. Even if you tried something physical with me," he gestures to the programmed augmented intelligence weapons on the walls to the right and left behind Koko and grins, "you'd be roasted before you hit the ground."

Koko looks up and sees the vacant barrels of the AI weapons squared lazily on her.

Man, she really needs to ramp up her game. How the hell did she miss those suckers? Koko settles her eyes back on Juke and lets her shoulders sag.

"Damn it. Okay, how about twelve hundred?"

"Fifteen."

"Fifteen hundred for a knife, a gun, and a holster? What am I? An idiot?"

"No, sweetie, you're a former corporate soldier-cum-madam with a bounty on your head."

"Jeez, for fifteen hundred credits throw in a pulse suppressor or at least a list of all the ships up here who are lax on customs and won't repossess my weapons like those nitpicking shits over on *Hesperus 6*."

"My, my, you do want fresh egg in your beer."

"C'mon, Juke. All those boywhores I comped you back down on The Sixty when you came to visit? I think you can cut me some slack here."

"Those revelries I believe were payback for favors already rendered. Sorry, but I do need to make a living up here too, you know. I'll throw in the suppressor but the price today stands."

"Miserable prick." Koko plants her hands on her hips. "Okay, how about thirteen-five?"

"Fourteen."

"Thirteen-seventy-five."

"Fourteen. Go ahead. You're welcome to take your chances unarmed. It doesn't matter to me."

Koko grinds her teeth and groans. Juke gloats happily.

"Excellent. Fourteen hundred credits it is. For the knife, the Sig, a suppressor, one holster, and a list of approved personal armament vessels in the Second Free Zone. Oh come, come, Koko. Don't be so cheerless. You're getting quite the special today. Look, I tell you what. How about I give you my word that if I see anybody slinking around *Alaungpaya* looking for you, especially some redhead, I'll give you a heads-up? Does that make you feel any better?"

"You're a real peach, Juke."

Juke tucks his head and munches another biscuit. "All this being bitter over a minor financial transaction could mean your life isn't very becoming."

Koko hands over nearly the last of her wad of credits. "Yeah, yeah," she says. "Hey, that reminds me. How's the casino on this tub? They play it on the square here?"

Juke sways. "*Alaungpaya*'s casino? It has one of the better reputations in the orbits. Why do you ask?"

"After this fleecing I think I'm going to need a little more run and gun money."

"Do you think that's wise?"

"What?"

"I mean, maybe you should focus on saving yourself. As you said, this redhead is still alive and aboard."

"Can't run without credits. And given that her being up here and running me down isn't exactly legal, engaging in the open with citizens around? I'll take my chances."

Juke sighs and finishes chewing. He picks up a data chit from the table and plugs the chit into a towered workstation humming on his right.

"While it's against my better judgment to give away anything for free, I like you, Koko." He ejects the chit and holds it out to her. "Here. Take this. Before I change my mind."

Koko takes the offered chit and reads the logo on its surface.

"DropSledz?"

"It's a coupon for a very reputable strat-sled rental outfit. If you're going to be so stubborn as to venture out in public, you might need it."

"Aw, thanks, Juke. I'm touched. I take back all the bad things I said about you."

"Yeah, I'm a big softie. Don't spread it around."

Juke then hands over the holster and a black velvet pouch containing a pulse suppressor. Koko shoves the strat-sled coupon into a pocket and removes the suppressor attachment from the pouch. After slaving the suppressor under the barrel on the Sig, she slides the weapon into the holster. Koko clips the holster onto a slit cut into the inside of her jacket and shimmies a bit from side to side to find the feel of the weapon hanging off her body. She draws, spins the gun on two fingers, and slides the weapon home beneath the jacket. In another pocket on her jacket she stashes the pouch and the weapon's extra power grids.

Tweaking the workstation prompts on his right some more, Juke downloads the vessel information she needs to a data plug. He then tosses the plug to Koko, and she pockets it too.

"After you hit the casino, you really should plan on leaving *Alaungpaya* before they initiate the Embrace lockdown."

"The Embrace lockdown? What the hell is the Embrace lockdown?"

Juke twists side to side in his sling like a child dawdling on a swing set. His bathrobe flaps open a bit, and it's a scope of hairy nakedness Koko wishes she hadn't seen.

"Oh, you must have heard about Embrace by now," he says. "Magnificent stuff, really. The current track has *Alaungpaya* on a descending orbit, and we'll be poised over the southern Pacific just after dawn. Those laid low by the dreaded Depressus will jump and commit mass suicide. They shut down all outgoing and incoming air traffic."

"They call that nonsense 'Embrace' here?"

"Branding." Juke shrugs. "Gives the whole spectacle a more secular feel." He indicates a thick, triangular window smudged with grime behind him. "I can see the tortured souls raining down from my little vantage point right here."

Of course Koko has heard about the sanctioned mass suicides. When Depressus first started affecting the population in the Second Free Zone, those suffering the affliction inexplicably sought to kill themselves in gruesome public displays. Headers into well-traveled social decks, setting themselves on fire, blowing themselves up with less than sophisticated bombs in publicly traveled areas. Ultimately the governing confederacies of the Second Free Zone insisted on mass-euthanizing days to quell the distractive carnage. Despite the protests of some hardcore humanist sects, patient advocacy groups applauded the measure and longtime sufferers found themselves relieved not to be alone in their final moments. Or so they claimed.

Not all Second Free Zone barges utilize jumps. Some have chosen massive hydrogen pyres, and others organize collective last suppers laced with poison. All of the more colorful, ghoulish proceedings are broadcast on the live feeds.

"Thanks for the heads-up," Koko says. She gives Juke a farewell salute and then pivots for the exit.

"Oh, one more thing…"

Koko turns.

"Yeah?"

"Where can I reach you if trouble does happen to rear its ugly head?"

Koko hesitates. Again she wonders whether she should trust Juke. If the redheaded bounty agent or someone else does come by, asking about her whereabouts, Juke might forget their "history" and sell her out if the credits are right. Then again, she's pretty sure Juke knows if she survives that kind of a double-cross she's capable of torturing him to death in any number of mind-staggering ways. *What the hell*, she thinks. *At least it won't be totally unexpected.*

"I've checked into a place on the far side of the lower concourse. Wonderwall. Do you know it?"

"Ewww."

"Yeah. My sentiments exactly. I might head back there, but believe me, as soon as I can I'm going to take your advice and get the hell out of here."

"As you should, my dear." Juke nods. "As you most definitely should."

RE-EUALUATE

Vincent Lee drops his head into his open hands and plants his elbows in the clutter atop his cubicle's desk. Clenching the tender flesh inside his cheeks with his teeth, he rolls a nugget of fizzy saliva back down his throat. He rereads the message on his screen prompt once more before erasing it.

Custom Pleasure Bureau Executive Offices
Date: 7.2.2521
To: Lee, Vincent T. (Tikayama) Employee 01124-18930
Contractor/Freelance Employee: Heinz, Cleo F. (Faye) Freelance 89713-99220
Subject: Status Report—Containment; Martstellar, Koko P. (Penelope) Vendor 456712-20189
Trans-Feed Code: 12-33-899 Executive Archive Routes Only (classified)

Following trace of Pod 288, Martstellar, Koko P. (KPM), arrived *Hesperus 6* and confirmed target. Weapons confiscated at Customs. Initiated pursuit of KPM to residential and leisure-class vessel *Alaungpaya*. Upon arrival target became aware of pursuit and target was engaged for containment and erasure. Engagement aborted—medical. Possible witness. Acquiring location of witness and legal enforcement contact for follow-up SOP erasure measure protocols. End transmission.

Lee takes a licorice-flavored hard candy from a dish to his right and crushes it between his molars.

Great. His day has just gone from bad to full-blown shit-puppet shambles.

Lee looks over his cubicle's partition and surveys the other CPB junior executives outside the senior staff offices that line the floor's glassy perimeter. Men and women of similar age to him attending to their assigned SI executive duties with the rote fervor of jacked-up wasps. He wonders how many of them have executive counts on their heads. From the drawn looks on many faces, he imagines more than quite a few. Comes with the territory.

It's not the first time Lee has drearily regretted his career choice. Lee could have pursued any number of reputable and less stressful fields of employment. After all, he possesses the mental proficiencies, raw intelligence, and skills for a livelihood in just about any field. But the glamour and excitement associated with the Custom Pleasure Bureau and The Sixty Islands … those temptations pulled him in like a seductive vortex. Now, with an executive count on his tenure, Lee feels that nagging wash of runny doubt and desperation that threatens to paralyze him.

Lee thinks of his lover, the merchant sailor. His lover has constantly cautioned and encouraged Lee to find other means of gainful employment, something that doesn't hang a deadly sword over even the most minor managerial blunders. *One day*, his sailor boy warned, *that boss of yours is just going to snap like a twig and kill you.*

Gosh, they don't execute accountants when they screw up, do they? Or lawyers, for that matter?

Well, they do execute lawyers when they screw up in most rebuild regions still.

Oh, relax, Lee tells himself. *Martstellar is a former soldier for hire, for crying out loud. She's practically steeped in suspicion and spent years fighting for the multinationals. She is out there scrabbling for her very life—is her winning one little skirmish any surprise? I mean, my word, can you blame the poor woman?*

So Heinz got checked by someone with better moves. It happens. And it's not like this bounty agent Heinz is dead or out of the game altogether, although she damn well should be. The transmission indicated that Heinz is still engaged in active pursuit post-medical. By the day's end? All of this? This whole debacle might be a laughable memory, and Lee will be able to shrug it off with a chilled glass of sparkling wine.

Lee quickly sets about sending Heinz additional instructions. First off, he informs Heinz that classified transmit protocols shall henceforth not be sent via executive archival routes. They are, indeed, engaged in sort of a quasi-illegal action, and he adds that all transmissions should be scrubbed clean of encoded tracers upon Heinz's receipt until the Martstellar situation is closed. And he tells her to forget the witnesses. More dead bodies means additional clean-up, and he'd rather not go through the headache. Lee also decides to up the stimulus on Heinz's assignment by upgrading Koko's elimination to Ultimate Sanction status, fixed credit transfers and percentage incentive bonuses secured upon completion.

There. That ought to motivate you.

The upgrade to Ultimate Sanction on the bounty is, of course, a total lie. Delacompte would never in a million years approve of such an additional measure. But if this all works out his boss will definitely cast an approving eye on Lee's being so cunning and deceitful. Oh, why not. It's not like they're going to make good on the bounty anyway. Lee encodes a note to himself to devise a fool-proof post-operational plan for Heinz's erasure as soon as Koko is eliminated.

Then Lee has a second brilliant idea. He encodes a restricted priority message to the CPB mainframe requesting additional freelance operative personnel files for review. Lee makes it clear he only wants freelance bounty operatives seasoned in the dark arts of taking care of business—ruthless, dedicated professionals who understand the value of zero blowback on assignment and who execute directives without question or mercy.

Moments after sending the request, Lee receives the files on his prompts. He pulls up Martstellar's personnel record as well to compare side by side each potential candidate against Koko's background, skill sets to lethal skill sets. It is good to exploit weaknesses. Lee's cumbrous time under Delacompte has at least taught him that.

In the corner of the projection in front of him, Lee also cues up a highlights archive of Koko's more colorful engagements. After a few minutes of examining the files, he narrows down the list to seven potential operatives and from that seven he shaves off three of the candidates to reach a final four. Then he sees that two of the best operatives (a couple of really good-looking men from the shores of the Black Sea) are unavailable for assignment, busy squelching re-civ insurgency factions in Greenland's copper strip-mine melts. Oh, well, such a pity. It would have been quite the vicarious thrill to have had a couple of macho men to boss around.

That leaves two contractor operatives available—both women. Even though Delacompte would frown on the extra measure of assigning additional agents for pursuit, having these two plus Heinz already up top on *Alaungpaya*—surely that would be enough to squash this wayward whoremonger, no?

Examining Martstellar's file some more, Lee discovers something else quite interesting. When Martstellar was still active and near the end of her private contractor career, she was reprimanded twice in the field on assignment. Her demotions for disciplinary issues outside of assignments, those were well recorded, but these in the field are worth noting. It appears that in two close-quarter situations when she was pitted against three or more assailants, Martstellar folded and needed to be rescued. One time in Uruguay during the South American water revolts and a second time during Geometronic International's hostile takeover of Core Dynamics.

Well, well. It appears his judgment is spot on. Three is better than one.

Finally, Lee feels the first significant surge of relief in his long, long day at the office.

MERCY IS FOR SUCKERS

Cupping her arms behind her head as a pillow, bounty agent Cleo Heinz stretches out on a slanted gurney in one of *Alaungpaya's* health clinics.

Above her a male nurse of Persian lineage meticulously plucks therapeutic narco-pins from Heinz's quickly healing leg. The nurse daintily drops each blood-tipped barb into a bio-hazard slit in the top of a clear plastic drum affixed to an aluminum, doughnut-shaped base. As each disposed needle falls to the bottom of the container it makes a small, distinct clink.

The nurse looks up, and Heinz catches his watery, dark eyes. Heinz immediately props herself up on her elbows.

"What?"

"Nothing," the nurse replies.

Although it's still throbbing with traces of dense pain, Heinz twitches her leg away from the nurse's gloved hands.

"You just fish-eyed me, boy. Don't tell me it's nothing. Hey! I'm talking to you."

The nurse tries to resume his task, but Heinz moves her leg further away. Then the nurse seems to notice that the skin on Heinz's face has darkened quite a bit. He bows his head apologetically, his voice rushing.

"I'm sorry. It really is nothing. It's only, I mean, it's just that—"

"Just that what?"

He gestures to the veritable porcupine that is Heinz's upper leg. "It's just that most patients feel major pain when these pins come out, yes-yes? Even with release narcotics you don't seem to feel any discomfort at all."

Heinz gives the nurse a flat look and throws her hair. No use telling this nutmeg-faced loser that she's had it a lot worse. Yeah, once you survive a sonic concussion pulse dissolving your kidney and endure ten months of muscle grafts and excruciating rehab in a sweltering West African hospital, doing the pins for a minor fracture in some Second Free Zone patch-and-go seems pretty fucking uneventful.

Heinz fingers the nylon bandage covering the bite mark around her eye. Beneath the gauze, the laceration froths in a slather of accelerant antibiotics as the torn flesh knits itself back together. Another scar for sure and an embarrassing one at that, but such is life in Heinz's chosen profession.

Damn it. She was positive she had Martstellar cornered in that tunnel, but the woman's surprising speed, the volant and sublime ferocity of Martstellar's countermoves, that really threw Heinz off her game. Yeah, Martstellar had once been a professional like herself, but wasn't that, like, years ago? Martstellar's file said she tended to overindulge in drink, plus she lazed around living the indolent good life and banged her own help. Shouldn't the girl have softened up some by now? Apparently not. Pretty humiliating.

"Just get on with it," Heinz tells the nurse.

The nurse bows again and jerks out another long pin. Heinz bites her lip.

Clink.

At least fifty more of these pins to go. Man, if this clown didn't pick up the pace she'd be here all day and Martstellar could be in the wind. Heinz starts to lie back and an incoming message patches directly into her field of vision via her ocular implant.

Custom Pleasure Bureau Executive Offices

Date: 7.2.2521

To: Heinz, Cleo F. (Faye) Freelance 89713-99220

Staff: Lee, Vincent T. (Tikayama) Employee 01124-18930

Subject: Status Report—Containment; Martstellar, Koko P. (Penelope). Vendor 456712-20189

Trans-feed Code: 12-33-770 Executive Archive Route Lee, Vincent T. (Tikayama) Only—(classified)

Understood. Forget witnesses. Continue pursuit post medical—two additional operatives assigned. Rendezvous 1.5 hours at *Alaungpaya* arrivals with Wire, J. (-Jackie-) Freelance 73213-55110, and Mu, L. G. (-Loa-) Freelance 77788-34562. Reevaluate COA. Bios and files attached. SPECIAL NOTE: Updated reward status approved—ULTIMATE SANCTION— fixed transfer credits with percentage incentive bonuses secured upon termination of target KPM. End transmission.

Heinz taps the side of her head to terminate the patch on her ocular. *Clink.*

In the cloudy and often shifting world of bounty-agent work, there are some pretty damaged individuals floating around—bloodthirsty borderline sociopaths who you wouldn't dare break bread with but you sure as hell would want as backup if things went gonzo on a gig. Heinz hasn't had the privilege of working with either Wire or Mu, but she knows their names and has heard plenty of unsavory stories. Skimming the attached bios and files, Heinz digests a raft of atrocities so horrific it takes her very breath away.

Like her, after a few years serving for the multinationals, Wire and Mu cycled out of the private army corporate bullshit and turned pro. Their files say that, besides practicing the time-honored tradition of biting out combatants' eyes, both Wire and Mu take the extra time to remove additional small trophies from their victims, even the ones that are to be handed over alive. Mostly fingers but also pieces of shaved skin, which Wire and Mu allegedly dry into crispy ornaments they wear around their necks. Heinz wonders how dried skin would look hooked to her neckbands. Maybe some earrings made from the bones of Martstellar's severed thumbs? Beyond the fading twangs of pain in her leg, Heinz feels a flush of excitement swirl in her belly and, not unlike sexual arousal, the feeling is warm and yielding.

Clink.

Even after her first disastrous meeting with Martstellar, successfully completing an erasure assignment with the likes of Wire and Mu would definitely raise Heinz's profile on the open market. True, in the end she'll have to split the bounty credits with the additional operatives, but that's entirely her fault.

For a moment, Heinz relives the blow that snapped her tibia and she swallows. That elbow of Martstellar's, God, what was it made of? Steel? Stung like a lightning strike.

No matter. If all this Martstellar business finishes clean, Heinz could really make some serious moves.

Plus the transmission from Lee said the bounty status on Martstellar has been upgraded to Ultimate Sanction. Well, hey, now we're talking. Why didn't they offer stakes like that in the first place?

No matter what happens, if Martstellar dies today, tomorrow, or ten years from now, with Ultimate Sanction status all credits are now secured with accrued interest and bonuses. The upgrade also means the contract on Martstellar's life is now permanent and irrevocable.

Guess CPB really wants this Martstellar bad.

Clink.

Heinz smiles slightly and eases back down on the gurney.

Now, if only this nurse here will show a little hustle on the pins she'll clean up and go meet the pros.

PRESSURE IS A FOUR-LETTER WORD

"So, Vice President Delacompte, you're telling us that this vendor matter is being handled?"

There is a small, penetrating silence as the CPB board of directors' projections look mirthlessly down at Portia Delacompte. Five men and five women in total; most appear as though they have been rousted out of bed by a bad smell, the jowly director from Buenos Aires in particular. For the last ten minutes the majority of the discourse has been a tête-à-tête with the jowly director.

"I'm expecting an update soon," Delacompte answers finally. "But I am confident this situation will be resolved within a few hours."

"How did this even happen?" the jowly director asks. "A pleasure vendor brazenly attacking resort security personnel out of the blue? Impertinence like this is absurd. How did this woman ever escape The Sixty?"

"The vendor in question used a contraband pod," Delacompte says. "We're not sure how she smuggled in the parts, but we believe she is now in the Second Free Zone and using the orbits as sanctuary, naturally."

"What about The Sixty's aerial defenses? Did you not engage?"

"By the time we realized what had gone wrong, she had cleared the long-range scope of our countermeasures. Nevertheless, I've authorized full incident containment and assigned a freelance operative for pursuit."

The jowly director bridles at this development. "You sent a freelance operative into the *Second Free Zone*?"

"Yes."

"Need I remind you, Vice President Delacompte, that our charter and commerce agreements with Second Free Zone confederacies stipulate—"

"Sir, I assure you this action will be discreet. You have my word."

"Your word," moans the jowly director. "I know all about your word. You know, Madam Vice President, this is by my count the second mismanagement incident on your current cycle."

Delacompte is taken aback by this accusation. *What? Her second incident?*

"I'm sorry, but I think you are mistaken. I believe this is the first incident on my current cycle."

"Well, then, let me refresh your less than precise memory. The ration hijackings last quarter?"

"Oh… that."

"Yes, oh… *that*. That disaster took us nearly a month to clear up. If it weren't for the trade elections clogging the feeds that particular week, international media interests would have had a field day with us. They might have ended up making those bloodsucking pirates into folk heroes. We were practically skinned alive buying up the entertainment rights on auction. And our CPB value hit? I don't have the numbers up here on my prompts. What did we lose again?"

One of the projections, a withered-looking matron from Rome in a black-lace pillbox hat, mumbles, "Eight to fifteen on worldwide trade markets."

The jowly director booms. "Eight to fifteen points!"

"Yes," Delacompte says, "that incident was unfortunate. For all of us. But I believe we rebounded from that hit with a surge a week later, cross stratum. Several points higher than the downgraded analysts' expectations, if I'm not mistaken."

"Only because the CPB board here authorized a full blitz on the discounts and adjusted to resort prime fees immediately."

"I disagree. Once we decided to hold public trials and allowed contest-winners to participate in the subsequent executions—an idea I came up with, I must add—I think the publicity of the whole affair strengthened CPB and The Sixty's inherent value."

Another one of the board, a drowsy-looking fop from flood-ravaged London, chimes in. "In Vice President Delacompte's defense, I believe her assessment of the correction is accurate. We have gotten quite a bit of meat off that bone."

The jowly director rolls his eyes to make his discontentment known to all.

Beneath the desk and out of the transmissions' view of her, Delacompte slides out the green vial of Q from her jacket pocket. As inconspicuously as possible, she pries off the lid and pinches out a capsule. Slipping the vial back into her jacket, she rises from her desk and crosses the office to a long wooden credenza braced against the far wall. With her back to the airborne faces, Delacompte pours some ice water from a pitcher into a crystal tumbler and then, faking a curt cough, slides the capsule under her tongue and flushes it on its merciful way.

"So," Delacompte says, turning, "if the ration hijackings actually helped CPB's overall value and The Sixty Islands' brand, wouldn't this incident be the first blemish on my current cycle?"

The jowly director scowls. "Don't be glib, Madam Vice President. All incidents affecting our inherent value are serious. You say you were just enforcing new amendments to the SI Decree Measures, the VDOMs, but this vendor... what did you say her name was again?"

"Koko Martstellar."

"Right. This makebate Martstellar, she just turns around and starts killing our security staff willy nilly?"

"Well, she is former private military. And I mean, I do know the woman. Or should I say I used to know the woman."

"And how is that again, exactly?"

"We served on several operations together back in my private military career. I was the one who recruited and hired her here, but I think she's come unglued somehow."

"Illuminate unglued."

"Too much vice and ease is my guess. Reports of erratic behavior, other disciplinary issues, and quite a few customer complaints. It is an unfortunate personnel situation. Because she was my recruit, though, I feel a personal responsibility to make certain the entire matter is brought to a close expediently. This is why I approved dispatching an asset into the Second Free Zone."

The feeds mute abruptly. In the weighty stillness, the board members transmit confidential messages to one another like school children passing notes in class. After a half-minute, the mute on the projection streams is released and the jowly director peers closer, his face looming large.

"Something is rotten here, Madam Delacompte. I don't know what it is, but I am recommending a full reassessment of your executive commitment to CPB and The Sixty."

"Wait—my executive commitment? Oh, no, no, no. My commitment to the CPB and The Sixty is absolute, directors. As all of you know, The Sixty is a massive operation and something like this? You must agree, a bump or two in the road with our day-to-day operations, this sort of thing can be expected."

The jowly director's face prunes. "Bump or two in the road, you say? Beyond the pirate incident, we've heard other similar dismissive excuses from you not too long ago, if I'm not mistaken. Need I remind you of the monkey attacks?"

Delacompte sighs. "Please, let's not bring up the monkey attacks."

"I will damn well bring up the monkey attacks!"

Delacompte squares herself. "With all due respect, director, those monkey attacks were a cybernetic anomaly. The subsequent inquiry exonerated us from all liability and proved this. And the monkey attacks' relevance to this current situation hardly seem—"

"Oh, just shut up."

More muted conferring amongst the directors. Delacompte isn't exactly certain but when the sound is switched on again it appears one of the board members, the foppish one from London, has fallen asleep and is lightly snoring like a dog.

The jowly director's face swells again as he leans further into the projection to make his point clear. He holds up one plump finger.

"I don't have to tell you what this means, do I?"

Delacompte hangs her head. "No, sir."

"Good."

The transmissions cease, faces vanishing in the air like so many ghosts, and Delacompte plops down in the chair behind her desk. After a troubled minute's worth of sulking, she picks up the shiny gun left on her desk when Lee reported the Martstellar debacle to her earlier. Giving herself a push with a foot, she clocks around in her chair until she faces the large window behind her. Looking out the thick glass, she takes in the blockish structures and parapets of the Custom Pleasure Bureau's central campus, the sylvan landscapes and pearly clouds further beyond. Delacompte asks her office's environmental systems for music, and soon the rich, relaxing notes of gently stroked cellos fill the room.

Delacompte raises the gun in her hand and tracks a bead on an unsuspecting SI employee hastily making his way across an exposed walkway stretched between two nearby campus buildings. Taking a careful lead with her aim, Delacompte pretends to let off a round as the warm endorphin rush of her fresh dose of Q takes hold.

PUNCHING THE TICKET

Meanwhile, up above at *Alaungpaya* Security Services' operational command, Jedidiah Flynn positions himself at one of the T-shaped duty pillars, jacks in, and starts to download his shift chronicle into the central security mainframe.

To Flynn's right and left other security deputies like him are also downloading their chronicles at similar T-shaped pillars bolted to the deck. Plenty of griping and grousing on both sides. On his immediate left, a female deputy with a chiseled scar on her cheek repeatedly slams the heel of her hand into the side of the pillar in an effort to mitigate her frustration.

A bit drifty with his Depressus medications, Flynn checks the time stamp on the prompts. It's only a few more hours until the Embrace ceremony, and he's thinking about what he is going to do once he returns to his quarters on this, his last night alive. Finish packing up his meager possessions for charitable donations for sure, but then what? Maybe numb himself with the last of that aged beauty he's been saving? Have a final fling down at *Alaungpaya*'s central casino? Yeah, that sounds like a plan. Get liquored up and bet recklessly. If he wins, maybe he'll give away the last of his credits to some poor rube down on his luck and go out of this world as someone's soused and generous angel. Flynn can almost taste the smooth aged beauty coursing down his throat, and he pictures the happy faces of the people taking the last of his credits off him.

Twenty minutes later Flynn has finished organizing the bulk of his shift download, and he grabs a lift upstairs to clean out his locker. Once upstairs, he finds next to his assorted toiletries in his locker's top half a wrapped present replete with a bow and a red envelope. He unwraps the package and discovers a mid-priced fifth of beauty. Gutting the envelope, he finds a card signed by nearly everyone in Flynn's division save for his jerk of a lieutenant and a few others who Flynn has always suspected kind of hate him for some odd reason. Lots of farewell best wishes on his upcoming jump. The card even contains a couple of doodles of sex acts, and when he shakes the envelope a coupon for a complimentary fellatio session at a massage parlor on the loop clatters to the floor. He picks up the chit and turns it over in his hands and studies the pulsing pornographic logo. Gee, how thoughtful. Kind of pitiful, but maybe there will be some fun on his last night alive after all.

After changing into his plain tan civilian coveralls, Flynn slumps down the hall to turn in his gear. The sergeant charged with collecting his official kit is a thick, brick-mugged hard case who over-juiced on frenetic physique tablets and now sits behind a wall of blast-proof caging in a globe of resentment for his troubles. When the sergeant speaks his voice is more than a little phlegmy, rough, and deep.

"Body armor…"

Flynn slides his lightweight chest protector across the counter through a partition cut in the bottom of the cage. The sergeant scoops the vest into a basket and checks Flynn's file on the prompt display stationed on his left.

"Says here you were issued a Beretta J-X Gamma series."

"Yes."

"Hand it over."

Flynn releases the grid chip on the weapon and gently lays

it down. He pushes the grid chip and the gun, butt-first, across beneath the partition. The sergeant checks the gun and sets it aside.

"Two hooded uniform jumpers, one duty belt, ten restraining cuffs with pouch, three aerosol acid canisters, one retractable, lightweight impact truncheon, and a verification recorder with case."

Flynn slides all the bundled clothing and devices across. The sergeant unclips the holster from Flynn's duty belt and spins the empty holster back beneath the partition.

"You can keep your holster," the sergeant says.

Flynn picks up the holster, a bit amazed. "Really? I can keep this? Seems you guys would want that back."

The sergeant sniffs hard and spits between his feet. "Upgrades," he says. "Those outdated holsters won't handle the wider barrel on the new Beretta series they're outfitting us with next week. Anyway, if you're like most around here you probably have an extra piece at home, am I right?"

Flynn in fact does, so he nods.

"Consider it a parting gift." The sergeant grins sarcastically.

"Oh. So, I guess you're going to de-chip me now, right?"

"Hold out your arm and slide it under the bar."

Flynn does as he's instructed. The sergeant finds the black oval tattoo centered on the soft side of Flynn's right forearm and sticks him with a reverse-suction syringe. Flynn feels a hot sting as the syringe pierces deep into his flesh. Suction pressurizes and his identification chip leaves his arm like a fat, buried tick. The sergeant tosses down a packet with an antiseptic pad, and Flynn picks up the packet and tears it open with his teeth.

Flynn swabs the oozing blood around the fresh, raw mark and remembers his upcoming suicide.

Antiseptic swab? In a few hours he's going to leap to his death. Why does he even bother?

Setting the reverse-suction syringe aside, the sergeant inserts the grid clip into Flynn's turned-in gun and frowns. With some irritation he tells Flynn that he is supposed to have more rounds loaded into the power grid clip. Flynn fashions a quick lie and says he hit the range recently and forgot to re-juice to the proper power levels. The truth is Flynn got bombed out of his mind a few nights back and, in a fit of self-pitying rage, decided to climb up a restricted topside platform. It was a foolish thing to do, going up top on *Alaungpaya* with only an emergency oxygen mask and without the full weighted safeties of a pressure suit, but the topside platform he selected is set into the barge's hull kind of like a foxhole. Recessed staging areas are used by maintenance technicians doing external hull work and at the time he honestly didn't care if he was sucked off into the sky, but he clipped into a safety harness anyway. It was ferociously cold up top, with a blaring wind, and he nearly blacked out. After all that effort, all Flynn ended up doing was taking pot shots at the silvery moon.

The Depressus afflicted, Flynn muses. *We do many a rash thing.*

The sergeant mumbles some more nonsense about not recharging after range time being a credit-punishable offense and adds that it's no wonder Depressus-afflicted knuckle-shufflers like Flynn wash out of ASS. The sergeant then makes a notation in Flynn's file on the prompt screen and tells him the full expense of a weapon recharge will be docked from his severance credit transfers. All in all it seems petty, but Flynn decides not to argue.

"You're free to go," the sergeant says.

"Thanks."

Flynn turns to go, but stops. The sergeant looks up.

"What now?"

Flynn shrugs. "I don't know. Good luck, I guess."

"Good luck? What do you mean, good luck? Good luck with what?"

"I don't know," Flynn answers. "Good luck with the rest of your life?"

The sergeant leans back and snickers. Then he balls his fists and rubs them in his eyes, mimicking a crying baby.

Wah-wah-wah.

WHAT A PIG KNOWS

On the seventy-fifth floor of a skyscraper overlooking the Plaza San Martin in Buenos Aires, the jowly CPB director retrieves Portia Delacompte's and Koko Martstellar's personnel files on his desk prompts. Predisposed to follow up meticulously on any and all suspicions in his business matters, the director scrutinizes the breadth of the two women's capabilities and accomplishments.

To the jowly director's dismay, it appears Vice President Delacompte was being truthful when she claimed Martstellar's disposition tends toward slovenliness and depraved, impetuous distraction. Martstellar's former private military career had as many demotions as it had commendations, with most reprimands attributed to reckless disregard to the conduct becoming a paid soldier. But if this Koko Martstellar is so scandalously irresponsible, why on earth would Delacompte recruit her to work on The Sixty, the crown jewel of CPB's resorts?

Leaning into the prompt projections, the director soon stumbles upon a singular possibility: a hostage-rescue operation on a supercore drilling platform off Ghana.

De-civ rebel factions had taken over the structure and

Martstellar's actions, in the face of extreme duress, were awarded quadruple bonus credit payout under her contract's valor clause. Using a variety of weapons and wounded after her team's insert aircraft crashed, Martstellar managed to suppress the de-civ rebels, free the company hostages, and disarm a major explosive device rigged to cripple the platform. Martstellar also consolidated and provided medical aid to the casualties under fire for two and a half hours until reinforcements arrived.

One of the wounded on the Ghana platform that day?

None other than one Portia Delacompte.

Hmm. Interesting.

But would Delacompte *really* order an eliminative action on someone who once saved her life in the field? Well, perhaps the jowly director judged Delacompte too quickly. Maybe her executive commitment to CPB management is absolute after all. The jowly director takes a fresh cigar from the steel box on his desk and chomps the cigar's tip between his teeth.

Maybe.

YOU, THE WE

INTERNATIONAL DEVELOPMENT ASSET/MERCENARY
RECRUITMENT FEED SOLICITATION/ADVERTISEMENT—0:45

CLIENT: Global Resource/Syndicate Deployment
Initiatives, LLP (GR/SDI)

PRODUCTION ENGAGEMENT: 2516 All Hemispheric Seasonal
Cycles

VISUAL FEED 1: BLACK SCREEN.

AUDIO: THRILLING, TRENDY BEATS AND/OR MUSIC
CUSTOMIZED TO FEED BROADCAST MARKETS/AGE/
DEMOGRAPHIC TARGETS—POWERFUL SOUND, RAGING TO
EARDRUM-TEARING CRESCENDO.

VISUAL FEED 1 (CONT.): BLACK SCREEN SLASHED AWAY TO
REVEAL RAPID, ICONIC, MIXED STILL AND MOTION MEDIA IN
LUSTY, SAFFRON TINT—ALMOST SUBLIMINAL NIGHTMARISH

FEEL. (Note: Client Suggested Inclusions: Third and
Fourth North America and Middle East Smartwars with
catastrophic regional devastation imagery, satellite
scans of once-dominant political/economic centers
marred, smoldering radioactive infrastructure ruin
(Beijing, US/California/New York, Eastern Mediterranean,
etc.), body-count clocks, riots and upheaval, etc.) AS
AUDIO VISUAL CRESCENDO CLIMAXES CUT TO BLACK.

AUDIO: SILENCE (hold—5 seconds).

VISUAL FEED 2 (CONT.): BLACK SCREEN SLICED LEFT
TO RIGHT BY EYE-POPPING GREEN LINE (HORIZONTAL)
WIDENING. AS GREEN BAND GROWS, THE BAND FRAMES A
DAZZLING MOSAIC OF FULL-COLOR MIX IMAGERY/MOTION—THE
CORPRATE AND SYNDICATE MERCENARY EXPERIENCE. DE-CIV
COMBAT ACTIONS, INTENSE FIELD-TRAINING PYROTECHNICS,
MARKET-TAMING MISSION ENGAGEMENTS. (Note: Client
requires footage of "happy" soldiers, solidarity
imagery, payday pillaging, and the like. Please review
attached creative brief for additional specifics.)

VOICEOVER: We are the peace. We are the order.

VISUAL FEED 2 (CONT.): FRAME OF THE CORPORATE AND
SYNDICATE EXPERIENCE MORPHS INTO EARTH SEEN FROM
OUTER SATELLITES.

VOICEOVER: Think you got what it takes to be *the we*?

VISUAL FEED 2 (CONT.) PAN FROM EARTH TO THE SUN. SUN
FILLS THE SCREEN. DISSOLVE AND FADE IN GR/SDI LOGO.

VOICEOVER: If born in the collectives, contact your

re-civ labor-assignment professional recruiter. A
message from Global Resource/Syndicate Deployment
Initiatives, its worldwide re-civ alliance nations, and
your future.

MEETING THE TEAM

Agents Wire and Mu whip off their sunglasses. The lenses of the sunglasses are shiny and green like the backs of dung beetles, and Wire's voice sounds as if she's just gargled a glass of shattered shale.

"Where is this problem child?"

Heinz and the two additional agents are in the buzzing pandemonium of *Alaungpaya*'s main arrival and departure terminal just outside of baggage claim and customs. In bellicose mannerisms and dress, Mu and Wire are practically carbon copies. Tight, olive-toned bodysuits and smooth, no-nonsense black assault shoes. Five foot even with ocular implants affixed to their temples and hair shorn convict-close. Heinz suspects Mu is engineered South American descent and Wire possibly a genetically engineered variation of Southern Mediterranean or perhaps Portuguese. Both women are blocky with cut muscle.

God, Heinz thinks, *I must look ridiculously feminine compared to these two stacked cans of homely, brawny butch.* Heinz pulls her ample red hair back and lets it fall generously over her sharp shoulders and then notices with some disappointment that no skin or finger trophies dangle around Wire's or Mu's thick necks.

So much for their files' descriptive accuracy.

Self-consciously Heinz touches the drying bandage over the bite mark encircling her left eye.

"Martstellar is still aboard," she begins.

Wire adjusts her bearing and sneers churlishly. "And just how are you so sure?"

Heinz shifts her eyes and places her hands on her hips. "Because no scheduled transports, merchant vessels, or personal craft are allowed off *Alaungpaya* until post-Embrace. They just gave the notice. You two are lucky you even landed. Your shuttle was one of the last arrivals, and the whole to-and-fro grid up here is now on lockdown until the Embrace ceremony concludes in a few hours."

"Embrace ceremony? What the hell is an Embrace ceremony?"

"You know, the Second Free Zone mass suicides? Depressus?"

"Oh, those yahoos."

"In any event," Heinz says, "before you two arrived I bribed a barge tech and scoured all outgoing flight manifests and transport logs archived since I came aboard. There's no record of a Martstellar departure. It's a pretty safe bet that she's still hiding out on *Alaungpaya*."

Wire glances at Mu and then both of the women look back at Heinz. Wire clears some of the sedimentary rock fragments from her throat and speaks teasingly.

"Gee, Heinz, so what happened up here, huh? That simpering little twit down at SI HQ gave us the rundown. This Martstellar, she's supposedly a has-been, and you're still up and about sucking air? How the hell did that happen? Your file made you out to be death's glammed-out little sister."

Heinz's face flushes. "Martstellar got lucky is all," she says. Once again, the shame of her brutal takedown burns, and she starts to raise a hand to touch the triangular bandage above her eye.

Wire giggles. "Set her teeth on you, huh? Wow, that has got to suck. Hey, don't sweat it, big red. Me and Mu are up here now, and this Martstellar? Trust me, that woman's heartbeats are numbered."

Mu takes a step forward and tosses a heavy rucksack at Heinz's feet. The rucksack is black nylon with multiple zippered openings and thick buckled straps, identical to the ones Wire and Mu have secured to their own shoulders.

"What's this?" Heinz asks.

"Your gear," Wire says. "That suit Lee said your guns were confiscated on *Hesperus 6* so we thought, you know, we'd bring you some gear. One reinforced plasma HK U-50, a Ruger combat application GPPG sub-cutter with collapsible polymer stock and sniper bipod stand, half a dozen pulse grenades, one thermal-imaging scanner, an uplink skimmer, plus a whole boatload of extra power clips. Happy birthday."

"Gee, you shouldn't have." Heinz crouches down and unzips the rucksack. She takes a look inside. "Any body armor?"

"What, you think we're made of credits? Get your own."

"Some birthday."

Heinz picks up the rucksack. She swings it over her shoulder and starts to limp away as Mu and Wire put on their sunglasses and follow behind her. Soon all three agents are walking as a unit through the crowds.

Past the outer arrival and departure area, they turn right down a glowing hallway and find a lift available to take them down to *Alaungpaya*'s commercial levels. A cheerful young man in a waiter's tunic looks late for work as he attempts to board the lift with them, but Wire steps forward and shoves the man backward with such force he hits the far wall and is knocked unconscious.

The doors to the lift whisk shut. As they begin their rapid descent, Mu and Wire can't contain themselves any longer. They crack up.

After they finally get a hold of themselves and calm down, Wire coughs and asks, "So, where do we start?"

Heinz looks straight ahead at their reflections in the lift's closed doors.

"I've been kind of sidelined getting my leg all fixed up, but the nurse who cleaned my pins post-op swore black-market weapons can be had on *Alaungpaya*, so I asked around. Apparently there's a fat man aboard. Some hustler with a hobby-game-maintenance front on Deck 7. Goes by the name of Juke."

LAST NIGHT OF THE REST OF YOUR LIFE

Bent at a blackjack hoop and considerably less intoxicated than the hordes around him, Flynn is up several thousand credits and he can't believe his luck. To be honest, it kind of pisses him off.

Doesn't that just beat all? The last few hours of my unexceptional existence winding away and now a streak of decent fortune finally falls my way?

Figures.

The blackjack dealer, a female uniformed in the orthodox manner for the *Alaungpaya* casinos (neutral gold tunic and kufi hat), is maybe a year past forty. With soft facial features, she offers Flynn a tight, saccharine smile as she moves a pile of winnings across the table toward him. Flynn takes his winnings and starts tidily arranging the credits in his growing pot. Albeit slightly addled from his Depressus medications and a few quick shots from that bottle of aged beauty he'd been saving back in his quarters, Flynn entertains a fleeting notion. This dealer? She might be the mother of that dopey kid who reported that fighting incident earlier today. Like an inquisitive terrier, Flynn angles his head and strains to see a resemblance. He supposes it might be possible. Then Flynn notes the possession beacon on the dealer's wrist pulsing out its dull bioluminescent strobe just below the surface of the skin—a warning of disease.

The dealer is a former prostitute.

Wait, didn't that kid say his mother was crazy religious?

Yeah, but can't former prostitutes be religious? Flynn argues with himself. *Pious fundamentalist types pimp those feel-good turnaround stories all the time, especially those New One Roman Church of the Most Holy Liberator nuts.*

Ah, don't be so judgmental. Besides, what does your opinion matter now anyway? In a few hours you'll be dead.

Flynn tosses the dealer a chip as a gratuity and the gesture is met with a brisk bow, immediately forgettable. Flynn indicates he wants a pass on the next hand and continues organizing his winnings. The dealer alerts the other players that Flynn is sitting out the round, and Flynn flags a floating hospitality robot. He orders some seltzer on ice, thinking maybe with his Depressus medications he should watch his intake on the sauce lest he end up passing out and missing Embrace. With a sizzle, the hospitality robot dispenses his non-alcoholic beverage into a plastic cup and then glides away to the next thirsty customer.

Swishing some fresh bubbly water in his mouth, Flynn turns his attention back to the table and watches the other players' winnings rise and fall on the next two hands. Soon a second and much skinnier dealer appears behind the first. The replacement table skipper is a bit on the androgynous side of the equation with his taciturn air and lip gloss, and Flynn wonders if the man lost all of his sense of humor as a child. Flynn pins the dealer swap-out as a bad omen, so he scoops up his winnings, stuffs the chips into his pockets, picks up his drink, and shoulders through the bodies toward the deeper, pricier pits at the casino's heart.

As Flynn moves through the crush, his eyes roam over the people heading past. All the disconsolate faces etched with angst, anger, and exhaustion. The pricier tables at the casino's center mean bigger risks. Flynn knows if his mental state was anywhere close to normal he would never have the guts to try his fortunes at the higher-staked tables, but acquiescing to suicide does have its advantages. A last-ditch hardening of nerve.

I am Jedidiah Flynn.

Former Alaungpaya *security deputy and one of the Depressus blind and brave.*

Bring it on, people. I die at dawn.

Flynn drops out of the flow and selects a table on his right garlanded in festive tinsel and spot-lit in soft rose. Sensing his presence, a jolly-looking dealer welcomes him and motions to a vacant stool.

"New player, new player," the jolly-looking dealer announces. "Coming in, coming in. Blackjack 5000, Blackjack 5000. Yeah-yeah, right-right."

Flynn greets the other players with a smile and a few quick nods of his head and plants himself on the empty stool. He takes another pull on his seltzer and sets the drink down on the felt. To Flynn's immediate right is a petite woman with a shock of spiky blue hair, dressed in a black bodysuit. The woman gives Flynn a quick appraisal and the vague scent of cinnamon and chemical smoke pirouettes toward him. Flynn catches the woman's assessing eyes when she laughs softly to herself.

"Something funny?" Flynn asks.

The woman glances across the table at the other players.

"Funny?" the woman replies. "Oh, no. Nothing funny at all, *lawman.*"

Flynn's eyes flick to the dealer and to the other patrons awaiting their cards. He taps the first cards dealt his way and glances briefly down at the Beretta hanging off his hip.

After leaving ASS operational command and heading back to his quarters, Flynn had caught a shower and poured himself a few stiff drinks while he dressed in his best jumper. He was almost out the door before he turned around and found his spare weapon, the one the sergeant who had collected his gear had assumed he owned. He slid the spare Beretta into the now outdated ASS holster the sergeant let him keep and clipped it to his belt. Even though he is officially retired, Flynn's carry permit is still valid for twenty-four hours and for some reason he felt sort of naked going out for his last evening unarmed. The truth is, he has always felt wearing a gun to be a habit and part of his identity. Of course the added benefit of having a gun on you is people tend to give you a wide berth and show you some respect. Flynn has to admit, it's not the first time he's been made.

"Good guess," Flynn says. "Actually, to be perfectly honest… I'm sort of retired."

"Retired?"

"Yeah. Today was my last day on the job."

"Congratulations."

Flynn shrugs. "No big deal."

"Kind of odd, though," the woman says, "you still toting in public like that."

"Well, my open carry permit is still valid."

The woman peers at her cards. "Drinking man, sporting a weapon with all these credits around, I don't know… kind of risky, don't you think?"

"Oh, you needn't worry about me. I'm a professional."

"Right."

"And this is seltzer, if you must know."

"Sure it is."

Flynn holds up his cup for her to inspect. "Take a whiff."

The blue-haired woman raises a hand, "No, no. I believe you." She lifts her chin and licks her lips as she continues to check her cards. "Beretta Gamma series, right?"

Flynn plants his forearms on the table and peeks at his hand. Folds.

"You know weapons?"

The woman answers with a sly smile. "You might say that." The woman folds too. "Private military training can be hard to shake.

You kind of learn to size up hardware pretty quick on sight."

Now Flynn is *definitely* intrigued. But this woman, she's so slight. She doesn't carry the hardened edginess Flynn has seen in other militarized types who've fought for the restructuring efforts. Self-assured without question, but all in all she seems kind of… nice? Maybe the multinationals were recruiting more of the minxish sylph-type for their operations nowadays. Then again, with his medications and the few drinks he had earlier, maybe his judgment is off. Aw, hell. What does he know.

"If you don't mind me asking," Flynn says, "what, uh, sort of work have you been involved in?"

The woman puffs out a bored sigh as they watch the action and wait on the next round of cards.

"Oh, this and that," she answers. "Did a bunch of forward combatant stuff. Quick-response inserts for M&As, environmental crisis support in devastated de-civ hot zones, and blah, blah, blah. Got traded around a lot, you know how it goes. But, like you, I'm retired. I left that life behind me a long time ago." With a beat of her chin, she motions to his gun. "Those itty-bitty Berettas are standard security issue so I pegged you for law enforcement straight up. Medium-round capacity. A good, basic service weapon. Tried one once or twice. They have some loose nip on the recoil when you crank the levels, but the durability is a plus. You can bury those Berettas in a vat of mud, rinse them off, and they'll still fire."

The jolly-looking dealer clears his throat to get Flynn's attention, and Flynn physically has to shake the look of curiosity from his face. The other players are glaring at them. They both wave a pass as the woman beside him laughs, all throaty and coy.

"I clean up nice," she says.

"No argument here."

"Ooh, are you flirting with me, officer?"

Flynn feels his face go red. "Flirting? Me? No, not at all. Just being friendly is all. Sorry."

"No need for sorries. It's okay if you are, it's just that… well… I'm kind of busy here." She rolls her eyes, indicating the game.

"Oh, right."

Another hand is dealt and Flynn glances at her as she pokes out her cheek with her tongue in concentration. Flynn notices a weak floating sensation in his stomach, and the feeling spreads upward to his chest. Flynn hasn't been with or felt attracted to a woman for quite a long time and is actually a bit stunned by the sensation. Is it just his medications stewing with the aged beauty he downed back at his quarters or is it actual desire? Oh, good grief. Is her judgment of him correct? Is he really flirting? He's going to kill himself in a few hours. *Good lord, man, get a grip*, Flynn thinks. *Get a grip.*

But as the game's hands progress, Flynn can't help himself. He ends up exchanging more idle shuttlecock chit-chat with the woman. They both win big on a few rounds, but after losing hard on a reckless triple split, the woman bangs her fist on the table and lets fly a string of virulent obscenities at the dealer. The dealer quickly reminds the woman of the casino's rules for decorum and she burns him an icy look and abruptly shoves off.

Flynn watches the woman weave away from the table and into the crowds. Suddenly a powerful, impulsive urge strikes him, and he makes a quick decision.

You planned on giving away your winnings to a stranger tonight, right? Man, she seemed so pissed off. What the hell, why not try to brighten her mood?

Cramming his chips into his pockets, Flynn apologizes to those remaining at the table. Then he jogs to catch up.

"Hey!" he calls out. "Hey! Wait up!"

The woman turns and, in an instant, all of the easygoing and cavalier manner she displayed earlier dissolves from her features. As Flynn approaches the woman drops back and braces herself into a ready position.

Flynn slams on the brakes and holds up both of his hands defensively.

"Whoa! Wait a second, take it easy."

The woman's eyes are hot, and her hands are balled and tight, ready to swing. Expecting some kind of a confrontation or worse, passing casino patrons spread out and muster to watch.

"What do you want?"

Flynn lowers his hands to his sides. "Listen, I know this is going to sound kind of bizarre and out of the blue, and I know you don't know me, I mean, we just met playing cards back there, but I was wondering—"

"You were wondering what? Leave me alone."

"Hold on a second, will you?"

"I don't care if you're a retired security or not, if you don't beat it in five seconds, I'll drop you."

What? Five seconds? Holy—what was this woman's *deal*? Here he is, just trying to make her day, just trying to be nice, and she wants to kick his butt? *The chips*, Flynn thinks. *Right. Quickly tell her about the chips.*

"Listen, do you, um, do you want my credits?"

"What?"

"I said, do you want my credits? My winnings."

The woman scrutinizes Flynn. Looks him up and down. "Is this some kind of a joke?"

"Not at all."

"Look, buddy, I'm not interested, okay?"

"But I'm serious."

"As am I. What the—who *are* you? Is this more of your sorry attempt at flirting with me?"

"No, it's not flirting at all. I swear it." Flynn slowly holds up one hand, and with the other he carefully reaches into his front pocket. He grabs a fistful of his chips and holds them out in his palm for the woman to see. "Here. Take them. Take them all. For real, I swear. It's not a joke. It's kind of hard to explain, but I'm sort of celebrating tonight."

"Celebrating? What do you mean, celebrating?"

"You know, my retirement."

"What kind of idiot celebrates his retirement by giving away credits to a complete stranger?"

"I guess I do."

"Drinking seltzer back there at the table and making conversation—I'll lay even odds you're blotto. Sheesh, who goes around doing something like this? Are you mental or something?"

Well, Flynn admits to himself, *there is that.*

"No," he says. "Well, not entirely. It's just that—if you could just listen to me for a second—I kind of made a promise to myself earlier tonight. I made a promise that if I won big at the casino I'd give at least some of my winnings to someone in need. I know it sounds sappy, but I thought, you know, maybe help somebody as a gesture of good will."

"A gesture of good will?"

"Yeah. Are you familiar with the concept of karma?"

"Come again?"

"I said are you familiar with the concept of—"

"I know what karma is."

"So you know what I'm talking about, right? The law of moral causation? Jeez, I know it must sound stupid, but I'd just really like for you to have the chips. You seemed pretty angry back there when you lost, so you're probably in an unfortunate financial situation, am I right? Think of them as a gift. From one human being to another. You never know, maybe some of my luck has rubbed off on them. They might be able to turn yours around."

The woman's tension eases a smidge, but she still gives the impression she's ready to break his neck or worse. One of the casino patrons who's stopped to watch the confrontation, a man duded up in furry jodhpurs, speaks up. "Hey, I'll take them if the little lady doesn't want 'em."

Flynn whirls around and jabs a finger at the man. "Fuck off."

The sudden wrath in Flynn's face makes Furry Jodhpurs draw back and disappear. The rest of the crowd follows the man's lead, deciding it might be for the best to disperse and move along.

When Flynn turns back, the blue-haired woman is pointing a finger at herself.

"You want to give your chips to me? Me?"

"Yeah."

"What's the angle?"

"No angle. Look, I totally understand if you're embarrassed."

"I'm not embarrassed."

"Then here. Just take them." Flynn scrunches his palm closed and turns his hand over, nodding for the woman to take the chips from him. The woman doesn't delaser her lock on his eyes, but gradually she extends one of her arms. Flynn takes a cautious step forward and smoothes the chips into her open palm.

"There. See? Was that so hard?"

She takes a step back. "Kind of a weird way to stack your karma, don't you think?"

"Well, when I say I'm going to do something I like to see it through." Flynn looks around. "So, um… you want to, I don't know, get a drink or something?"

The woman hoots. "See? I knew this was some kind of ruse. Freakin' creep."

"Hey, I'm a perfect gentleman."

"Sure, a perfect gentleman all hot and on the make."

"That's easily twelve hundred credits I gave you right there."

"Oh, so now I'm, what? Some kind of whore? Forgive me if I don't fall all over myself in gratitude, but what happened to all that karma jive you were just on about?"

Flynn looks down, blushing again. "You're right. This is really stupid. Forget it. Forget I even asked."

The woman relaxes her shoulders, rolling her eyes and head in the same motion. "Oh, c'mon. That's it? That's the best you've got? And here I was starting to enjoy our witty repartee. You're just going to quit? Man, I was actually considering your offer."

"You were?"

"I don't know, maybe. But let me ask you something. Free

credits aside, if you're supposedly celebrating tonight shouldn't, I don't know, your colleagues be giving you some kind of send-off or something?"

Flynn offers a weak smile. "Well, they did give me a nice card."

"A nice card?"

"Well, a card and a bottle of discount hooch." Flynn figures it might not be best to mention the massage-parlor coupon his fellow deputies gave him.

"Got to say, that sounds pretty pathetic."

"Yeah. My former employers are not exactly known for being generous. Hell, I'll be lucky if they even transfer my final credits to my account."

"So, tell me… do you always suck this bad at picking up women?"

"I suppose that depends on your answer. Am I down for the count?"

The woman tapers her eyes and shakes her head. "Look, you seem like a really nice guy, albeit a tad odd. And I'm not really one to look a gift horse in the mouth. But I've got to tell you—"

Flynn presents a hand. "I'm Jedidiah, by the way."

"Huh?"

"I said my name is Jedidiah."

"Jedidiah?"

"Yeah, Jedidiah Flynn. Although most people just call me Flynn because Jedidiah is really sort of a pain in the ass to pronounce."

"Hmm, Jedidiah. Not Jed for short?"

"Nope. Not Jed for short. Just Flynn."

Sighing, the woman shakes her head and warily takes his offered hand in her own. As she squeezes, Flynn is more than a little surprised and intimidated by the intensity of the woman's grip.

"I know I'm probably going to regret this," she says, "but all right. Nice to meet you, Flynn. People call me Koko."

EXIT THE FAT MAN

Swaying in his paraplegic swing, Juke Ramirez sweats like it's nobody's business.

Between heaping spoons of honey-flavored *prik khee nu* mash and deep siphons from a jumbo jug of Diet Orange Quake, he eyeballs the three sour-pussed women standing before him.

Juke isn't a fool. Just shopping for black-market weapons on some vague, happenstance referral? Please. Ocular implants, the blunt statures and squared-off shoulders, plus the neck-banded redhead… it's no great mystery who this surly trio is after.

To ease his nagging conscience, Juke tells himself he'll warn Koko right after the women leave his shop. However, for now potential credits are in play, and it is in Juke's nature to run both sides of any and all fiscal opportunities.

Juke burps into his fist and chortles. "I'm sorry, I don't have any of the Styer models you've mentioned in stock," he says, "but if we close a deal this evening, how about I include some strat-sled coupon chits to make up for it, hmm? Perceptive women like yourselves, up here and on the go in the Second Free Zone, strat-sled rentals might come in handy, yes-yes?"

The redhead with the neckbands sets down a small pulse gun she's been examining as Juke picks up three chits from the table. Plugging them into the towered workstation next to him in succession, he downloads the strat-sled coupon verifications as the redhead cocks a hip.

"Let me ask you something…"

"By all means," Juke answers merrily. "Fire away. It's the customer's right to ask as many questions as she wishes. I do love making my special clientele happy."

"Yeah," the redhead says, trailing off. "You haven't by chance happened to sell any weapons to a female aboard recently, have you?"

Juke pauses. "A female?"

"Uh-huh. Someone like us who looks like she's been around? About yay high. Long dark hair, probably tan?"

Juke remembers Koko's new frisky blue shag, so he feels secure in thickening his bluff. He taps a finger against his chin contemplatively. "Well, let's see… I do recall selling a Daewoo Precision T-278 to an elderly female recently. But that was, oh, some days ago. A refined, sophisticated lady. Exceptional taste in collectibles."

"No. This would've been in the last few hours."

Juke busies himself with some disassembled housing on a metal table to his immediate right. "Oh, well, then I'm afraid not," he says. "No, you three have been, ahem, my only customers in quite some time. Alas, there's not much interest in weapons up here on *Alaungpaya* these days, but I do keep myself busy. Plenty of hobby-game maintenance, you know. Rarely a shortage of that type of tedious work with the kids' novel cravings nowadays."

The redhead glances back at her companions. "Oh, I so don't like it when people lie to me…"

"I beg your pardon?"

The redhead turns back. "You. You're lying. I can tell. So, why don't we stop wasting each other's time. Where is she? Where is Koko Martstellar?"

As the redhead asks this, bit by bit Juke slides a hand to the panel switches affixed to the right side of his paraplegic sling, searching for the remote controls for his wall-mounted security measures. Juke is fairly certain the weapons are still online, but given the threatening tone of the redhead's voice he wants to be sure.

All three see Juke's move.

As the other two women dive for cover, the redhead springs deep and soars through the air. Flying like a spread-eagled amoeba, she lands and latches onto Juke's front and shatters his nose with a quick head-butt.

The hammer blow to Juke's nose is a starburst of pain and a delta wash of blood squirts down his sweaty face. Swinging with him on the sling, the redhead reaches around and squeezes Juke's neck in the crook of one arm while her other hand digs beneath his robe into the deep, ample folds of his flesh. Her fingers grip the lower edge of his rib cage, and Juke bellows like a stuck bull. The programmed weapons on the shop walls whine and revolve on their hydraulics, effectively unable to target.

"Shut those off," the redhead hisses.

Hot tears trickle from the corners of Juke's eyes. He flaps his meaty arms and slaps blindly at the controls as the redhead digs her fingers deeper. The pain in his side is excruciating, unlike anything he has ever felt before. Like five canine teeth set on bone.

Juke finds the weapons' kill switch and, on command, the weapons on the walls lower and lock off with simultaneous, loud clacks. He weeps.

"Please! Just take everything! Just take it all! There's more, much more in the back.

Whole crates of weapons, an entire arsenal if that's what you're after, just don't—"

"Where is Koko Martstellar?"

"I don't know who you're talking about!"

"This is so unproductive."

With a twist, the woman yanks back and two of Juke's ribs snap like brittle roots. Juke nearly blacks out from the veritable supernova of pain and wishes with all his might he just would.

"GAHHHH! Wonderwall! Oh God! Oh God! Martstellar booked a room at a place on the loop called Wonderwall! For the love of— please let go of me!"

"What did you sell her?" the redhead demands.

"What?"

The redhead switches arms, grabs the ribs on Juke's other side, and holds on as he squirms. Five more precise teeth set on bone.

"Weapons, fat boy. What did she buy off of you?"

"One knife. One knife and a gun. Please—"

"What kind?"

"What?"

"I said, what kind?"

"A Sig Sauer. The knife was a lightweight stiletto model. Iberian."

"That's it?"

"That's it, I swear. She's traveling light. She didn't have enough credits for anything else. She may even have gone off-barge by now because I gave her a strat-sled coupon too. Please, that's all I know, I swear. She told me she booked a room over at Wonderwall."

The redhead stares into Juke's greasy, beseeching eyes. She appears to relax and releases her hold on his ribs.

Oh dear God, Juke thinks. Maybe if he just gives these women everything. Maybe then they'll let him be. Juke wants to tell them he could help them, but with the throbbing pain and immobilizing fear washing up and down his body he has trouble finding the words.

Sure, he could help them. Juke could help set Koko up, maybe even help them lay a trap for her. He could talk her into coming back here or perhaps advise them on the best place to ambush Koko over at Wonderwall. Let her think she was safe, and these three psychopaths could squash her like a bug. They're in the game; they can be bargained and reasoned with. Of course, he owes Koko nothing. All of this? Koko's problems? This was none of his affair.

Juke feels woozy as he dares a peep into the redhead's cruel eyes.

He offers a look begging that he is not one above betrayal. The redhead nods and pats Juke's damp, bloody cheek.

"Thank you," she says.

There is a sliver of a moment when Juke believes that he is in the clear, that all is forgiven, that these women want nothing more from him and that something unspoken has been worked out. But then it's as though someone has thrown a soft switch and hurled his soul into a dark abyss.

The last thing Juke hears is the crisp snap of his own neck.

EMBRACE ON THE FEEDS

EMBRACE CEREMONY PROMO FEED—0:30

CLIENT: *Alaungpaya* Oversight Collective—Second Free
Zone Host Barge Class Vessel *Alaungpaya*

PRODUCTION ENGAGEMENT: 2516- Spring/Summer Current
Hemispheric Cycles

VISUAL FEED 1: PANNING IN SUCCESSION, SERENE FACES LIFT
THEIR HEADS HOODED IN EMBRACE CEREMONIAL ROBES. WOMEN,
MEN, CHILDREN, YOUNG, OLD, DISFIGURED, MIXED RACES.
FACES SHOULD BE STRONG YET TRANQUIL, LOOKING OUTWARD,
RESILIENT AND STEADFAST.

[CUT TO] VISUAL FEED 2: SHAFTS OF SUN BREAKING THROUGH
HEAVENLY BILLOWING CIRRO-CUMULUS CLOUDS. CAMERA
SWEEPS FROM *ALAUNGPAYA'S* STERN TO THE CROWN WHERE
DEPRESSUS GROUP HOLD HANDS IN CIRCLES ON THE STILL-
SEALED, TRANSPARENT EXTENSION PULPIT PLATFORM. CAMERA

PANS OVER THE FACES OF LOVED ONES IN THE WITNESS-
SEATING WINDOWS AROUND THE EXTENSION PULPIT. CAMERA
PANS UPWARD TO THE SUN BREAKING THROUGH THE CLOUDS.

AUDIO: THE SOUND OF GENTLE, HOLLOW WINDS. FAINT,
SLOW VIOLINS PLAYING SOFTLY. ONE BY ONE, ORCHESTRAL
INSTRUMENTS JOIN THE VIOLINS. MUSIC GROWS MORE
TRIUMPHANT.

VISUAL FEED 2 (CONT.) FADE IN—LOGO: *EMBRACE*

[CUT TO] VISUAL FEED 3: OVERHEAD SHOT OF *ALAUNGPAYA'S*
EXTENSION PULPIT AS THE TRANSPARENT SAFETY SEALS ARE
DRAWN BACK AND EMBRACE PARTICIPANTS RACE INTO THE AIR
IN THE OVERPOWERING RUSH OF WIND, BLOWN TOWARD THE
PULPIT EDGE IN ONE MASS. THE LEAP BEGINS.

[CUT TO] VISUAL FEED 4: THE FACE OF ONE EMBRACE
PARTICIPANT (FEMALE), WIND IN HER HAIR, EYES DAZZLED
WITH JOYOUS RELIEF. (DISOLVE INTO A CLOUDLESS BLUE SKY.
FADE IN LOGO): *EMBRACE*

VOICEOVER: (*Whispering*) Time to Embrace is now (INSERT
COUNTDOWN TIME) [PROMO NOTE: Feed Embrace promo will
sync with updated schedule times and approved flight
status.] Good spectator seats are still available. Contact
Alaungpaya Valet Services for witness-seat pricing and
availability.

GIMME SOME SAKE, GIMME SOME SNACKS

Koko's cheeks are chipmunked with food.

"Wow," she says, muffled, and then swallows. "Got to hand it to you, Flynn. When you're right, you're right. This place? They lay out some really great chow."

Delighted by her enthusiasm for the meal, Flynn admires Koko's profile as he neatly lines up his chopsticks on the outer rim of his plate. The restaurant they're in is an inexpensive Indo-Pac-Rim joint just off the starboard side of *Alaungpaya*'s central casino, with red walls and drapes of gold metallic bunting across the ceiling. The restaurant has two long seated bars framing an oval dining area with a forty-seat capacity. Small-plate menu options. Tanked micro-fish sashimi. Synthetic game skewers. Lots of soy noodles with fortified insect mash on rice. Upon entering, Koko said the zesty aromas of charred lemongrass, smashed garlic, and powerful chilies were making her mouth water, and she and Flynn elected to eat at one of the bars. Flynn knows one of the cooks behind the counter, a hulking Asian-looking fellow, and Flynn and the big man joke as he sets dish after tasty dish before them. The cook even sneaks them a free carafe of high-priced sake on the sly. They've nearly finished devouring a warm, fermented *mechi-katsu* plate, and Flynn feels remarkably sober with the food. He raises his cup.

"To my retirement," he says.

Koko wipes her mouth with a balled-up napkin and lifts her own sake.

"To your retirement."

They tap and sip.

"So," Koko asks, "what're you going to do now?"

Flynn sets down his cup and shifts on his stool. "Huh? Oh, you mean now that I'm retired? That's a really good question. I'm not sure what I'm in for, actually."

Koko uses a chopstick to lance a cube of tempura off one of the plates in front of Flynn and pops it into her mouth.

"You know, there's plenty of corporate syndicate outfits looking for seasoned security pros if you're interested. I mean, have you thought about a little part-time work like that? Re-civ worker oversight and the like? Pretty boring work, but the pay isn't too shabby."

Flynn takes another slurp of sake. "Oh, I think I'm all done with that sort of thing."

Koko nods her head approvingly. "That's cool. Setting out as a full-on lad of leisure, I can dig that. Kick back and take life as it comes at you for a while, right? Hell, you're still pretty young. What're you? Thirty-six or something?"

"Thirty-three."

"Still a pup. You've got plenty of time to work out what you really want to do."

Thinking of how young he actually is and how little he has accomplished with his life causes a small hitch of gloom in Flynn's chest. He debates whether he should take a moment to sneak some more of his Depressus medication, but decides instead to will himself past it.

"So, you have any travel plans with your free time?" Koko asks.

Flynn looks away. "In a manner of speaking you might say that…"

"Hey, if you really don't want to talk specifics that's fine by me. But if you haven't noticed, I'm a pretty good listener. Hell, in my business it's important to lend a generous ear from time to time."

Flynn looks confused. "Private mercenaries lend ears?"

"Oh, that. I told you, I *used* to work for the syndicates, but I don't really do that stuff anymore."

"Oh. So, um, what is it you do now?"

"Promise not to laugh if I tell you?"

"I promise."

"I'm in the hospitality business."

Flynn laughs. "Get out."

Koko shakes her head. "You said you wouldn't laugh! But it's the truth. I'm up here on holiday from other people's holidays." She looks around and adds sarcastically, "Hitting the atmospheric glamour of Second Free Zone to get away from it all."

"But here? On *Alaungpaya*? I mean, it's nice enough, but it's not exactly a raging party vessel."

Koko prods a chopstick into the air to accentuate her point. "Yeah, but we seem to be having a good enough time. *Alaungpaya* isn't all that bad, and anyway it's just a stopover for me. Freebooting my itinerary, you know. Making things up as I go along."

"Ah, an organic holiday method."

"Exactly."

Flynn scoots forward a bit. "I see. Well, if you don't mind me asking, what part of the hospitality business are you in now? I mean, with your militarized background one could only wonder. Are you in executive protection? Site defense? Something along those lines?"

"Not really," Koko shrugs. "Well, that's not entirely true. I mean, I used to teach a few classes on the side—you know, resistance training and such—but I kind of got tired of greenhorns accidentally shooting themselves and blowing themselves up. Mostly I just work as a bartender these days."

"A bartender?"

"A bartender and a manager."

"Wow, that is different."

"Hey, I kind of like it. It's fun, straightforward work. And it's a whole lot better than stomping out de-civs on directives for the man, that's for sure. Pour somebody a tall one, listen to his tales of woe. Plus, I'm pretty handy with a shaker. The Blue Fist, that's my signature drink."

"What's in it?"

"One hundred sixty proof rum, mango extract concentrate, and coconut milk. I use a couple of drops of narcotic dye to give it a blue tint, but that's just between you and me. It'll knock you on your fanny, that's for sure."

Flynn rotates his cup of sake between his palms. "Kind of a big downshift from gun slinging for the multinationals, but I guess a good ear is important, then."

"You can't imagine," Koko says. With a flourish Koko throws back the rest of her rice wine and sets down the cup. She rubs her hands together and dips her head. After a short, awkward pause she lowers her voice. "Hey, Flynn?"

"Yeah?"

"I'm sorry to bring this up, but um… I really have to go."

Despite his intentions to play it cool, Flynn feels his face cave into an exaggerated look of disappointment. He strokes his beard.

"You need to take off? Damn, I knew I was boring you and this was too good to last. I suppose you want to head back to the casino, right? Try your luck some more. That's cool. I mean, I've taken up enough of your time. I understand."

Koko pokes his shoulder. "You're not boring me, Flynn. It's just that, well, I need to use the restaurant's head for a minute." Koko points left and right, miming for directions to the bathroom.

"Oh!" Flynn can't help but perk up, and he indicates right. "It's just around the corner, past those two potted plants over there."

"Thanks." Koko pats his arm and climbs off her stool.

As Flynn watches Koko leave, he lifts his sake cup to his lips and the glum swell of despair that bubbled up earlier washes back. She's probably just lying to him, looking for an easy exit. What did he expect? Give away his credits and buy her dinner and drinks? He feels awkward and foolish. Goddamn, he wishes he was drunk.

Above the bar, the feed screens have been streaking constant advertisements for the upcoming event broadcast of the Embrace ceremony. During dinner Flynn has done his best to ignore the glossy feed images, but now he finds his eyes glued to the screens. He watches footage of bodies falling through the digitally enhanced heavens, intercut with shots of faces showing expressions of blissful relief, all of it soundtracked with calming songs. Flynn doubts the glossy depictions are accurate. Sure, barge doctors are supposed to inject Embrace thanatophobics with anodyne psychopharmaceuticals to make the jump all the more enticing. And there's been no shortage of assurances that there is no real terror at all. But despite his knowing all of this, doubt nags at him.

Really? No fear? Falling to your death from a ridiculous altitude? Whatever drugs they use had better be really good.

Flynn's thoughts switch back to Koko. Well, he has to admit, she is really something. Pretty and provocative as hell with a ferocious appetite. Quite engaging despite their clumsy start and his hokey, aw-shucks-miss ploys. All in all, a hell of a way to end things. A dinner date before doom.

Flynn sullenly recalls when the first of several ship physicians advised him of his Depressus condition. It would be untruthful to say he didn't have his suspicions that something deep down was wrong for several months before he finally worked up the courage to make an appointment. The crashing mood swings and rattled nerves plagued him daily, and he prepared himself for the worst. But even with all that, the acute demoralizing blow of the final diagnosis unhinged his knees.

* * *

"I've found it's better to be forthright with information like this..."

Flynn plunked himself down in a chair next to an examination table and let the doctor shoot him up with a sedative. After the sedative had dulled and relaxed him enough, Flynn willed himself to speak.

"Are all Depressus cases terminal, doc?"

The doctor looked up at the ceiling and then dropped his eyes.

A warm, practiced smile.

"As far as we know, yes. Naturally, with proper medications we can blunt and pacify your more troublesome symptoms as your condition progresses."

Flynn's throat swelled shut. God, it was all so unfair. What did he do to deserve this? Him? He'd been healthy his whole life. Flynn took care of himself, damn it. He really didn't but he told himself he had plans. He deserved better than what this doctor was telling him.

"So what do I do? I mean just how long before it... you know?"

"Before it becomes intolerable? Well, that depends. From the tests and lab work it appears you're just a few nudges beyond Stage 2. You explained you are somewhat active and stay fit because of your security deputy responsibilities, so that probably has helped mask your initial symptoms for some time." The doctor rubbed his chin thoughtfully. "Maybe a month or so?"

"A *month*?"

"Mmmhmm. Would you like some more sedative?" the doctor asked quietly.

The guy had to ask? The doctor juiced him up, but good.

Flynn's mind lurches back to the present.

He debates whether, if and when Koko does return from the bathroom, he should tell her about his diagnosis. Maybe then she might understand why he wanted to give his credits away. A genuine medical condition. Makes more sense than all that karma babble.

No, he decides. *Just leave it alone.* If Koko doesn't ditch him, just try to have a good time. Maybe go and order something obscenely calorific for dessert. Keep things light. She already thinks he's a bit off as it is, why ruin her evening with his psychosis?

KOKO, INDISPOSED

Meanwhile, alone in the restaurant's bathroom, Koko flushes a steam toilet and cleans her hands at one of two metal trough sinks.

Looking at her reflection in a gilded teardrop-shaped mirror, she barely recognizes herself as she works tiny yellow disinfectant crystals off her hands.

God, she thinks. *Hate the hair. As soon as I'm clear of all this craziness I am so going to shave this spiky blue mess right off my skull and go basic.* Jeez, what was she thinking? Blue? She should have gone with white or blonde or maybe even pink. Pink is all the rage these days, isn't it? *Really, really hate the hair.*

Koko shakes off the excess moisture and dries her fingertips under a sanitizing heater. As she readjusts her folded back gloves over her hands, she studies her face in the mirror some more. She toggles the zipper fob on her bodysuit beneath the flaps of her new jacket. Turns sideways.

And these clothes? Yuck. Juke was right. These clothes make her look like a preacher.

She closes her eyes and settles herself with a breath.

What is she doing? She must be out of her mind. She should be gone by now. Gone. She should be in hiding, in motion, or at least be figuring out how to drop off Delacompte's scope altogether. And she's, what? Allowing herself to get talked into dinner with an ex-sky cop who's throwing money around? Slamming back free sake? Yeah, okay. Not the smartest thing in the world, but she did crater on that last hand and then there Flynn was, offering her all those credits. Hard to run without bank, so where's the harm in a little free dinner and conversation? Flynn seems easygoing enough. But that whole karma line, that sounded more than a little cornball. Perhaps he's overcompensating. Now that dinner is over she suspects Flynn will change his tactics and make some feeble pass at her for sex. Koko decides if Flynn does go all horndog on her, she'll just say thanks for everything and bail on him.

Koko opens her eyes. She runs a thumb over her lower lip, and sucks off a dab of garlic sauce sticking to the back of her glove. The gingery hot flavor lights up the taste buds in her mouth.

Oh, man. This stuff is just amazing. Maybe Flynn's chef buddy will give her the recipe. Yeah, drizzle that on some braised suckling boar? Koko bets she could move the living hell out of that back down at her—

Memories of her bar in flames seize her.

Goddamn it.

Goddamn Delacompte. Goddamn her and her stupid corporate ambitions. Koko swears an oath that when she finds Delacompte again she will definitely take *both* of that woman's eyes. Fry that goldbricking backstabber over an open pit and feed her charred flesh to the fucking Komodos. Make a picture frame with her bones.

Then again, Koko realizes her present predicament is all her own fault. She is in this mess because she went against her gut and trusted Delacompte. She should have known better. She used to be smarter. Stupid. Stupid, stupid, stupid.

She thinks back to when Delacompte first contacted her about the opportunity on The Sixty. Koko was in Manitoba on an assignment quelling re-civ rioters up in the re-established Canadian territories. The incident back in Finland had been a few years prior, and in the time that had gone by Koko had done her best to put the mess behind her and get some distance. Standing there in front of the mirror, Koko replays the precise moment when Delacompte patched into her ocular with the offer. Koko was hoisting a bazooka to her shoulder, and she thought it was some kind of a joke.

"Hey, Martstellar! The hell you up to, girl?"

What the—Delacompte? How the hell did Delacompte get access to my ocular frequency on assignment?

Okay, yeah, it wasn't a clandestine or covert operation, but this was just plain sloppy. Of course, then Koko reminded herself who she was working for.

Frigging nouveau riche Canucks.

Koko peered down the sights of the bazooka and tapped the side of her head to respond to the audio stream.

"Same shit, different part of the planet, Big D," Koko said. "Been a long time…"

The transmission in Koko's skull squelched and crackled. "That it has," Delacompte replied. "That it most certainly has. Can't believe you're up in the territories, though. So depressing. You're telling me you're that hard up for a little scratch these days?"

Truth was, Koko was always hard up. Fiscal responsibility had never been part of her mindset. She couldn't believe she'd taken the shitty assignment either.

"Hey, we can't all be so business-minded like you," answered Koko. "So, what can I do for you, D? I'm kind of busy here. Rioters getting ready to pop."

"I had the hardest time tracking you down…"

"Well, I figured, you know, maybe it was for the best, considering."

Delacompte's response muted as contractor oversight interrupted their patch. Operation command informed Koko that she needed to move to the south end of the roof, stat. The rioters were taking up a cornering position and command wanted to squelch that advance first. Koko confirmed the order, and Delacompte's patch resumed after another garbled burst of static.

"Considering?" Delacompte asked. "For the best considering what?"

Delacompte couldn't be serious. Considering what? Hello? Your gargantuan screw-up back in Finland, you dumbass.

"Look," Koko answered brusquely, "we're cool, D, okay? Everything's cool. Just forget it. All that stuff that happened back in Helsinki was just one of those things, you know? Some BSGD."

Bad shit, going down.

Delacompte squawked. "Helsinki? What the hell are you talking about, girl? By Helsinki you mean Helsinki fucking Finland? When were you in Finland? Sorry, I've had some SMTs recently, and there's a whole bunch of stuff I can't recall…"

SMTs? *Well, shit*, Koko thought. Selective memory treatments. That explained Delacompte's confusion. Not that Koko blamed her. Hell, who wouldn't sign up for selective memory treatments given the fact that Delacompte—

A massive, rolling explosion shattered to the right of Koko's rooftop position. When Koko turned her head back, she saw that the explosion had taken out an entire floor of an adjacent office building. Crouched with her bazooka, she duck-walked to the south end of the roof, a silhouette moving fast and low in the smoke.

Another follow-up fizzle of squelching static and Delacompte's voice sliced into her skull again.

"Take a guess where I am now," she teased merrily.

"I really don't have time for this, Big D. Could I, like, patch you later to catch up or something?"

"C'mon, take one little guess."

Koko leveled the bazooka in her arms on a ventilation unit. She aimed at the advancing throngs below and fired.

"I don't know. Mombasa?"

"Try about ten thousand kilometers east-northeast. You remember that time when you said you thought you could run a bar?"

* * *

Oh, yeah.

I so remember now.

Bitch.

In a burst of speed, Koko cross-draws the Sig from the holster inside her jacket and levels the sights at her own reflection.

Daring and staring back.

COVER ME

At the bar, Flynn looks relieved and positions himself next to his stool as Koko makes her way back across the room. Cheerfully, Koko holds her chin high.

"Well, either you aced your civil courses at whatever passes for a security academy up here," she says, "or whoever raised you had a shred of class."

Flynn laughs. "The latter. I'm one of the engineered populace."

As she takes her seat, Koko's eyes widen. "Oh, yeah?" she says. "Engineered? Hey, me too. Were you bred up here or in one of the collectives down below?"

"Up here. Been skying in the confederacies most of my life. How about you?"

"Came out of one of the Oceania cooperatives. Humble beginnings—rolled right into basic at seventeen and never looked back, really. Count yourself lucky you were bred up here. Not a lot of exciting labor options for conventional re-civs bred down below."

Flynn wags a finger. "Ta, ta, commercial efficiency is for the greater good…"

"Yeah, yeah. You sound like a public service announcement on the feeds. Given the choices for menial waging down below, a life policing re-civ order seemed the best option for me."

"And now you're loving life as a bartender. Wow, life sure does have a way of working itself out, doesn't it?"

"That it does."

"More sake?"

"Please."

Flynn picks up the white bulbous carafe from the bar and pours a generous dollop of the rice wine into Koko's cup. Placing his hands together, he mutters something and bows slightly over her poured drink. He picks up the cup and hands it to Koko.

"What was that?" she asks.

Flynn gives the carafe to Koko, and she pours him a serving.

"What was what?"

"That bowing stuff."

"Oh that. It's supposedly Japanese. My cook buddy over there, he's a stickler for dying languages. He told me I'm supposed to show sake a little more respect and say something profound. Gave me a whole spiel of grief while you were in the head. Apparently he thinks I'm not reverent enough."

"So, what does it mean?"

"What? Oh, honestly, I forget, and he just told me a minute ago. Hang on a sec, and I'll find out."

Flynn flags down his friend, and the big cook and Flynn confer across the bar. Koko can't hear their low exchange over the surrounding restaurant noise so she rotates on her bar stool and checks out the room while they talk. Out of habit she takes in everything in a pattern. Evaluates the layout. Tracks her eyes over potential cover and exits. There is a large unobstructed view of the passing crowds outside the restaurant and occasionally there's a curious glance from a patron considering the bill of fare posted near the restaurant's entrance. Seems like most people in the place are abuzz and having a good time. Across the room, a couple claps with delight as their waiter proudly hands over two skewers of blazing meatballs.

Flynn brushes Koko's hand. When she turns back to face him, he holds up his cup.

"*Au nowa wakari no hajimari.*"

Koko snickers. "You sound like you're choking. Try saying that ten times fast."

"I'd rather not. Roughly translated, it means 'to meet is the beginning of parting'. Kind of a thought on the transient nature of things."

"Pretty deep for a chef."

"Well, like I said, the big guy is a sucker for dying languages." Flynn's eyes drift left for a second and then return. "Hey, can I ask you something?"

"Sure."

"When you were active—I mean, back when you were working for the multinationals—did you have to wear one of those," Flynn scratches his temple, squints a bit, and looks past her shoulder again, "one of those imbedded contraptions?"

"You mean an ocular implant? Yeah, sure. All militarized personnel do. Mine was one of the original series and a bit on the clunky side, but I had it surgically removed when I finished up. Why?"

"Did it hurt?"

"Not really. After the adhesives set into the cranial bones, you sort of just get used to it. Like I said, I had mine removed when I cycled out. Why?"

Flynn polishes off the rest of his sake. "Oh, nothing. It's just that there's a woman with one over by the entrance, and, man, she looks like she wants to burn this whole place down."

Koko's spine turns to ice. Instinctively, she slides her right hand under her jacket, eyes drawing inward.

"Inside or out?"

"Pardon?"

Her voice is steady and low. "The woman by the entrance. Is she inside or outside the restaurant?"

Flynn casually bobs right and then bobs back. He studies the look on Koko's face. "Is something wrong?"

In less than three seconds, Koko's brain falls through the angles of the restaurant, cover, and possible collateral damage. Her heart slams in her chest.

Good God, she thinks. *Get a hold of yourself.* Ocular implants aren't all that uncommon—hell, plenty of militarized personnel travel in the Second Free Zone all the time. An imbed means nothing.

But what if it's the redhead? No, Flynn would have described her like that right away; those neckbands make a big statement. Then again, could it be a second agent? Beneath her jacket Koko depresses the safety on the Sig.

She needs to look to be sure. A distraction, shit, she needs a distraction.

While she knows she might regret it, Koko settles on the play. She leans over toward Flynn and places a hand on his knee.

"Kiss me," she says.

Flynn blinks at Koko as though he's not heard her correctly.

"Come again?"

"I said kiss me, Flynn. Kiss me."

Flynn dithers so Koko doesn't wait for him. With a rush Koko leans closer and presses her lips to his. To encourage him, she zooms her resting hand quickly up his leg and cups his crotch.

Flynn shudders and stiffens beneath her hand. Koko responds by giving the bulge in his pants an upward stroke. Hot and slightly sour from the sake they've enjoyed, Koko's tongue bores into his mouth. Deeply.

As their tongues intertwine, Koko hooks a leg around Flynn's hip, covering his Beretta. Meshing her body into his, she angles them backward to the point it feels she might topple the both of them right off their bar stools. Koko's hand leaves Flynn's crotch and slides around to the holster on his hip.

No matter what, if this is a go Koko sure as hell is going to have two guns.

Koko cracks an eyelid and takes in warped reflections in the bar's decorative chrome. Slowly and clockwise, she shifts both of their bodies around on their stools.

Focus, Koko.

Imbedded ocular. Find it.

More funhouse reflections turning in the bar's chrome and glass. Turn, turn.

Koko thinks she sees the shoulders and head of someone moving away—short hair and built, but she can't be sure. From the back she knows there's no visible proof of an imbedded ocular, as even the most archaic devices lay close to flat against the skull.

Was it the woman Flynn said he saw? Hard to say, but it definitely is not that redhead with the neckbands. Aw, hell. Koko asks herself what she's still doing here. She needs to move.

Koko breaks off their kiss. As she tries to slither away from Flynn, to her surprise she discovers Flynn is now holding fast to the flesh of her ass. Koko has to clear her throat to get his attention.

Flynn opens his eyes.

"Wowza."

Koko reaches around her back and pushes down on his arms until he lets go.

"Hey, Flynn?"

"Yeah?"

"You don't by any chance live close by, do you?"

Flynn raises a hand for the check.

A MU WITH A VIEW

This is going to be so easy, Mu thinks.

Look at these two. Arm in arm, not a shred of care in the world. Like a couple of lovebirds out for a post-dinner stroll.

Suckers.

Mu is totally positive they didn't make her at the restaurant. A close call, yeah, but luckily she turned around at just the right moment and became another unexceptional head in the *Alaungpaya* hordes. No, these two have no idea they're being followed. No idea at all.

Mu hangs back and allows some of the people along the promenade to buffer the distance between her and her targets. She falls in behind a pack of chatty teens whooping it up, getting their evening party on.

What the hell? Mu thinks. *What is it with this Martstellar?*

A few hours ago she goes all tiger-on-tiger with Heinz and now the woman decides it's okay to pick up a little man meat for some shift and shake?

Well, the file did say Martstellar had gone soft. All that oversexed living down on The Sixty. Not to mention the guy she's with is packing heat. The fat man said she was low on credits. Maybe she's looking to score another weapon. Whatever. Girl is a total loser, and she's totally in Mu's sights.

Now if only these two would take a small detour. Yeah, that would be choice. Perhaps slip into another bar. Someplace dark. Mu could just sidle up behind them and slit both of their throats with one speedy pull of that blade she took when they killed the fat man. Let both their bodies fall and take their eyes while the life drained from them, maybe take an extra ear each.

Oh, yeah. That would make things so easy.

Mu is about to update the others on her location when a personal audio message crashes in via her ocular.

Oh, who the—Now? *Now*? Damn it to hell…

The audio patch is from Mu's grandmother.

"Bootsy, dear?"

Mu attempts to sound upbeat and cheerful as she taps in to respond.

"Hey, Nana…"

Mu's grandmother is ninety-six years of age and has no idea what Mu does now. To be honest, it has been more than a wearisome inconvenience for Mu to conceal her secondary career and new identity from the old woman all these years, but Mu has always been afraid that if her grandmother knew the truth of what she now does for a living or how she's changed her name it would crush the old woman's heart. Mu's grandmother was so proud of her when she played football for the South American Coalition, and after she retired from professional sports it thrilled Grandmother no end that she went back to school to pursue a professional degree. Her grandmother actually believes that Mu is now an accountant. A bit of a half-truth. Balancing ledgers for the powerful, only with a quick hand of death, all under her new alias, Loa Mu.

"I'm not bothering you at the office, am I, dear?"

Looking over and past the shoulders in front of her, Mu twists through the crowds with her eyes locked on her targets ahead.

"No, Nana," Mu says. "You're not bothering me at all. I'm just, you know, crunching the numbers, your busy little girl as always. Are you all right? Is something wrong?"

"Well, I hate to trouble you at work," her grandmother says, "but I'm having trouble with my medical payments again."

Mu sighs. "Nana, I think I took care of that."

"You did," Mu's grandmother says. "Well, you told me you did anyway. But my health axis administrators, they're saying they never received the credit transfer for my last two treatments."

This news pisses Mu off. She's been handling all the mind-numbing ins and outs associated with her grandmother's recent medical condition and is certain she received confirmation of receipt of payment for her latest treatments. Why those data-pushing, lazy-ass, little—

"Did you check your advocacy representative's records, Nana?"

"I did," the old woman answers. "But they said the same thing. They said the credits haven't shown up in their account silos. Of course, now they won't let me schedule a time for my follow-up treatments because they say I'm carrying an insufficient balance. I'm very worried, dear. My tumors feel funny."

As much as she loves her dear old Nana, Mu doesn't have time for her reedy prattling. She notes that Martstellar and her armed friend have dropped out of the flow up ahead. Quickly, Mu takes cover behind a three-dimensional advertising hologram shooting upward from the deck. Easing her head incrementally around the hologram's projection, she sees that Martstellar and her man-panion have stopped to be part of a small crowd waiting for a lift. Both of them look upward as a lift slides down the inner atrium wall to their location.

Not good, Mu thinks. If those two board that lift she will more than likely lose them. Of course, Mu could just slam aboard the lift at the last moment before the doors close and go all close-quarter on them, but there are almost a dozen additional people waiting with them for a ride. The lift will be brimmed. Yes, Mu isn't above a little hand-to-hand or smoking a couple of bystanders, but that jerk Lee down at CPB gave specific orders. He stressed discretion.

Mu has a brilliant idea.

She taps in. "Oh, I'm sorry you're not feeling up to snuff, Nana. I'm sure I can get this issue all sorted out, but I'm kind of needed in a meeting right now down the hall. Can I patch you back in a few minutes?"

"Oh, of course, dear," her grandmother answers. "I don't want to cause you any trouble."

"No trouble at all," says Mu. "Just give me fifteen minutes or so and I'll get back to you straight away, all right?"

Right, Mu thinks. *Right after I kill these two bozos.*

Her grandmother's tone brightens. "Oh, that would be so helpful. I love you, sweetie. Be a good girl, Bootsy. Smooches!"

"Smooches to you, Nana. Bye."

Mu terminates the patch. Bending her elbow and reaching back, she jerks back a zipper on her rucksack and paws inside, and immediately she finds what she's looking for: a small translucent bag of microelectronic tracking chips. Edged with miniscule adhesive barbs, each chip is no bigger than a fleck of party confetti. She pinches out one of the chips from the bag and holds it to the side of her skull. The chip beeps softly in response to confirm synchronization with Mu's ocular frequency.

Now all Mu needs is a diversion. Something simple that will allow her to get close. Mu remembers she has a sizable amount of credits in her pack, enough to bribe a small army if need be. She opens a second zipper on her pack and takes about half of her credits, figuring half will have to do. After she collects the bounty, hell, she'll bill the outlay to CPB as a field expense.

Mu rolls left and around the hologram. She shimmies through the crowds, keeping her face averted, and moves ahead. When she believes she has enough distance, she hurls all the credits into the air behind her like a tossed wedding bouquet.

The diversion works. Once people on the concourse realize what's fluttering down all around them, the scene becomes feeding time at the jackal cage. Shrieks and squeals, diving bodies lunging every which way in an all-out scramble of greed. Some people wrestle and even come to blows, and Mu couldn't be happier when she sees a teenage busker wielding his pipe guitar at people's heads like a battle axe. She sees Martstellar and her friend get shoved about in the crowd of people waiting for the lift. Mu slips past behind them and hooks back, planting the tracking chip on the tall bearded man's waist with a passing tap.

Mu jogs ahead, patting the side of her skull to check the tracking sync on her ocular. A locater beacon echo flashes clear in her field of vision, and she can't help but pump a victory fist. When enough distance is between her and her targets, Mu finds cover in a shop doorway and catches her breath.

Pulling up a previously uploaded file of *Alaungpaya*'s barge architecture and using an overlay, she cross-checks the chip's location beacon. She sees the transmitting beacon board the lift and power upward. It takes eight minutes longer to assess the final location.

Deck 20, personal quarters of Flynn, Jedidiah; SFZ Citizen Identification 821612403.

Pay dirt.

INTO FLYNN'S

After a moment of insisting that he enter his quarters ahead of her (no way in hell is she going to have her back to anybody, not even Mr. Nice Guy former lawman with the ass-grabbing hands), the first thing that strikes Koko about Flynn's quarters is the number of packing crates and recycled cardboard boxes lying about.

Most of the storage boxes are sealed with clear packing tape and all appear to be labeled in thick black marker for shipment to the same location. Strangely enough, it's the name of an organization that Koko is somehow familiar with:

new liberty international relief services (nlirs)
depressus donation division (d3)—second free zone

"Charity?" Koko asks, not turning around.

The unit's augmented managerial intelligence system senses Flynn's presence and adjusts the lighting and ambient background noise to suit his predilections. The soft carbonated bubbling of a meditative fountain rises in the background, and Flynn seals the entry's magnetic locks with a soft click.

"Just unloading some clutter," he says.

Koko puckers her lips.

Just past a cubby sitting area with a C-shaped settee and foot table is an accordion screen made of synthetic sandalwood and pale, gossamer fabric. The fabric-lined sections are animated, painted with moving abstract shapes, and just beyond the accordion screen Koko spies an unmade full-sized bed with wrinkled black sheets. A series of framed prints are hung on the wall above the bed. Enlarged images of nanometer processing chips in a succession that go from orderly and new to completely scorched and destroyed. Koko has seen the prints before. It's an antique tongue-in-cheek pop-art series referencing the aggressive stages of the Radix3 electro-virus. Unleashed by an alliance of quasi-political and devout malcontents hundreds of years ago, Radix3 decimated global power grids, obliterated the Internet and wireless spectrums, and initiated Earth's first foray into small-scale thermonuclear smartwars.

One of the recycled boxes resting on the foot of the bed isn't sealed. Koko uses a sharpened fingernail to peel back the flap, leans over, and peeks inside. Neatly folded towels and assorted labeled toiletries. She doesn't turn to face Flynn, but angles her chin upward to point.

"Is this the window view you mentioned?"

Just off the unit's tiny galley kitchen, Flynn is busy emptying his pockets onto a table planking out from the wall. His habit-driven hands unclip his gun holster from the belt around his waist, and he sets it down on the table.

"It is," he answers. "Pretty lucky I snagged a bulkhead unit, but like I said in the lift on the way up, I nailed this place on foreclosure a few years back. Sky views on this deck are pretty steep price-wise. If it hadn't been for the foreclosure, I could've never afforded it. Here, let me open the protective shade for you." Flynn raises his voice slightly to address the unit's AMI system. "Window. Open, please."

With a flat click, the protective housing covering the reinforced window releases and withdraws like a reptile retreating into a hole. Once uncovered, the window is about the length and thickness of Koko's leg. Koko glances out the narrow window just as one of the bright columns of *Alaungpaya*'s outer klieg lights slashes through the clouds.

"Cool."

"Well, there's some stars shining through here and there," Flynn says. "It's much better in daylight."

"I'll bet."

Flynn puts his hands on the small of his back and stretches. "When *Alaungpaya* tracks over the poles you really get a good show, particularly entering dawn or leaving any major climate systems. Last year's triple typhoon that obliterated what's left of India's eastern coast? The most amazing sunrises."

Koko turns and waits until Flynn looks her in the eye.

"Listen, Flynn," she says, "About before… down at the restaurant…"

"Yeah?"

"Well, there's no easy way to say this, but I think that kiss was a mistake."

"A mistake?"

"Yeah. I'm afraid I haven't been exactly forthcoming with you."

"Oh? And how's that exactly?"

"Well, for starters I'm not really on holiday from the holidays up here."

"You're not?"

"No. See, most of what I told you before was true. I mean, I used to do hardcore contractor stuff for real and for a long time, and up until recently I also used to be in the hospitality business too. But I'm not in the hospitality business either. To tell you the truth, I'm not really anything anymore, and now," Koko's voice trails off and she blows out a breath, "I'm in a bit of a muddle."

Flynn hooks his thumbs into his front pockets like a farmer.

"A bit of a muddle?"

"Yeah, and that may be understating matters a bit."

Flynn looks down at his boots in a thoughtful way and then looks up again.

"Well, as long as we are being candid with each other here, I sort of had a feeling."

"You did?"

"Yeah. And while we're tossing around honesty here, I knew something was up. That outburst at the table and even at dinner. You kind of gave the impression that whatever muddle you say you're in, it's not good. You're sort of distracted."

Koko crosses her arms and cranks a single eyebrow. "Really."

Flynn shrugs. "Not that that's a big deal or anything. Like I said, at first I thought it was because you'd lost so many credits at the tables. I mean, who wouldn't be ticked off by a big loss like that? But then I thought you were just shining me, going from telling me you're going to kick my butt to being all friendly, waiting for your chance to skip out. Which is fine too, but—"

A bell softly bongs twice behind him. The unit's AMI system addresses Flynn—a raspy, feminine voice:

Jedidiah. Single visitor present at entry. Female. Do you wish to grant access?

Puzzled, Flynn swings his head to look at the unit's door and then turns back to Koko. The expression on Koko's face and her now-drawn weapon say it all.

Holy shit. Where'd that come from?

Koko vaults sideways and takes cover on the opposite side of Flynn's unmade bed. Crouching down, she levels her weapon past Flynn's hip and directly at the door behind him. The indicators on Koko's gun glare red like the eyes perched on the snout of a demon.

Flynn lunges for his holster on the planking table and spins into the unit's open bathroom area just as the front door pops with a suppressed *whump*. The muffled detonation sounds like a large pillow being punched.

Flynn draws back on his footing as a snapping shower of electrical sparks streak inward into his quarters. Sliding down the bathroom's doorway, he pulls his Beretta and discovers the safety has already been released.

What the—

He flashes back on Koko's sudden kiss at the bar.

Oh, that's just perfect.

Flynn smears a forearm across his forehead and curses himself for being so stupid just as a body rushes past him. The AMI system announces the alarm. "Intrusion, Jedidiah. Intrusion."

Flynn looks across the room and sees Koko and a second woman grappling. The second woman is shorter than Koko, forged in muscle, and has a gun. Each grips the other's gun hand while her second hand attempts to execute attack strikes. The sound of flesh smacking flesh without pause or pity is sharp and quick.

The intruder reaches behind her back and withdraws a hidden blade. As the blade snicks open, the intruder whirls it around toward Koko's side. Koko anticipates the stick, arching her body. The intruder's knife misses Koko by a mere fraction, and to Flynn it doesn't seem real. Koko bends her body in such an impossible angle, it's as though she's made of rubber.

Whipping her head around and down, Koko seizes her attacker's knife hand in her front teeth and rips away a small sheet of flesh. The woman drops the knife instantly, but astoundingly she does not scream.

The AMI system continues: "Jedidiah? Intrusion and smoke detected within quarters. Repeat, smoke detected within quarters. Are you safe, Jedidiah? Ten seconds before alarm engagement and security notification."

Flynn falters and panics. He doesn't know what to do. He wants to squeeze off a round to at least clip the intruder, but he can't get a bead on Koko alone, and he fears he'll end up shooting them both. As the two women continue to thrash violently around, Flynn gets to his feet and sidesteps from the bathroom to the kitchen area. He keeps his gun up and his sights trained and hopes for a break, but it doesn't come. The two women's moves are so fast, so blinding, it's almost as though the two are one blurred animal. A fusion of unstoppable limbs.

The assailant lifts a leg and stomps on Koko's instep, and Koko throws her head back and roars. Reeling around, Koko claws a hand down and across the woman's face and gouges four precise, deep grooves. Koko's follow-through screws her free, and she backhands the side of her weapon across her attacker's forehead. On sickening impact, the woman tilts for a second, and Koko plants the barrel of her gun into the woman's side. Koko pulls the trigger.

The muted blue whelp pierces the intruder just under her kidney, swelling and lifting the woman clean off her feet and onto Flynn's bed. The heated energy of the discharged round roams inside the woman's body like a monstrous, squirming creature seeking an exit, and a split second later a chunky, wet, cough-like pop renders the assailant messily across the bed.

Something wet and hot splashes on Flynn's face, and he knows it is showering viscera. Bits and pieces of the intruder have painted his quarters like a ruptured can of bright red tomatoes, and the exiting round has vaporized the entire right side of the dead woman's body.

"Jedidiah? Alarm and security notification imminent. Five seconds to reply."

Koko staggers backward. "Turn it off!"

Three seconds before alarm and security notification.

"*Flynn!*"

Flynn stammers past the hard ache in his throat. "Clear! Do not engage alarm! Repeat! Do not engage alarm!"

The AMI system's voice waits a beat. The meditation fountain trickles in the background, and sparks from the blown-in front door fizzle on the floor.

Alarm engagement deactivated.

A heaving, blood-soaked creature, Koko crashes back against the far wall near the window and swings her gun back toward the door and then over at Flynn standing in the kitchen with his raised Beretta.

A dribble of the intruder's blood winds into the corner of Flynn's mouth, and instantly he feels sick. With a loud retch, Flynn twirls about and brings up all the dissolving medications, beauty, seltzer, sake, and food in his belly into the sink. When Flynn finishes puking, he wipes the vomit from his mouth and turns. Koko is on him. She throws a power cross across his chin, and Flynn splashes to the floor.

When Flynn comes to he's not sure how long he's been unconscious. Possibly five seconds, possibly five hours. When he rolls over and looks up, Koko is pointing his Beretta and her own gun down at his face.

"I guess I owe you an explanation," Koko says.

WELL, GEE, THIS IS AWKWARD

With most of the gore swabbed off with a few purple towels dampened in the kitchen sink, Koko strips out of her bloody jacket and bodysuit and shucks them aside. She steps into and tugs on an old canvas jumper Flynn has pulled from one of the packing boxes marked for donation. The jumper is more than a little roomy on her so she cuffs the fabric around her boots and squares off the sleeves high on her biceps. Settling the zipper of the canvas jumper a few inches above the middle of her breasts, she locks the zipper off with a twist. Flynn offers her one of his smallest belts and she cinches it around her waist. She clips Flynn's gun in its holster and her own holster to the belt and holds the Sig in her right hand.

Now fully sober and changed into fresh clothes himself, Flynn needs all of his fogged-up mental capacities to process the insanity of her tale so far.

"So, there's got to be others," Koko says. "If I were going to deploy a team up here and try to keep it quiet on a Second Free Zone barge as big as *Alaungpaya* I'd send a minimum of three, maybe five. Enough to take care of business, but not enough to rustle up too much attention. Best bet is they've already found my room over at Wonderwall and the second team is holed up there, waiting for an update from this one. Price on my head, they may or may not have agreed to check in with each other—as I imagine Delacompte has put a load of credits in play. One thing's for sure, though: This woman is definitely not the agent I boxed down earlier. Damn, not taking that crazy redhead out was a big mistake."

Flynn rubs his aching jaw and withers. "This redhead… she wouldn't happen to be wearing neck extension bands, would she?"

"Why? You've seen her?"

Flynn sighs. "Never mind…"

Rummaging through the open box at the foot of the bed, Flynn finds a small kit containing first-aid supplies. In the kit, wedged up against some antiseptic bandages and tape, he locates an adrenaline-sustainer capsule the size of a caterpillar's chrysalis and offers it out to Koko like a little boy sharing a discovery. Koko pinches the capsule from his outstretched palm and jabs the sustainer into her neck. The needle discharges its adrenaline with a deflating buzz, and Koko tosses the spent capsule to the floor.

"Thanks. I guess I should thank my lucky stars I'm no longer in the presence of an actual, licensed Alaungpayan lawman, huh?"

"God, what did you do that's so bad someone would illegally send a couple of cold-blooded killers after you?"

"Would you believe it's because I helped her out of a tight spot in Finland?"

"Huh? A tight spot in Finland? What the hell is that supposed to mean?"

"I really don't have time to elaborate. And right now it's probably better if you don't know, because I sure as hell wish I could forget." Koko picks up the intruder's knife from where it dropped to the floor earlier. "Hey, wait a second. I know this knife. This knife is just like the one I got from…" Koko's face angles off with the revelation. "Oh, no. Juke."

"Juke? Who the heck is Juke?"

"Do I have to connect all the dots for you, Flynn? C'mon, you're going to tell me you security go-getters aren't wise to a fat man aboard who runs a hobby-game-maintenance front?"

"There's a lot of hobby-game-maintenance vendors on *Alaungpaya*."

"Well, let's just say this particular chubby little hugger sidelines. Juke used to sell black-market weapons down below years ago, but a pissed-off customer sort of took his legs."

Flynn puffs out his cheeks and shakes his head. "Goddamn." He recalls overhearing something about an arms trafficking investigation a while back, but since he wasn't part of the investigation he never gave it a second thought. Flynn crosses down the hallway and starts to insert the unit's blown-in door back into its housing.

Koko gestures to the boxes marked for donation.

"So, I guess you were going to Embrace, huh?"

Flynn leans a shoulder into the entry door and pops it back onto its track. The door holds in a makeshift way, and when he turns around he half expects Koko to have her gun pointed at him again. Instead he sees Koko picking through the sticky corpse on the bed.

From a zippered crease on the dead woman's sleeve, Koko removes a credentials plug. She stabs the plug into the wall processor above the right side of Flynn's bed, and a yellowish holographic slab of light projects out of the wall and rotates between them. Koko passes her fingers through the light's display but the cues don't respond.

"Do you mind unlocking this thing?"

Flynn looks up and addresses the unit's AMI system. "Visitor system access, please."

Visitor access granted.

Koko opens the files in the gyratory beam and blandly scours the information. "Loa Mu. Took part in the West African civil war takeovers," she says matter-of-factly. "Operation Buzzsaw. Operation Happy Safari. Usual de-civ merc cycles and typical conglomerate rebuild shakedowns. Hmm. Did a major stint on the Antarctic pontoon drilling settlements. Ooh, impressive body counts on that one. Yadda, yadda, yadda…" Koko looks over and studies the dead woman's face. "Hang on a second…"

"What?"

"No way. It couldn't be." Koko address the AMI system. "Please retrieve all files for soccer World Cup league standings."

"The World Cup?"

"Shhh." Koko pulls up a mass of data in the beam, team rosters and photos, and looks over a waterfall of statistics. "If I didn't know any better, I'd say this girl is a dead ringer for that fullback on the South American Coalition team, Bootsy Starr." A video of highlights from several soccer matches streams with a hushed audio of cheers. "Hey, you follow the bread and circus much?"

Flynn's eyes dart to the players running around multi-decked fields gyrating in the projection.

"Only to bet on the occasional over or under," he says vaguely.

"Oh yeah? Best game ever invented. Whoa, I'm telling you, there's such an uncanny resemblance. See? That's Bootsy Starr right there. Look at that girl run. Of course, the names don't match, but that doesn't mean anything. Aliases are easy to spin, and maybe she's had some work done on her cheekbones and nose."

"How does a soccer player get into private bounty-hunting work?"

"That's just it. They can't. All corporate mercs are supposed to be bred-engineered."

"And bio-engineered competitors were banned years ago."

"Precisely."

Flynn watches the beam as Koko keeps sorting through the data. A minute later she wrinkles her nose and shuts down the hologram. She ejects the credentials plug from the wall, tosses the device onto the dead woman's body. Wiggles her gun.

"So, you. All these boxes all packed up for donation. You're checking out with the big decision, then?"

"I'm afraid this is the case."

"So what the hell was all that down at the casino and at dinner, huh? Some pre-suicide revelry and last-breath largesse? Or was it an attempt to rock a little shift and shake as a last hurrah before you offed yourself?"

Flynn objects avidly. "No! That's not it at all. I was, I mean, we were just talking. We were just having a good time. I was down in the casino because I was bored and figured I'd try to go out on a high note, you know? And I really did win big tonight and swear I was planning on giving my winnings away. Anyway, you're the one who made a pass at me, if I remember correctly. You're the one who asked if I lived nearby."

"Don't flatter yourself," Koko says. "I thought you made a second agent in the window of the restaurant. Boy, I'll tell you, *that* threw me for a loop. I thought it might be best to lay low for a while. So us coming back here to your quarters? I was just using you as a shield."

"Gee, thanks for that."

"Hey, if it makes you feel any better, you're not that bad of a kisser. Maybe hung a little smaller than I usually like, but I'm sure you make up for it with scads of charisma, what with your fancy bachelor-pad view and all."

"Now you're just being mean."

"So, tell me. Is Depressus really that bad?"

"Yeah. It really is that bad."

"I'm sorry for your troubles."

"Spare me your patronizing concern."

"Oh, and I'm the one accused of being mean?"

"They say the odds are getting better on convalescence and life extensions," Flynn says, "but like everybody else I guess I was in denial from the get-go, hoping they'd come up with a miracle cure. The drugs are getting better, but the pharmacology keeps changing. I was good for a while, but then you get to this point of no return where you're not sure of yourself and everything closes in like a heavy curtain. Caring about yourself or anything else doesn't even enter the equation. You take more drugs just to stave off the mood swings and keep the darkest thoughts at bay, and they say that's the tipping point. Now, with the second and third generations afflicted up here, some theorize Depressus is gripping the genomes and getting passed down. But like I said, I'm an engineered birth like you, so who knows about the genome thing."

Koko has stopped listening. She looks down disgustedly at the corpse spread out on the bed.

"God, the head is still on this one. Do you mind?"

"Mind what?"

Koko takes one of the purple towels and wipes the face of the dead intruder. In one swift motion she dips her head and chomps on the corpse's skull. She bites out the woman's eye with a squishy shred of flesh.

Flynn's stomach backflips and he dry-heaves. Koko bolts upright and spits the eyeball out in a streaming arc. The eye wetly smacks the floor and tumbles to a rest beneath the love settee.

"Rules of hand-to-hand engagement," Koko says. "Sorry."

Another wambling roll in Flynn's belly. "God! How can you do that?"

Koko inspects the damp purple towel for a clean spot and then wipes her mouth and tongue. Buffs her front teeth with vigor.

"How can you kill yourself?" she counters.

"That's Depressus. That's different."

"Not to me it's not. If you ask me, a bunch of mopey whiners doing a lemming dive off a sky barge beats battle-marking any ol' day."

"Listen, Koko…"

"Hey, I'm sure I don't really understand what you've been through, and I'd love to hear more about your sob story because you've really done me a solid here, not accidentally shooting me and giving me new duds and all. But you have to understand, Flynn. I'm out of here. I'm not going to finish out my life being hunted, and I'm damn sure not going to be taken down by a bunch of credit-grubbing killers out for an easy payday." Koko inhales tightly. "I need to get off *Alaungpaya*, like, now. Like yesterday. Out of the Second Free Zone orbits completely. Back down to Earth."

"I think *Alaungpaya* is already on lockdown until after Embrace."

"What? That's already happened? Shit, when does Embrace go off?"

Flynn addresses the unit's AMI system once more. "How much time until the Embrace ceremony on *Alaungpaya*?"

Embrace countdown is now at one hour, thirty-two minutes, and twenty-three seconds.

"There you go," Flynn says.

Koko looks down and fiddles with the gun in her hand. Flynn watches her, and suddenly his chest feels very, very heavy.

"So, I suppose you're just going to kill me now, right? Tie up a loose end?"

Koko looks up. "I'd rather not, but I think it'd be more convenient."

"Yeah, but I was kind of looking forward to the Embrace ceremony."

"Mmm, the Embrace ceremony," Koko says. "Do you have any idea what happens to a body on terminal velocity? Splits open just like this girl here, only in a thousand tiny pieces."

"But it's quick."

"Quick."

"And they say it's a beautiful flight."

Koko makes a face. "Who says that? The survivors?"

"Ha-ha, very funny. The doctors are supposed to sedate you with a calming hallucinogenic, so the word is the whole jump is kind of exhilarating and peaceful. We'll be over the southern Pacific. I had my last words picked out and everything."

"Let me guess. Poetry?"

"More like a curse, actually." Flynn rubs his face with both hands. "Look, Koko. I get it. I mean, I do. I'm a liability to you, and you need to move quickly. No matter what I swear to or promise right here, I know you shouldn't trust me. But listen, if you're going to kill me, can you at least allow me the courtesy of clearing my thoughts first?"

"What the hell for?"

"I don't know. To be civilized."

"Don't be such a baby."

"I'm not a baby."

"Oh, yeah? I suppose you want a blindfold too. I'd give you a stick of crinkle-flake for dramatic effect, but my smokes are ruined thanks to this dead one here." Koko cranks the levels on her gun, cocks her head, and crosses her arms. "Fine. You've got one minute to clear your thoughts. But listen up, okay? Fair warning. If you even think about making a move or try some kind of hero antics here, I promise your last moments alive will be so painful you'll wish you'd never been born."

Flynn nods. "I understand."

"Good."

Flynn shifts on his feet and glances around his quarters. Not much to speak of, his mundane life's slovenly trappings and belongings. He considers his donations to NLI Relief Services and his dismal legacy—molecular traces of skin, sweat, and bodily oils soon to be cleaned from the items given to those in need. Time seems to undulate radically, speeds up and slows, and his hands start to shake. Is this really it? Really? After all his inconsequential striving and meager, senseless achievements, this is how he is going to die? At the hands of a trained corporate killer bartender? It's all so absurd. Flynn wants to laugh but he can't. God, he thought he'd at least see some memories flash by in his mind, but he doesn't and Flynn finds that more than a little disappointing. Should he say a prayer? No, his intention is to be brave in the face of his mortality and curse. He looks up as Koko levels a reticent look. Those eyes. Such a remarkable shade. So impassive and green.

Wait. Does he really want to be shot? Shouldn't he, well, shouldn't he have some say in how he dies? Perhaps Koko knows something less messy. Something painless, something dreamt up in some clammy Hapkido den that could take him from this world with a measure of kindness. Flynn starts to utter something, but he can't find his voice, let alone his breath.

Slowly, he forces himself to open his palms at his sides as Koko meanders from around the bed. Over the funk of death, Flynn catches a faint whiff of her cinnamony scent as she moves closer. Soon twenty feet becomes fifteen. Then ten.

All of Flynn's nerves are frenzied, and the elation blended with sheer terror in his heart is beyond electrifying.

Koko is seven feet away now, and Flynn believes he can feel the warmth emanating from her body. As she enters his comfort zone, he squeezes his eyes shut. A tight, hard knot presses the skin above his sternum. The barrel of her gun.

Here it comes, Flynn thinks. The flash, the inconceivable rush of killing heat.

Here it comes, here it comes, here it comes…

The barrel leaves his chest and lifts the soft space beneath his whiskered chin. Startled, Flynn opens his eyes. Koko tips back slightly and with her free hand thumbs away a tear streaming down the side of Flynn's face. No. It can't be. She's actually smiling at him.

Smiling?

"You know what?"

A croak escapes Flynn's throat.

"I think I've got a better idea," Koko says.

MOVING OUT

Ten minutes later Flynn is hustling Koko up a protracted climb on the curving outer maintenance passages, decks, and ladders that skirt *Alaungpaya*'s massive hull.

Even with his turned-in credentials, Flynn knows how to bypass security access panels on alternating decks. To ward off the cold, he's provisioned them both with the heaviest coats and gloves he could find from his scanty packed-up possessions. But despite these extra layers, the freezing, less-oxygenated air near the hull is cruel. The sub-zero infrastructure appears endless, skeletal, and utterly confusing to Koko. Sometimes it looks as though the two of them are heading up and other times it seems they are awkwardly galumphing their way back down. Tree-trunk-thick stanchions of cable web out from the walls, and longitudinal pipes jacketed with dense,dripping stalactites of frost elbow out at almost every turn. Now and then, massive crisscrossing spars twang above them with great creaks of turbulence.

Koko's leg muscles burn and her lungs ache from the climb's exertion. She wants to keep at least one of her hands on a gun, but in the narrow, grated passageways it is more than a little difficult. They found the dead bounty agent's rucksack outside Flynn's quarters and discovered it was crammed full of weapons. Koko took the extra power clips for both her Sig Sauer and his confiscated Beretta and threw the rest back inside Flynn's quarters.

On the next passageway they bustle past a handful of worker-drones in heavy hooded oil coats. A couple of the maintenance workers appear to recognize Flynn and assume he is trafficking through the area on official ASS business.

Koko can't stop her teeth from chattering.

"C-c-can you move any f-f-faster? My nipples are about t-to snap off."

Flynn glances over his shoulder. "Any faster and we might draw unwanted attention. Word travels fast up here, and someone might get suspicious. Just be cool, all right?"

Koko gestures to the icy surfaces around them. "Be cool, he says. That's got to be the understatement of the twenty-sixth freakin' century. It's a meat locker out here, Flynn." Koko compresses her hands into tight balls to keep the blood flowing to her fingertips. "Damn, how many decks more do we have to climb?"

"Forty. Maybe forty-five."

Forty-five? Koko shivers. Goddamn, how she misses The Sixty. The oppressive soggy heat, the vibrant hyper-growth tangle and succulent blooming flora. Annoying as they were, she finds herself missing those crazy Gibbon monkeys that hung around her bar.

"Had to live on top of the world didn't you, Depressus boy?"

"Hey," Flynn chides, "you could have blown my head off back at my quarters. I'm doing you a favor here."

"How about a lift? Any of those bad boys around?"

Flynn shakes his head and keeps moving. There are tiny sweat icicles beading the hairs of his beard. "Lifts always empty out onto public decks," he says. "It's too risky. Just keep moving, and we'll be there before you know it. Man, I thought you diehard mercenary types were supposed to be tough."

"Tougher than you."

"And yet who's the one complaining?"

On a stretch of scaffolding up ahead a group of dark-goggled maintenance technicians in full-length oily parkas are taking a break. With ear-protection headsets looped around their necks, they sip steaming tea from reservoir thermoses strapped beneath their coats and nibble on buttery triangular biscuits. Koko and Flynn start to hew their way through the group, and Flynn gives the men and women a busied look. Koko keeps her head down.

"Excuse us, friends," Flynn announces. "Security Services. Be out of your way in just a second. Got us an urgent classified breach infraction, degree-code seven."

The group moves apart as best they can, cramming themselves back against the narrow passage's frosted rails. Flynn and Koko are almost through when a burly parka on the end of the group blocks Flynn's path with a raised arm. Koko bumps into Flynn's back like a halted caboose.

"Restricted area here, officer," the burly parka growls, his breath fogging the air. "Can I see your credentials?"

Flynn dead-eyes a stare forward and doesn't move.

The burly parka continues. "Hey, I'm sorry, but I'm master chief here. Not busting your chops or nothing, but like I said, this section is restricted. Breach infraction or not, I still need to see identification."

Flynn is still looking forward when he finally speaks. His voice is unemotional and restrained.

"Officer Jedidiah Flynn, C-class. Badge number two-two-nine-four."

One of the techs behind Koko chuckles hollowly into her tea about the bogus nature of breach infractions, and the rest of the crew don't even bother to suppress their commiserating laughter. Koko clamps her cheek with her back teeth and bites down.

The big parka doesn't lower his beefy arm. "Regulations," he snarls. "Yeah, I know they can be a hassle and all, but I still got to see identification no matter who you say you are. Nothing personal."

Bit by bit Flynn turns his head. Over the tilt of his shoulder,

Koko can see Flynn's eyes reflected in the burly parka's protective goggles. It's an irritated look she's seen plenty of times on senior officers in the field—a heady mixture of contempt, calm civility, and aggravation. If she didn't know Flynn was a bit of a cardsharp and somewhat skilled at the bluff, it would appear that the big man blocking their way had just kicked a snake.

The burly parka shoves Flynn back a little. "Hey, you deaf?"

"What?"

"I said, are you deaf? The ears. Hard of hearing. The noise out here near *Alaungpaya*'s hull, I know it does a number on the eardrums over time. That's why techs like us are supposed to wear ear protection. Anyway, I still got to see your creds, man."

"Step aside, sir," Flynn says.

"Hey. I don't make the rules, buddy, I just follow 'em. If you don't present proper identification I'm afraid you're going to have to turn around and go back the way you came." Burly parka finishes chewing some of a biscuit in his cheek and passes a fleeting look at the other workers in his crew. Flynn's darkened look doesn't waver.

Subtle and slow, Koko moves her fingers under her coat, her mind percolating. The massive network of ducts and pipes around them, who knows what hydrogen fusion magic is whisking through them to keep *Alaungpaya* aloft? Drawing her gun could be a big mistake. Her mind downshifts to tactical defaults. Six techs on two. Clipping leg sweeps, incapacitating breaks of bone, and crushed windpipes. But what then to do with all their bodies? No, she needs to wait for Flynn's call. Flynn then utters something so quiet that none of them can hear.

The burly parka grunts. "What did you say?"

Flynn speaks louder. "I said, regulations got your back, huh?"

"That they do," the burly man answers. "That they do."

Flynn moves his face five inches from the big man's bulbous nose. "So I suppose then, as the master chief of this crew, you are familiar with the penalties for impeding a Security Services emergency."

"Huh?"

"Sure, yeah," Flynn says. "It's pretty laughable stuff now here in front of your crew, but interfering with an officer like me on an issue like this? Do you really think your precious regulations will have your back?"

"Now, hold on a second…"

"No, you hold on. I don't have time for this. This is an emergency and it's classified, you got that? All wrapped up in that fragile ego of yours, you just thought—hey, let me swing some attitude around, be the big man and mouth off to a guy just trying to do his job. You know what? I really hate that. How about I drop some background probes into your and your buddies' files here? Specified and careful work, rig engineering, hard to erase the taint of even a minor inquiry."

"Are you threatening me?"

"What do you think?"

"I think I don't have to take shit like that from you, that's what I think."

Flynn's voice is louder and even more mocking. "Oh, really, now? And who do you think they'll believe if you report it, huh? Me or some jerk who doesn't have the good sense to get out of the way?"

Reluctantly the burly parka ponders this as the other technicians in his crew grow still. Flynn reaches out and puts his hand on the burly parka's obstructing arm.

"Show me how smart you are," he says.

A few minutes later Koko and Flynn are scaling up four more deck levels, taking the metal stairs two steps at a time.

"Urgent breach infraction degree-code seven?" Koko asks.

Flynn bats a hand in the air like he's swatting away an annoying fly.

"Give some meathead a PhD in fusion propulsion and anti-gravity physics and he kind of gets dopey on the details."

PEDDLING THE FAITH

NEW ONE ROMAN CHURCH OF THE MOST HOLY LIBERATOR
RECRUITMENT FEED ADVERTISEMENT "FOG SPOT"—0:60

CLIENT: New One Roman Church of the Most Holy Liberator
(NORC/MHL) Division of Populace Assessment and Public
Affairs

PRODUCTION ENGAGEMENT: 2516 All Hemispheric Seasonal
Cycles

VISUAL FEED 1: USING CELEBRITY STAND-IN AVATAR
INSERTIONS. (See attached creative brief for available
endorsers with fees, demographic specifics, languages,
and agent contact information.) NARRATOR, IN WHITE,
EMERGES LIKE A SPIRIT FROM THE MIST AND STEPS
INTO A ROCKY, BARREN FOREGROUND. THE SCENE IS OF
INDETERMINABLE ORIGIN, NEITHER COLD NOR WARM IN
NUANCE. CAMERA DRAWS IN SLOWLY AS NARRATOR STOPS AND
LEANS THOUGHTFULLY AGAINST A LARGE BOULDER IN THE

FOREGROUND. NARRATOR SMILES AT CAMERA, TENDERLY.

AUDIO: GENTLE, SOOTHING, SOFT WIND SOUNDS. BARELY
DISCERNABLE WHISPERS OF DEITY NAMES IN SUCCESSION.
[Yahweh, Allah, Mulungu Christ, Bhagavan, etc. See
attached creative brief for specific names and
pronunciations.]

NARRATOR: Questions. Since the beginning, the hearts of
many have struggled to attain answers. Questions defining
our very existence. Some speculate this is an egocentric
flaw in our very natures—to ponder such deep questions.
Yet questioning one's meaning in and of itself is arguably
part of what makes us human. You know this. I know this.
And we both know in the past few centuries the world has
survived [PAUSE]...

[CUT TO] VISUAL FEED 3: NEW ANGLE ON NARRATOR.

NARRATOR (CONT.): ...*trying times.*

[CUT TO] VISUAL FEED 4: NEW ANGLE ON NARRATOR.

NARRATOR (CONT.): In the past hundred-plus years, from
the despicable heaps of deliberate destruction, all
shades of worship and manners of faith are surging again.
A commitment to rebirth, to faith and moral absolutes—
this is hardly something to be ashamed of. The challenge,
however, is to humble yourself before omnipresent
truths. To accept and marvel at the grace of humankind's
miraculous survival. For one to wallow in dissolute
confusion in the face of our unlikely persistence is
(LAUGHS GENTLY, BUT NOT DERISIVELY) absurd.

[CUT TO] VISUAL FEED 5: TRACKING, CIRCULAR PAN AROUND NARRATOR.

NARRATOR (CONT.): No, my friends, you feel, as I do, the turning. A yearning to fill the hollow ache within yourself. A calling to higher matters of the spirit, yes-yes. But how do you choose the right path? The best faith? An introspective soul like your own deserves better. The most encompassing credence for peace and success. All I can ask you today is that you consider. Consider the right way and the life. And join us.

[CUT TO] VISUAL FEED 6: CLOSE UP NARRATOR'S FACE. NARRATOR HOLDS UP A NORC/MHL MEDALLION.

NARRATOR (CONT.): Good news and prosperity to you. I'm [CELEBRITY NAME] and I endorse this feed.

VISUAL FEED 7: [DISSOLVE, LOGO UP—NORC/MHL]

KNEEL BEFORE YOU RISE

While waiting for news on Koko, Portia Delacompte contemplates popping back yet another hit of Q just as the glowing orange projections above her desk bleat to remind her it is time for her daily supplication.

Delacompte mutters a curse out loud but stops herself. She knows that once the notification is locked in on her location the Church is likely listening.

Shit, this keeping up appearances is getting stale, she thinks miserably.

Supplications are unavoidable. As an aspirant to the New One Roman Church of the Most Holy Liberator, Delacompte is mandatorily required to log in for the daily sacrament. Even with 79-million-plus members and millions more like her going through the acolyte process worldwide, the sanctimonious bean-counters kept track of every single detail of her application. How many prayers. How many deficient confessions, how many credits she's tithed and how often she's attended their boring collective missionary mobs, the fasting and all the post-flagellate medical anointments—ticking off her faithful affirmations and inadequate stumbles like so many hash marks on a scoreboard. The Church keeps track of everything. *Everything.*

It makes Delacompte feel so tired.

You'd think they'd have better things to do than ride fresh applicants like this. She doesn't know—maybe, instead of engaging directives they have conveniently extrapolated from their pruned ancient scriptures, they could spend their time helping those crushed in the embattled disease- and famine-ridden regions. Perhaps feed the plebeian re-civ minions who actually believe in their revamped, monotheistic mumbo jumbo and huckster platitudes.

But of course not. That would mean work, and who wants to work when you can lie back and roll around in devout fantasy like a pack of overfed dogs?

Really, the reinvention and resurgence of organized religions across the globe after centuries of human-made sub-apocalyptic cataclysm defies logic. Take the best of the world's bankrupt faiths and cobble them into a unified belief that supports and espouses status and commerce—all of one cast and yet anonymous at the same time, inclusive yet formless. Pure genius in terms of mass control, and no doubt admirable. But after the razing of the planet, after technology's meltdown and generations of effort patchworking scattered nations' corrupt power structures back into a tenuous workable engine, after all the suffering, environmental collapse, contagion, war, and moral dearth… don't you think the Most Holy Liberator—or any deity, for that matter—would have shown up by now? Powered down on some superstar cloud flanked by a bunch of bored-silly angels and said, "Okay, idiots. That's enough. Knock this shit off right now."

Doesn't matter.

Delacompte knows there is no way she is going to move up the CPB corporate ladder without stomaching it all. Every top executive in the managerial echelon of the CPB board wears his or her NORC/MHL faith like a cabalistic badge, and if she is going to continue to the top level she needs to gulp down the fabled garbage whole.

Still, it constantly amazes Delacompte how nobody dares to acknowledge the two-ton elephant decomposing in the corner of the room. Which is, given the secular and violent desires at the core of the Custom Pleasure Bureau's commercial efforts, the insistence that board-level executives be active in the Church really makes no sense at all.

Talk about compartmentalization.

Delacompte ticks in her salvation identification codes and works her way past the Church's central mainframe firewalls. Logging in past the gateways takes only a few seconds but the music while waiting is always the worst to her. Country-fried paean hymns and chants moaned by hairless monks living in deep fallout caves in what used to be northern Peru. Like listening to the tone-deaf crooning of humping baboons.

Just get through this, Delacompte tells herself. *It gets easier every day.*

Easier every day.

A greeter welcomes her through the engaged stream. The greeter is a chinless, harsh-looking female with straw-colored hair tightly drawn back; she cuddles an infant in a pale blue blanket like a prop. Usually it's some feeble old loon jacked high on the Church's long YOU CAN HAVE IT ALL! con, so seeing this woman with her child certainly is a new one. The conviction of fanaticism sparkles in the greeter's jittery eyes.

"Good news to you, Sister Delacompte! The Liberator welcomes you to the new covenant and blesses you and yours always! The right way and the life!"

Yeah, right, Delacompte thinks. *You don't know me, lady. The things I've done, the things I am capable of. If you did, I'm sure your head would pop like a blister. The right way and the life? Why don't you do that kid a favor and smother him while you have the chance?*

The thought of the woman smothering the baby wobbles a cold feeling through Delacompte, as though a circuit has been inadvertently tripped inside her. The dim sensation fogs her brain for a few moments before Delacompte forces a tight-lipped smile and nods her head.

"And good news to you, sister," she replies.

"Are you ready? Is your medallion ready?"

Her medallion—*shit*.

Delacompte opens the top drawer in her desk and retrieves an oblong black velvet box. She undoes a brass hook fastening the box closed and removes the plain silver medallion of the faithful. The NORC/MHL medallion is secured to a brown leather lanyard, and she drapes the lanyard over her head. When the medallion is centered against the skin just above her collarbones, an internal mechanism begins to hum quietly like an insect, growing stronger in response to her body heat. Delacompte pushes herself up from her desk chair and strikes a pose mimicking the meek. She turns over her hands and opens her arms.

When she first applied to the Church years before, pharisaic policymakers and archbishops still required kneeling on something hard to increase the presence of pain. Delacompte is grateful they scrapped that primitive part of the daily ritual at least. Now all she has to do is check in, stand there, and wait for the locator currents to lance through her body.

"The service will begin in thirty seconds. Prime yourself, Sister Delacompte. The glory of the right way and the life are with you this day!"

The elapsing pace of the throbbing vibrations in the medallion harmonize with the greeter's countdown and expand outward in Portia's muscles with increasing intensity. Delacompte shuts her eyes and tries to focus on something else that will allow her to put herself beyond the dreary hair-shirt discomfort. She hones in on an image of Koko. Koko being hacked to pieces by the blades and gears of indifferent machinery. The mental picture is good; however, thinking of Koko stirs a second wobbly sensation, stimulating the blank voids from her SMT therapy.

Why is she so bent on killing Koko, again?

Forget it, here it comes.

The pain coursing through her body increases in strength, and she has to fight against bucking back and forth on her feet in full seizure lest her organs malfunction. Again, Delacompte compels herself to recall the pixie-like sharpness of Koko's mercurial features. Her green and quizzical eyes. Delacompte imagines herself holding Koko's head in between her own two hands and feels her mouth parting on reflex, teeth ready to mark her former comrade blind before she squeezes the spark from her pretty little skull.

Oddly enough, it helps.

TEAM WONDERWALL

Meanwhile, six thousand meters above, Heinz looks at Wire from the bathroom in Koko's Wonderwall hotel room.

Propped on a single elbow, Wire stretches out on the room's bed with her rucksack next to her. Suddenly the walls shake as though the barge itself has a bout of indigestive gas.

Wire tenses. "What the hell is that?"

Heinz sighs. "I think *Alaungpaya* is entering a lower altitude. Prep measures for the Embrace ceremony. The service ceilings on these babies are pretty high, and I think they have to descend to a little under four kilometers for the jump. Or so I hear."

"Crazy bastards."

"I suppose so."

Wire flops back and sweeps the sights on her HK across the ceiling.

"This is dumb," Wire says. "No way is this Martstellar coming back here. I mean, here? To all this? Just look at this place. Not exactly the St. Regis or the Ritz, am I right? Her reserving a room in a dump like this could be a false flag."

"A false flag?"

"Yeah, a dodge. A false flag. Think about it. Our guest record hack told us Martstellar booked this room, grabbed a shower, got her head together with a couple of drinks, and then split. I don't know about you, but to me that spells reboot and on the move. Look around—the woman doesn't even have any frigging gear here."

Heinz roams her eyes around the room. Hmm. Wire does have a point.

Heinz steps out of the bathroom and checks the window. Parting the blinds, she looks down on the weltering rucks of people on the *Alaungpaya* concourse below.

"Look, we had to check it out," Heinz says, turning. "Yeah, I get what you're saying, but this place being that easy might just be Martstellar's thinking too. She might think we'd see it as a false flag and blow it off too."

Wire frowns. "Yeah, right. I think we'd be better off covering the arrival and departure areas up top and just trap her there. No way is she sticking around *Alaungpaya*, not after she chose not to finish you off."

"I told you," Heinz says, "no passenger transports or personal craft are allowed on or off *Alaungpaya* until after the Embrace ceremony. Your and Mu's shuttle was the last incoming transport. If Martstellar can't leave until after Embrace concludes, she might come back here to rest up before she does."

"Oh, sure. A bounty operative attacks her, she gets some weapons from that chubby paralyzed scumbucket, and she's just going to come back here to this place? To what? Grab a little shuteye? Holy smokes, Heinz, are you always this obtuse?"

Heinz snaps the blinds closed and steps away from the window.

"Look," Wire says, "all I'm saying is that this woman used to be a pro. She could have even stowed away on a freighter by now. Might be hiding out on a layover trawler or Helium-3 tanker and biding her time, waiting for the Embrace lockdown to be lifted. I mean, have you even thought of that possibility? It's not a completely original idea." Wire ejects the power chip on her HK and rams it home. "From the look on your face I can tell you didn't even consider that. Whatever, Heinz. You want to bungle this all up, it's your reputation—not ours. Unlike you, Mu and I have plenty of other assignments in our queues."

Stung by Wire's accusation, Heinz watches as Wire taps in on her ocular. Heinz motions to the device with a flick of her hand.

"What gives? Anything from The Sixty?"

Wire shakes her head.

"How about Mu?"

Another shake.

"Huh. You don't think that maybe Mu might have—"

"Might have what? Done Martstellar all by herself and shafted us out of our end of the bounty? No way. Me and Mu go way back. We racked up ten tours together for the syndicates before we stepped up for the bounty game."

"Ten tours, huh? Am I supposed to be all impressed by that or something?"

Wire grips her breast. "Oh, suck this, beauty queen. It was a real tight ten. We came up together through the Antarctica outpost campaigns. I mean, have you any idea how hairy that was? Our body counts on those nation-building corpse fields alone peaked past twenty-five hundred each, so why don't you keep the attitude in check. Anyway, I saved Mu's ass more than once. That woman owes me."

"So you trust her."

"Does anybody trust anyone?"

"No."

"Exactly my point. Hell, no. But I do know Mu has a weak spot, and believe me, I can always leverage that if and when she ever decides she wants to spin the tables." Wire shifts. "You know what? To be perfectly honest here, I don't mind telling you about her Achilles heel because eventually—after we get Martstellar and take her eye?—one of us is probably going to kill you too."

"What?"

"Oh, don't stand there and tell me you're not planning on taking us out for all the reward credits yourself."

"The thought hadn't even crossed my mind."

"Really?"

"Really."

"Gee, you should be in a museum."

"You don't believe in professional honor?"

Wire throws her head back, hoots at the absurdity of the suggestion. "Professional honor? I suppose you believe in ethical morality and pink unicorns too. Holy smokes, Heinz, this ain't like we're back working for the syndicate despots, touting all that 'mission priority over the individual' jazz. These days the only thing a girl like me believes in is me."

Incensed and dumbfounded by Wire's arrogance, Heinz attempts to regain her composure. Why the conceited, greedy, little—kill her? *Her?* Heinz then makes a promise to herself. Once Koko is eighty-sixed, she vows to rip off both Wire's and Mu's heads and take all four of their eyes. Cut off their hands for good measure. Maybe their feet too.

Heinz shakes her shoulders and clears off the rest of her anger.

"So what is this chink in Mu's armor she's supposedly hiding?"

Wire chuckles. "Oh, you will positively love this." Like a teenage girl sharing a secret at a slumber party, she rolls over with an excited grin. "Okay, get this. Mu has a sickly grandmother she dotes on back on Earth."

"She has a *what*?"

"You heard me. She has a grandmother."

"Like grandmother as in actual blood-family grandmother?"

"The same."

"No way. How the hell did Mu ever get past the syndicate military entrance requirements? I thought all operative recruits have to be collective engineered."

"We do," Wire says. "But Mu worked some angles. Bribed some programmer or something. In any event, she got her re-civ records falsified. She confessed to me she did it because she didn't like the prospects of being another low-waging chump once she retired from playing football. In fact, Loa Mu isn't even Mu's real name. Her real name is Bootsy Starr."

"Bootsy Starr?"

"God, Heinz, she played in the World Cup on the South American Coalition. Fullback. Girl has, like, thighs of iron and crazy ball skills. You know how hard it is to get a decent credit-earning job when your glory days on the professional playing fields are over? C'mon, you saw her. She's not exactly a beauty like you, so once her meager endorsement packages dried up she had no marketable skills whatsoever. Hell, the private military hiring process is all so convoluted Mu knew no one would even care once she proved herself in the field, and she did that in spades."

Heinz's eyes flit back and forth as she processes this news.

"Wow. An actual real-life, living grandmother."

"I mean, how old-fashioned is that?"

"How do you even know this?"

Wire snorts back some snot, spits, and bull's-eyes a blank feed screen across the room. The phlegm slides down the screen like a pasty slug.

"One night off assignment we both got wicked wasted in some club and she just blathered. I was pretty toasty myself and pretended I didn't notice or care about what she shared with me, but I sure as hell squirreled that little nugget away for a rainy day. Mu may be a tough soldier, a solid tiger fighter, and a clean shot in a firefight, but she's also a sneak and a liar. She crosses me, I'll gut that wrinkly bag of skin of hers like a piece of rotten fruit."

Wire nuzzles the dark barrel slit of her HK softly under her chin. She winks at Heinz and imitates the look of a terrified child.

"You're one sick pup, Wire."

"That may be true," Wire says drily. "But unlike Mu, I'm not stupid enough to leave myself exposed. Not in the long game."

"And yet you lie there on that bed and tell me you're going to kill me when we get Martstellar."

"Did I also happen to mention I'm a confident bitch as well?"

Heinz contemplates drawing on Wire and blazing a pulse round right through her heart. Wire acknowledges the simmering menace behind Heinz's eyes, and the two stagnate in measured silence for a full minute before Heinz breaks off their stalemate. They need each other. For now.

Heinz crosses the room. She unzips her new rucksack and removes two pulse grenades. After she depresses buttons on the sides of each, attachment prongs spring open. Charges from the two pulse grenades will fry the entire hotel room out clean.

"Cover the hall," Heinz says, tapping in the armament codes. "I've got these."

Wire sits up. "Hey, so we are going proactive, then?"

"What, you need a written invitation?"

Wire jumps to her feet. "But what about housekeeping? That Lee down on The Sixty stressed discretion."

Heinz looks around for a place to plug the grenades into the walls. "You're not squeamish about leveraging some old woman, why should I care about some loser housekeeper? The whole place is probably maintained by drones anyway."

Wire beams. "Now we're talking!" She grabs her rucksack from the bed and bounces happily toward the door. "Redhead honey finally got her pretty little head in the game. Man oh man, I just love that. Ooh, yeah-yeah. Ooh, right-right."

ON THE MOVE

"Do you have respiratory issues or something?"

Flynn and Koko are in front of a six-foot-high curved metal hatchway. Hands splayed and planted on her knees, Koko looks up at him. If eyes were daggers, Flynn is pretty sure he'd be harpooned to the wall like a bug.

Koko wheezes, "Just… tell me… we're done… climbing."

"We're done climbing."

"It's about freakin' time."

Flynn explains that the hatchway accesses one of the least-populated areas of *Alaungpaya*'s incoming cargo and transport baggage holds. Flynn tells Koko that he has passed this way plenty of times before and that the hold is stacked with shipping containers managed by unmanned systemized robotics. The air about them is warmer and bitter with the pungent odor of scorched metal. Vibrations from the machine activity nearby shake the flooring beneath them. The whole area backs up to *Alaungpaya*'s arrival and departure decks and is a restricted section where, Flynn assures Koko, they are unlikely to encounter any additional techs. There are security image sweeps, naturally, but only one visual monitor trained on a bad angle and that had a cracked lens and frayed wires the last time Flynn passed through. He tells Koko to keep her head down anyway.

"I h-hate having my picture taken."

"Just move fast," Flynn says above the rumbling noise. The icicles in his beard have melted in the warmer temperature, and his face drips. "If somebody gives us any static, just keep quiet and let me handle it. I'm somewhat of a familiar face, and I'll power us through." He reaches over and starts to undo the seals and buckles on Koko's coat.

"Hey! I'm still freezing," Koko protests.

"You won't need it," Flynn says. "Take off the gloves I gave you too."

Flynn takes her coat and his own and stuffs them both behind a dark cross-sectioned nest of winding rubberized cable. As he takes her gloves from her, one of Koko's sharpened fingernails slashes the plump flesh on his exposed thumb. With the abating cold Flynn doesn't feel the cut at all.

Flynn sees the sluggish red glob leaking from his tingling digit and looks at Koko, bewildered. He sticks his bleeding thumb in his mouth and sucks.

Koko bunches her shoulders. Lets them fall.

"Sorry."

A wheel a foot and half in diameter is centered on the hatchway, and on the count of three Flynn rolls the wheel counterclockwise and pulls back on two locking bolts. As soon as he tugs the heavy door inward a brash screech undulates, indicating their presence. Oily gusts of balmy air muscle past them, and Flynn guides Koko inside. They huddle like two pilgrims lost in a storm, and he uses both arms and his full body weight to pull the hatchway shut behind them. When the door closes the alarm's screech goes silent. Flynn locks off the bolts and signals for Koko to stay close.

He presses his lips close to her ear. "Fifty meters right and we're clear."

* * *

The cargo hold is, indeed, vast and filled with the thundering sounds of chaos—hissing belts, grinding gears, and powerful slams of metal on metal. When a large chained container clamped in magnetic claws whizzes by overhead, Koko has to fight the urge to look up.

The next thing she knows they are in a low-ceilinged tubular passage lined with horizontal sleeves of wire and a floor brightly illuminated from beneath and so heavily scuffed it resembles marble. Flynn races ahead to a door on the right and taps a keypad. The door unlocks with a small snap. As Flynn drags Koko inside by her wrist, she catches sight of shelves with jugs and plastic storage crates. As the door shuts behind them, they are swallowed in darkness.

"Be quiet," Flynn whispers.

"What the hell is this place?"

"A custodial closet."

"Oh, for the love of…"

"Shhh," Flynn scolds. "The alarm. If anybody noticed, the SOP is to send a security check in under eight minutes." He drags her right and lifts the lid off a large plastic bin braced against the wall. "Here. Get in."

"You've got to be kidding me."

Koko curses herself for trusting this suicidal whacko. She should have just shot him in the head and taken her chances. Her itching hands fall, and she feels the plastic edge of the large bin in front of her. Insistent, Flynn's hands press in on the back of her waist.

"Just get inside," he says. "I'll climb in on top of you."

Koko wants to jab a pointed elbow into his ribs. Maybe a little higher up his chest and stop his heart cold. "This is stupid," she argues. "We'll be cornered in this stupid thing."

Koko turns her head and desperately tries to see Flynn's face in the inky black, but she can't. All she feels are his hands behind her right knee, urging and lifting.

"If they suspect any kind of a breach, it's over," Flynn says. "I don't care how good you think you are, you'll never get off *Alaungpaya*. They'll lock down every exit and might even depressurize the whole cargo area and surrounding flight decks just to be sure."

Koko groans with frustration and hoists herself over the edge and into the large plastic container. In a squat, she feels the stifling interior dimensions. The bin is empty, and the funk inside smells of burnt chemicals and putrid wet waste. Flynn climbs in next to her and lowers the lid on top of them. There is a buzz as the latch on the bin locks itself.

Flynn shushes her. "Quiet now…"

"Are we locked in here?"

"Yes."

That's it. Koko pulls her Sig from her belt as her other hand finds Flynn's throat. She chokes him, and he starts to gag. Koko feels the edges of her nails break the skin and mark his neck as she buries a gun muzzle firmly against his cheekbone.

"How are we going to get out of here, bright boy?"

Flynn seems to be holding his breath. The slightest of moves on his part and her nails will make him gush out like a stuck pig.

"If no one comes," he squeaks, "we'll… cut our way out."

Just for spite Koko considers ending Flynn right then and there, but she releases his neck.

"Boy, you sure know how to show a girl a good time, don't you?"

Flynn rubs his throat and coughs. "Thank me later."

Tucked inside the bin, they listen hard. Turns out, no one comes down the hallway to check on the alarm or the custodial closet. When they agree the coast is clear, Flynn instructs Koko to set her gun to the lowest pulse setting and squeeze off a reduced incendiary round to melt the lock. She does as he suggests, and the lid pops free. Koko throws back the lid and scrambles out of the bin as quickly as she can, but she trips and tumbles out onto the floor. Rolling over, she jumps up and finds her feet.

* * *

Flynn starts to hoist himself out of the bin, but he sees the dim red lights ornamenting the sides of her gun pointed directly at him.

"Put that away," he says.

The gun indicators hold steady in the gloom.

"You know," Koko says, "maybe I should just take my chances and get rid of you right here. Hell, you're in that stupid trash bin already, what do you care? It'll make a fine coffin. I'll be doing you a favor. I can find my way from here."

"Oh, yeah?"

"Yeah."

"Okay, but good luck with the rest of your little escapade trying to get off *Alaungpaya*."

"I don't need you, lawman."

"Are you so sure?"

The indicator lights on the gun move and settle again. "This is my finger applying pressure on a weapon I'm not so familiar with," Koko says.

"You know, you're right. What do I care? Go ahead. Shoot me."

"You think I won't?"

"No," Flynn answers, "I know you can. But you're smarter than that. Tactically speaking, it makes no sense at all. Think about it. You know you can still use me for at least a little while longer."

Flynn finishes fishing his lanky body out of the bin and straightens. He draws up a hand and rubs the neat, tenderized cuts scored beneath the stubble of his neck.

The red eyes on Koko's gun abruptly swirl and disappear as Koko shoves her weapon back in her belt.

"You are something else, you know that?"

"I do have my moments," Flynn says.

In the darkness, they go over the next steps of their plan and then head out.

TRAVEL ARRANGEMENTS

"Welcome to DwopSwedz, twhere convenience twis our motto, thwherever your twavels may lead. May I help you, fwiends?"

The blonde, perky sales clerk working the DropSledz rental counter in *Alaungpaya*'s arrival and departure area adjusts the tilt of her skullcap as she addresses the two unamused women before her. The clerk's tongue has recently been pierced with a waffle stud and gives the girl a heavily whistling lisp.

Wire hips past Heinz and cocks an elbow breast-high on the counter. She drops a couple of strat-sled coupons they took off Juke Ramirez on the counter between them.

"We have these strat-sled coupons…"

With an inspecting lift of her chin, the clerk leans forward and picks up the chits with dainty fingers.

"Oh yeth-yeth," the clerk chimes, examining the chits beneath a scanner. "Our economy swed special with exthenwed wawanty. Pwart of our way-test pwomotion."

Wire nods. "Yeah, terrific. Listen, maybe you can help us. We're sort of looking for a friend of ours."

"Oh?"

"Yeah. We're supposed to meet up and travel together, but there's been a bit of a miscommunication and now we can't reach her. She may have come by earlier and booked a strat-sled. Has anybody come by and checked in under the name of Martstellar, first name Koko?"

The clerk's blinking eyes ping between the two women. Heinz strokes the ribs of her neckbands and scrunches her nose.

"Oh. I don't thwink so," the clerk replies with cookie-cutter eagerness. "No, no one by the name of Koko. I thwink I'd wemember a name like that, and I've been on thwis shift for a while. Thorry. When would you two wike to departh Awaungpaya?"

Wire grumbles and takes the chits back from the clerk. "Never mind," she says. Then Wire reaches into her rucksack and peels off a bunch of credits from a banded roll. "Here. This is for you. We'll check back in a bit. If anyone named Martstellar shows up to book a rental, maybe you can let us know. Oh, and one more thing. Our friend doesn't know about my red-haired friend here. It's sort of a surprise, so if you see her don't say anything until we talk with you." Wire gooses Heinz's ass, makes kissy noises, and winks. "Ain't that right, sweetie?"

Heinz glares.

The clerk looks at the credits held out to her in Wire's hand. The credits are easily more than the clerk pulls down in a week. The clerk leans over.

"I can't accthep tipth," she whispers.

"Just take it," Wire says.

The clerk looks around and quickly palms the credits with a hasty nod.

Heinz has already turned away from the strat-sled rental desk and is scrutinizing the terminal area as Wire joins her, chuckling. In the arrival and departure area there are dozens of zig-zagged queues jammed with cattle-bored people awaiting transport. Most faces are upturned and glued to feed screens that hang at nearly every turn, and on a filmy blue membrane rotating above the entire area, a large scrolling display lists times, origins, and destinations of all departing and arriving aircraft. All listings on the blue membrane are underlined in red and marked CANCELLED UNTIL POST-EMBRACE.

Heinz gestures to a busy café a mere story above the whole place packed with travelers.

"We should probably set up surveillance there," she observes. "Looks to have a pretty good view, fore and aft. I could take the port side; you could take starboard. Martstellar comes through here, we'll spot her and cut her off."

Wire agrees, and they go up a short flight of stairs to the café. It is noisy in the café, and the cone-domed ceiling above the centralized bar is lit by thousands of tiny twinkling blue sequins of light. Bulling their shoulders through the patrons, they purchase a couple of large coffees and then position themselves at hover tables in their agreed-upon positions and begin their watch

Twenty minutes later, Heinz's ocular flutters on her skull with an incoming message from Vincent Lee down on The Sixty. From the communiqué's tone it seems Lee is less than pleased and freaking out. Heinz immediately buzzes Wire.

"Talk to me."

"Lee back at SI HQ wants an update on our status."

"He can bite me. Did Lee mention anything going down over at Wonderwall?"

"Hold on." A few moments later Heinz follows up. "Negative on Wonderwall, but that doesn't mean anything. Maybe Mu is flushing her to us."

"Yeah, or maybe she's already dead. I'm going to see if my uplink skimmer can probe the security coms. See if anything hinky has gone down anywhere aboard and run it back."

"I'm telling you—"

"Yeah-yeah," Wire says. "No other way off *Alaungpaya* unless she comes through here and blah, blah, blah. Just keep your post and stay sharp. We don't want her slipping through the choke point."

Someone behind Wire laughs heartily. Wire has the distinct

feeling the man is laughing at what she just conveyed to Heinz, so she turns around. She sees a dark-skinned, bare-armed man wearing a white wooly vest and drinking a pint of solar ale.

"Is something funny?" Wire asks.

The dark-skinned man sets down his drink. His head is enormous, like the head of a lion, and he is not the least bit intimidated by the stony look in Wire's eyes. The man leans forward on his well-developed and folded arms.

"There is always one other way off *Alaungpaya*," he says.

Wire lets her eyes drift down onto the departure and arrival area.

"Oh, yeah? And how's that exactly?" She looks back to the man.

The dark-skinned man leans back and makes a sad face and then flutters his thick fingers down through the air and makes a small screaming noise. The amber-colored ale in his glass jumps as he smacks the table in front of him hard.

He laughs even harder.

THE JUNIOR EXECUTIVE WAITS

As Vincent Lee sends his message to the bounty agent Heinz, he tries to put his boss's warbling moans out of his head. Just behind the polished blonde shine of her wooden office door, Portia Delacompte is going through the required supplication service for the faithful.

Lee frowns.

New One Roman Church of the Most Holy Liberator.

What a friggin' joke.

Lee has never understood the attraction of religion, particularly fundamentalist, hard-liner sects, and deep down he secretly dreads a future day when he will have to slurp up all the sanctimonious drivel like the rest of the CPB myrmidons with a big ol' straw. Yes, he realizes it has to be part of his long-term plan if he wants to survive and get ahead; many of his peers at CPB have already entered the NORC/MHL aspirant process and shamelessly adopted the dogma. But to Lee, the notion of turning his back on cold-bath sensibleness, secular reason, and the broader discoveries of universe-based physics sits about as well as a ball of foul cheese in the back of his throat.

The worst part is NORC/MHL's weaselly metaphysical

framework. Sheesh, if you're going to pick a massive delusional farce to cocoon yourself up in, at least have a backbone. You want to follow Mohamed to Allah? Terrific. Follow Mohamed to Allah. You want to flex your legs, get to know the chunky, mellow-looking guy breathing shallow? Have at it. But from the outset, the New One Roman Church of the Most Holy Liberator recognized the destructive nature of such antiquated limitations. Hell, even the breeziest study of antiquity could illustrate the fact that 99.9 percent of humanity's blood-spattered plunges down the commode were caused by religious fraction. So, to avoid this, the church founders forged a new path of aggregated non-exclusivity, accepting all arguments, parables, taboos, and truths of convenience. To Lee, the crippling truth is that it's all a snow job. A con. A ruse of solace designed specifically to justify the intentions of greed and power and to bless those in charge with the ability to shape and manipulate the future.

The most encompassing credence for peace and success?
The right way and the life?

People can be so stupid, Lee thinks. Like a flock to slaughter, like a flock to bloody slaughter.

Just beyond the door, Delacompte brays and Lee's chest spins out a sigh. It's all so ludicrous. Delacompte going through that crazy medallion ritual? Of course his boss is totally faking it. She's a former mercenary, and she has a ridiculous tolerance for pain. Lee has personally seen the woman take an incredible beating in CPB fitness center's sparring octagon and brush it off with indifference.

Still, he supposes, Delacompte has to sell it. The myopic, self-righteous NORC/MHL officials would only believe her if she quaked daily for absolution.

Bunch of masochistic maniacs.

Anyway, what on earth is taking these bounty agents so long? Why won't Heinz answer his messages? This whole affair should be completed by now. Where is this Koko Martstellar?

Lee tries to send another message to Heinz but the transmission again goes unanswered. He attempts secondary priority communications with both Mu and Wire and still receives no response.

In disgust, Lee pushes away from his desk, stands, and proceeds down the hall toward the floor's break room. His status as Portia Delacompte's right arm has always given Lee a slight edge over his fellow office workers, but the day's souring events have sucked all the haughty marrow from Lee's usual smugness. Avoiding others' eyes in the break room, he makes himself a large green tea and then heads back to his desk as quickly as possible.

Upon his return Delacompte's cries are in full swing, and he gulches down a burning swig of tea. Not that he'd know, but from the sound of the woman's histrionics if someone were to pass by just then Lee is sure they'd think his boss was thrashing through one very intense and protracted orgasm.

Lee shudders and tries the *Alaungpaya* team again.

TRAVEL ARRANGEMENTS, PART 2

In a half-squat, Flynn leans his back against a wall next to a smudged metal door that opens out onto the *Alaungpaya*'s main arrival and departure terminal. Koko squats next to him in a *wushu* rest stance.

"Let me see that strat-sled coupon you told me about," Flynn says, pulsing his fingers.

Koko removes the coupon Juke Ramirez gave her from her borrowed jumper's breast pocket and hands it over. Flynn examines the logo lettering on the chit: *DropSledz*. Flynn recalls seeing the strat-sled rental company's advertisements on the feeds. Smartly groomed, sophisticated men and women encapsulated in the personal propulsion crafts winging through a graphically enhanced atmosphere like angry hornets. Flynn slides up the wall and drops his hand to a bar that opens a perpendicular slit in the doorway just off to his left. He scans the view and eases the door closed again, keeping it slightly ajar.

"Wait here. I'll be right back."

Koko clutches his arm.

"Wait a second. Wait here? What do you mean, wait here? No, no, no. Uh-uh, I'm going with you."

Flynn eases the gap in the door closed and leans toward her. "They're looking for you out there, Koko, not me, remember? Me? They probably don't know about me or what I look like yet. Listen, I'll just go over and secure your strat-sled rental with this coupon. After the Embrace lockdown is lifted, you can take a strat-sled and take off out of here."

"Maybe we should think of something else," Koko says. "There might be a better way."

Flynn shakes his head. "Not unless you want to join me at the sunrise lemming ceremony. Shuttles are too conspicuous and freighters are completely out of the question. Too many tracer scans and cross-checks. Trust me, a strat-sled is the call."

Koko looks down. She wrinkles her brow and frowns.

"So, just how long is it until the... um..."

"What?"

"You know."

"The Embrace ceremony?"

"Yeah. When do you need to check in for your jump?"

In his head, Flynn tallies. He estimates the time since they left the dead agent down in his quarters, plus their interrupted lengthy climb out near the vessel's hull and their hiding out in the custodial closet.

"It's probably just over twenty minutes before they release the first wave of jumpers, give or take. The Embrace organizers are pretty flexible on participant check-ins, and they're supposed to stagger the jumps. I'm probably late for the first and second calls and dosage allotments, but they're kind of used to people dragging their feet at the last second."

Koko closes her eyes and slowly shakes her head. "Man, that's so *weird*."

"What now?"

"How can you be so laid back about ending it all?"

"Hey, it's not like I haven't been thinking about this for a while, you know. Embrace is not some random impulse buy. After you make your initial commitment and encode your personal contract, you sort of get used to the idea of your death just being out there. Like a big clock winding down."

"Oh, give me a break. Listen to you. Like a big clock winding down. Could you be any more unoriginal?"

"It's just a simile."

"Simile, schmimile. Here's a feed flash for you, Flynn. Everybody's big clock is winding down. The thing is most people just choose to ignore it. Anybody who isn't aware that their life can end at any second, that their tenuous existence is nothing but a fleeting notion, is a fool. You know what? Under different circumstances and if we had more time, I bet I could cure you of this big bad Depressus you allegedly think you have."

"Oh, is that so?"

"Yeah."

"Tell me, Doctor Koko, where did you go to medical school?"

"Oh, get over yourself. I'm talking about living here. I'm talking flat-out *joie de vivre*. I mean, look at you now. Just look at you. Mister Action Man. Mister All Chivalrous and Rising to the Occasion. And why? Just because I decided not to kill you and asked for your help? Before I told you my idea of using your knowledge to get off *Alaungpaya* you were a blubbering mess. And you could have blown off my idea and taken a quick shot to the head back at your quarters. But you didn't. No, you made a choice. You decided to help me, and that, my man, took will. That took guts. Not to mention you're a former security officer. Hell, I half expected you to try to make a stand against me, but again you didn't. Do you know what I saw in your eyes back there when I asked you to help me out?"

"No, what?"

"I saw a light, Flynn."

Flynn snorts. "A light."

"Yeah, sure, it was kind of dim, but I know I saw something. I saw somebody who wants more and no doubt deserves more, but somehow thinks big bad fate has dealt him a crappy hand. My hunch is that maybe you've just been up here in the Second Free Zone for too long. This whole weirdo Depressus thing? Sounds like a big scam to me. If you were anyplace else down on Earth, I'd say all you have is a mere spat of the blues."

"It's not a scam."

"Really? So, did you actually go to medical school?"

"I really don't want to get into this."

"Tough," Koko says. "I think like some dope you took those doctors' words as gospel and just gave up. Where's your self-respect, man? Where's your freakin' dignity? Have you even considered that maybe your problem is that no one has ever taken the time to show you how to stop taking it all inside? Hell, I've never met anyone worth a damn who hasn't at least once contemplated suicide at some point in their lives. Seriously, if you really sat down and thought about it, I bet you'd be surprised to find you don't really want to kill yourself at all. You only want to end your life."

"There's a difference?"

"Hell, yes, there's a difference. I'm talking about change. I'm talking about pride and taking charge of your destiny. Doctors are human too, you know. They can be wrong like anybody else."

"You're entitled to your own opinion."

Koko's face sours. "You're damn right I'm entitled to my own opinion. Stodgy shrinks and pompous quacks, I've seen my share of those flim-flam artists, and you know what I think? I'd say the vast majority of those self-aggrandizers were only good at three things: making junkies, lining their own pockets, and shoring up the aura of their precious profession. Cripes, Flynn, if I wasn't in such a jam here, I could show you a thing or two about really living."

"I bet you could, but like it or not it's too late for me now."

Koko harrumphs.

"Look, Koko, we just met. You really don't know anything about me or what I've been through. Don't give me that look, I'm serious. This condition has taken a real physical toll on me. You want to call it some half-baked conspiracy? Fine, get in line. There's plenty of people who argue that Depressus is some way of curbing the Second Free Zone populations. But I don't care at all about conspiracy theories. I'm just tired. I'm just sick and tired of suffering day in and day out. I'm tired of all the drugs that make me feel like I'm drowning in mud, tired of being irritable and angry, tired of seeing nothing good in this world anymore. The stagnant meaninglessness of it all. How today feels like tomorrow and spins around and feels like yesterday. How it's all so… fruitless. My life is over, so deal with it. I certainly have."

"Man, you *do* need to get laid."

"Will you stop it?"

"Not in my nature."

"Well, could you at least try? God, if there was any proof of me actually being off my rocker, helping the likes of you with a cockamamie plan like this definitely takes the cake. I must be off my nut altogether."

Flynn widens the crack in the door and peeks out. Koko chews her lip.

"I still don't like this," she says.

"What is wrong with you? I'm trying to help you here. Stop worrying. It'll be fine."

Koko gets to her feet and pulls both the Sig and Flynn's Beretta from her belt. "I'm going to cover you anyway."

"No!" Flynn scolds. "Just stay put. I'll be back in a minute. And put those guns away. If someone comes by, just pretend you're sick or something. I'll be back before you know it."

Before Koko can object further, Flynn pushes open the door and slips through. Picking his way through the crowds, he breezes up to the DropSledz rental counter centered in the terminal.

"Welcome to DwopSwedz, twhere convenience twis our motto, thwherever your twavels may lead. Hi, may I help you?"

Flynn lays the chit Koko gave him on the counter.

"Uh, it seems I have this rental coupon here…"

The blonde clerk picks up the chit and swipes it under the scanner squared in front of her. "Yeth-yeth, you do. Indeed, you do. Let'th look now…" The clerk stops.

"Is something wrong?" Flynn asks.

The clerk looks up and bats her eyes. "Oh, no-no. It'th nothing."

"Boy, I sure hope nothing's wrong," Flynn haws. "I know how expensive these strat-sled rentals can be, but my boss gave me the coupon as sort of a retirement gift. See, I recently left *Alaungpaya* Security Services."

The clerk busies herself with the screens in front of her. "Weally? Thwat's nice. And thwhere are you twaveling today, offither?"

Flynn thinks, *Is a world of cascading trouble a destination?*

Damn it. He forgot to ask Koko where she wanted to go, and he knows in order to secure a rental off *Alaungpaya* he must declare a final point of destination. But, knowing Koko's skills, she can probably hack the strat-sled's onboard navigational systems and reprogram a flight plan once she's clear, so Flynn blurts out the first vessel that pops into his head. A nearby entertainment ark that has been tracking the same orbit as *Alaungpaya* for the last year and a half—a barge known as *Desalus 5*.

"Oooh," the clerk croons. "Thwat sounds funny-fun. A whimsy wetirement pwesent, thwen? Pwenty of high-happy over on Dethalus, wight-wight. My girlfwiend? She go on holiday thwere wast year. Did her some of thwose cwazy gwoup massages."

Flynn realizes now why the woman lisps. A waffled tongue piercing.

"To be perfectly honest," Flynn says, playing things light, "I'd actually like to book the rental for a friend of mine. That's not a problem is it? What I mean to say is I can't really use it because I have other plans, but I'd really hate to see it go to waste."

The clerk leans across the desk and whispers surreptitiously, "Well, your fwiend is not by any chance named Koko, ith she?"

Flynn forces an uneasy laugh. The laugh sounds completely phony, even to him.

"Koko? No. Why?"

The clerk tilts her head. "Well, thome beefy wadies were here a few minutes ago snatching all clever-wike about thomebody named Koko. Kind of thuthpicious, you know? One of thwem, the pwetty wed-haired one? Had thwose things," the clerk strokes her throat. "Neck extenthions? They're kind of gwoss, but who's to thay what's fwashion? Qwuite wude, they were."

Flynn nods. "People were rude to me all the time when I was a deputy. I imagine you must get your fair share of rough-tempered boors, what with all the people passing through here day in and day out." He pauses and drums his fingers on the counter in a nonchalant manner. "So, umm, these women you mentioned, are they still around? The only reason I ask is, even though I'm no longer active in *Alaungpaya* security, I can still put in a priority patch transmission to command and have them checked out."

The clerk twitches. Flynn can tell by the roaming of her eyes that she discerns a presence, off to his left at eleven o'clock.

"Well, I think I twhee the neck extenthionz one ith up top in the café."

"The café? Where?"

The clerk points. Flynn snaps out his hand to stop her, but it's too late.

As Flynn turns, he looks up and marks a harsh-lipped redhead with the neck-extension bands standing motionless a floor above in the café. The redhead is close to the terrace piping overlooking the flight arrival and departure area and, honestly, the clerk is accurate in her assessment. If it weren't for the neckbands and the somewhat rakish, Jolly Roger bandage over her eye, the redhead is a bit of a knockout.

Flynn quickly surveys the crowd and sees a second fearsome-looking woman with an ocular implant glaring straight at him.

A knockout?

Mmm, not so much.

COVER BLOWN

Heinz immediately checks in with Wire via her ocular.

"Oh, man, did you just see that?"

Wire taps a finger to the side of her temple. "Hell, yeah. Popped out of a restricted doorway looking all kinds of suspicious. Crossed to the rental desk and got chatty with that clerk and she totally pointed you out. That *hombre* down there be throwing out the big vibe."

"Kind of looks like a security dork."

"My thinking too."

"Maybe something went down with Mu?"

"She still hasn't checked in."

"What if somebody discovered the fat man?"

"Screw it. Even on a barge as lame as this, they'd mobilize more than one asset if they found that tub of pus. This whole place would be swimming with pork."

"Try Mu again and keep an eye on him."

"Roger that," responds Wire. "Wait! Hang on."

"What is it?"

"Oh, are we lucky or what?"

"What?"

"There are nail marks on that guy's neck."

"You're kidding me."

"Ah, that's a negative. Yeah, and if I'm not mistaken that's, like, a total scorpion hold. I've used that hold plenty of times myself. Well, I'll be damned. It looks like this target of ours has had her nails done recently. Razor claws."

Heinz's eyes narrow with the good news.

"Well, hello, Koko…"

NOW WHAT?

After spinning away from the rental counter, Flynn threads and crisscrosses his way through the chockablock crowds of travelers. The fresh nail marks on his neck itch under his panicking flop sweat, and he pats them with the pads of his fingers.

Oh, man. This is so not good.

Not good at all.

Flynn feels miserable. Utterly impotent. An ineffective, wet pile of unmanly mush. *You've blown it,* he berates himself. *They've seen you and you've blown it, and now they're going to track down and kill Koko.*

He should just walk away. Go and find the nearest damn bar. Slam back as many double shots of the best booze he can afford, gobble the rest of his medications, and then stumble up to the Embrace check-in. Go ahead, do it. Do it, you limp-dicked wuss. Fire up an anonymous patch to ASS command and forget all this helping some damsel in distress nonsense.

Damsel in distress? Now, that's a laugh.

Like Koko can't handle herself.

But two highly trained operatives in pursuit? This business is about to get a whole lot worse, and innocent civilians are probably going to get hurt.

Shilly-shally, waver, waver.

Go. Stay.

Report it. No.

Report it now, don't be an idiot.

Flynn's mouth dries, and his temples pound. But what if he did patch it in and ASS somehow managed to trace the communication back to him before he checked in at Embrace? What then? Probably yank his butt right out of the suicide queue. Then Flynn would have to explain himself and why there's an eviscerated woman stinking up his personal quarters. Oh boy, he'd definitely miss the Embrace ceremony then for sure. They'd probably frog-march him in chains straight onto a shuttle and whiz him over to a holding brig on a Second Free Zone correctional vessel.

Flynn bleakly pictures the holding brigs in orbiting correctional facilities. In his time as a security deputy, he's helped lock up a whole host of unsavory miscreants and he knows if he ends up in brig population for even a few hours and the box assortment *du jour* gets wind of the fact he's a former security deputy, hell—they'll rip him to pieces. Sure, that would be a means to an end, but it wouldn't be at all like tripping his brains out through the cloud-bound dawn.

Out of the corner of his eye, Flynn notes that the two bounty agents have given up their sentry positions and are now quickly moving through the café crowds. Both carry heavy-looking rucksacks over their shoulders and are heading for the stairs that lead down to the main arrival and departure area.

Damn, he has to throw them off the scent.

He sees an open vestibule restroom facility is directly across the way. He dashes across and careens inside, his mind racing.

They saw me. They saw me, and now Koko is dead meat.

Goddamn it, Flynn. For once in your pathetic life get real.

You're dead meat.

And you so suck.

Flynn has to find another way. He has to get back to Koko right now to warn her before she figures something has gone wrong and makes a move. God, they've probably seen him entering this bathroom and one of them or maybe both are closing in on him right now. Two trained professional killers? Even with his security background and meager tactical training, he doesn't stand a chance.

Quickly Flynn considers alternative ways of getting back to Koko, but he realizes, without official ASS credentials, if he takes another roundabout way to the corridor where he left Koko he won't get very far. This isn't like bluffing a bunch of maintenance and rigging techs or sneaking up the back ways of *Alaungpaya*. The quickest way back to Koko's location is exactly the way he entered. Right through the access door and right in plain sight.

With a sucking roar, a steam toilet flushes behind him and Flynn jumps.

Time to go.

Go now. Be a man.

Be a—

Hero?

WAITING ON FLYNN

Koko withdraws from the crack in the access door.

What the hell, Flynn? You decide now is a good time to take a leak?

Koko rises from her *wushu* crouch. She swivels her head, intently scoping the empty corridor in both directions.

She should just take off. Someone could come by at any second and this half-assed plan of Flynn's to use a strat-sled is totally hosed. Flynn be damned, Koko can find another way off *Alaungpaya*. After all, it's just a residential orbital—how hard could it possibly be?

Sorry, Flynn, she thinks. *Thanks a lot and it's been great and all, but I'm not waiting around for your moody ass to botch this all up. That is, if you haven't already.*

Koko gives her shoulders a shake to prime herself. Her hands reach out, and she's almost touching the access door bar when Flynn bursts in and pulls the door shut behind him. The door locks, and Flynn's eyes are wide. His face—bloodless.

"We've got company," he says.

They run.

Like hell.

PURSUIT

Kneeling, Wire retrieves a small acetylene cutting tool from her rucksack and uses it on the access door lock. Heinz has her back to Wire to provide cover, and she has her new HK out and concealed under her armpit. A flight security team of three are moving quickly through the crowds toward them, assessing the two women as a credible threat.

"Three on our six," observes Heinz.

"Oh, c'mon, are you friggin' kidding me?"

"Negative. How much longer on the lock?"

"Five seconds, tops."

"No sweat. I'm on it."

Heinz bends down and snatches one of the pulse grenades from inside her rucksack. With a casual flip of her thumb, she arms the device. Then she slings the grenade across the floor of the arrival and departure area, toward the quickly approaching security detail. The grenade emits a wobbly red light as it winds off its countdown. The security detail rush forward, unsheathing their weapons and taking aim at Heinz's and Wire's heads as they traverse the floor. One shouts halt, and another yells for people to get down. A deafening alarm revs to a whoop, and large corrugated doors begin to wrap around and descend, quarantining the entire terminal area.

Screaming people scuttle every which way in an all-out scattershot stampede, and Heinz and Wire move inside the access door just as the pulse grenade releases its deadly payload. The keening alarm squelches silent upon the grenade's detonation, and almost every single life within a fifty-meter radius of the fiery blast is liquefied.

Inside, Heinz and Wire bounce off the corridor walls as the concussion knocks them to the floor. Both recover quickly and pounce forward, ears ringing. Crawling first, then running.

Guns up and out.

OUTWARD BOUND

"What the hell was that?"

Koko lands a blow between Flynn's shoulder blades, propelling him forward with a hard shove. "Pulse grenade! Just go! Move!"

They bound down a short staircase and run flat out through a steaming transfer tunnel beneath the central flight deck. Flashing orange caution lights swirl like sabers, and alternating drafts of metallic-smelling heat and frigid air push against them like unseen brutes.

Fifty meters in front of their advance two helmeted flight technicians run, their arms wildly pumping in cartoonish terror. One of the techs looks back and sees Koko and Flynn barreling down the tightening passage. The technician reaches and fumbles for a wall-mounted button that will probably seal off the section and lock them inside. Koko bares her teeth and doesn't falter. She draws the Sig from her belt, fires two silent bursts past Flynn's ear, and pulps both technicians hideously against the walls.

"Goddamn it!" Flynn cries.

"Move!"

"You can't just do that! They're—God! They're just doing their jobs!"

"Like I care. How many agents were back there in the terminal area?"

"I think I saw two. One with short hair and the redhead with the neckbands for sure."

"Oh, for the love of—that redhead again?" Koko spits. "Never mind. Two I can handle."

"Deck three has the strat-sleds."

"I'm thinking bigger than that now."

A warning booms through the air:

"Attention. Emergency sequence initiated. All *Alaungpaya* flight personnel clear all platforms. Security depressurization imminent—one hundred and fifty-five seconds. All personnel heads to secure areas immediately. Repeat. Flight deck emergency sequence initiated and security depressurization imminent—one hundred and fifty seconds—"

An alarm blasts to Koko's immediate right and her ears pop like they've been jabbed with a spoon. Wincing, she jostles Flynn forward, egging him on to move faster.

"How quickly do the outer hangar doors close?" she asks.

Flynn ducks beneath a low-hanging pipe. "I don't remember. I think the flight decks have to be completely sealed off and cross-checked before the hangars shut off completely. I've only been in a couple of drills before, and they were achingly slow. The outer doors are really big, and they need to completely seal off the pressure membrane." The floor beneath them shakes as though struck by a small, shifting earthquake. "You feel that? That probably means the outer hangar doors have just been released from their storage slots. There's no time! Here! Through here!"

"Flynn—"

"We get aboard a transport or something else and we should be okay to ride the depressurization out. Here, go. Up this ladder. I think it'll take us to the main deck."

Koko doesn't have time to argue. Flynn lets her by, and she takes the ladder first. She climbs toothed rungs quickly and comes to a round hatch painted with yellow and white zebra stripes. The hatch is locked off by two manual screw hinges that take all the strength in her wrists to spin down and undo. When the latches are free, Koko shoulders up two heaving whacks until the hatch slams open. Koko finds purchase on a grimy ledge and cautiously raises her head. They are directly beneath a large crescent wing of a cargo frigate, and the frigate's scorched and travel-beaten belly and wings stretch out left and right. The open hatch is hidden behind one of the ship's landing-gear wheels, the wheel as big as a rolled bale of hay.

Koko slithers out of the hole, followed shortly by Flynn belly-flopping out beside her.

"Addendum—today's Embrace ceremony has been suspended until further notification. One hundred seconds to completed emergency sequence and full security depressurization. All personnel move immediately to secure areas. Ninety-six seconds..."

Flynn rolls over and scans the craft's belly on his back. He points.

"There! Thirty meters down, a ship engineering portal. You can blow the lock with an incendiary round, and it should lead up to the hold. It's our only chance."

Koko groans and clambers in the direction Flynn indicates.

"This better fucking work," she says.

Flynn gets to his feet and follows. When they are under the engineering portal, Koko takes careful aim at the lock with her Sig and then both of them look away to shield their eyes. The short blue burst from Koko's gun splits the panel's lock with a shower of white-hot sparks and reveals yet another toothed ladder leading up and into the dark, unlit bowels of the frigate.

"You first," Koko says. "I'll cover us."

"No, you go."

"Go now, Flynn, or I swear I'll shoot you right here."

"Ninety seconds. Outer hangar doors closing, outer hangar doors closing. All personnel—"

Flynn's eyes flit to and fro. Koko raises her gun to the center of Flynn's forehead to focus the issue.

"Go, Flynn. Now."

Flynn nods and pushes Koko aside. He jumps up, grabs the ladder, and swings himself upward in a leg-kicking pull-up. Drawing Flynn's Beretta from her belt, Koko spins around in a low squat with both guns in her hands, searching for targets, but it seems anyone left up top on the main flight deck is gone, hauling ass for cover.

God.

Fucking Delacompte.

Fucking Finland.

I should have never, ever, ever, ever...

Flynn yells down the portal tube. "Koko, hurry!"

Koko doesn't want to lower her weapons, but she knows she has to. She jams both guns into her belt and looks up for a place to fit her hands for the climb up the ladder. That's when, hot-eyed from the hatch Flynn and Koko just climbed out of, the redhead with the neck-extension bands prairie-dogs. The woman seems so close Koko thinks she can even hear the soft, wet click of saliva in the woman's mouth as she curses and pulls herself out of the hole.

Koko can't believe it's going to be so easy. She yanks the Sig from her belt just as the redhead locks her one unbandaged eye on her. Koko aims clean.

Gotcha.

The discharged pulse from Koko's gun severs the redhead's neck just above her collarbones. The woman's long-locked skull flops backward across the open deck before it finally comes to a rest against a snaking section of ribbed fueling hose. Neckbands from the dead woman's throat scatter everywhere, and the rest of her bucking, decapitated body slams back into the hole and plummets down the shaft. A livid wail of irritation follows, and

Koko knows the second agent in pursuit is going to be busy, at least for a little while.

Koko drops the hot weapon into the open zippered space on her canvas jumpsuit and launches herself upward, catching the ladder halfway up in her grip. Koko scales the rungs, looking up while the hot suppressor attachment of the recently fired Sig blisters the naked skin on her front as it fishes its way down to her waist. She sees Flynn reaching down to her with the fingers of his right hand splayed wide.

"Seventy seconds to depressurization, sixty-nine, sixty-eight—"

"Seal this!" Koko snaps.

"Get in here, then!"

Flynn grabs her hand, pulls Koko through the passage, and together they both slam the hatch shut behind her. Flynn works the hatch locks, and when he raises his head Koko is heaving next to him on her knees. Koko's jumpsuit is fully unzipped as she fumbles inside for the Sig. She rips the hot weapon from down near her hip and, with her arm extended, swings the gun ready for who or whatever is next.

The hold is freezing and the stench inside is hellacious.

"My God, Flynn, what is that *smell*?"

"I don't know!"

"Sixty-five seconds—outer *Alaungpaya* hangar doors closing—repeat—outer *Alaungpaya* hangar doors closing—sixty-three seconds—"

As Koko scans ahead, she targets a tiny female in an oversized filthy flight suit. The girl—not more than a day past her teenage aero-cadet comps—flattens herself against a barely open hatchway in the bulkhead leading to the frigate's main cockpit; she has her hands up in a trembling gesture of surrender. The young woman's face is half pleading mercy and half pure terror, but she beckons them.

"Please! The hold isn't airtight! Come on! Get in here now or you're both dead!"

Koko grabs Flynn by the scruff of his collar and yanks him to his feet. With simultaneous frustrated moans, they charge forward.

It is, after all, what's next.

ON THE FEEDS

Albeit briefly, the terabyte bedlam of the worldwide media feeds glisten with recent *Alaungpaya* developments:

<newest> explosion aboard second free zone host barge class ALAUNGPAYA...reports indicate extensive damage and significant casualties <newest> restriction travel alerts amended for the all orbital craft in the second free zone <newest> superpopstar shelanza ki indicted on multiple organ copyright charges <newest> fifty-plus de-civ terror groups are taking responsibility for second free zone host barge class ALAUNGPAYA's casualties <newest> core lithium mining futures down sharply <newest> feed broadcast of EMBRACE aboard ALAUNGPAYA suspended pending all clear notifications <newest> the north african mineral alliance announces recall elections <newest> mega-tsunami and crash alerts issued across the southern pacific as a precautionary

measure regarding developments aboard ALAUNGPAYA
<u>newest</u> somalia republic crushes the european alliance's
lead by 312 runs with 4 wickets remaining <<u>newest</u>>…

THIRD STRIKE

"LEEEEEE!"

Lee gulps and dives for Delacompte's office door. When he stumbles inside, he finds Delacompte rigid behind her desk. Like a dueler, she points a gun directly at his head.

"What the hell is going on up there, Lee?" she screeches. "The feeds say there's an emergency sequence in progress on *Alaungpaya*. This is what you call cleaning up?"

"I-I-I…"

"Shut that door now!"

Lee hastily shuts the door behind him and whimpers. To his sudden horror, he senses a small, warmish trickle of urine leaking from his penis. As the dark spot on his pants blooms, he turns around on jellied legs to face his boss.

"What the hell is happening up there?"

Lee babbles, "I-I don't know. They weren't, I mean, the orders I laid out were specifically parametered not to… well… what I mean to say is—"

"What? What, Lee? Out with it. What?"

"Discretion!" he gushes. "I was specific. Very specific, Madam

Delacompte. I mean, all this, this might not even be related to the Martstellar situation at all. It could be something else entirely. Something that has nothing to do with… God. Oh God, oh God, oh God—"

"Don't you *dare* blaspheme in front of me!"

Lee is aghast to feel his urine flowing freely now, and his shame at wetting himself is compounded by the stirring pressure against his clenched anus. But, oddly enough, the sensation of warm piss leaving his body feels good. Humiliating, of course, but it's a welcome relief finally to let go of all the endless job tension and stress.

Lee finds himself praying for the precision of a headshot. He wonders sadly if his merchant sailor will mourn his loss and remember to water their plants.

Across the room, Delacompte's floating prompt screens flash white, alerting her to an incoming message from the Custom Pleasure Bureau's board of directors—marked URGENT. Delacompte's fuming eyes fall to her prompts, and she lowers her weapon with disgust, slapping the gun against the hard meat of her thigh.

"Oh, lovely," she says sarcastically. "This is going to be just great. *Just* great. Way to jam me up here, Lee. My word, this is turning out to be one hell of a day."

Urine puddles around Lee's shoes, and he shakes a foot. "I sent a communiqué only minutes ago, but the team members were unresponsive. If something has gone wrong, I know it can be fixed. I mean, yes, I understand you're upset and naturally this is a major screw-up on my part but—"

"Wait a second. Hold on."

"What?"

"What did you just say?"

"When?"

"Before. Did you just say 'team members'?"

"Uhhh…"

"*TEAM MEMBERS*?!"

"Yes! Yes. I didn't want to bother you. I mean, I was going to tell you about sending a few additional operatives to take care of the Martstellar situation, but with everything that's happened—if you just give me another chance I swear I can fix this."

Delacompte drapes a hand over her aching eyes. She can't believe this. How does one simple little chore like getting rid of someone spiral so quickly out of her control? The board members will be furious with her. Perhaps the jowly director was right after all. Maybe her executive chops are truly the pits. Delacompte's shoulders sag, and she blows out a long, cleansing breath.

"You can't fix this."

There's a merciful pause before Delacompte brings the gun up and fires. The pulse cuts Lee in half at the hips.

The exquisite look of astonishment on Lee's face is almost comical, and he doesn't make a sound as both sections of his body fall in opposite directions and hit the floor with simultaneous thuds like the sound of dropped luggage.

Delacompte resets the safety on her weapon and lays it down on her desk. After taking a moment she crosses the room and stands above the two sections of Lee's corpse. She takes in the sulfuric reek of fried intestinal waste and disemboweled guts. Delacompte frowns. *Oh, this just gets better and better*, she thinks. The antique Persian carpet beneath Lee's exploded core is absolutely ruined.

Passionlessly, Delacompte gazes down into Lee's flat, lifeless eyes staring blankly up at the ceiling. With an aimless, dying impulse, his left foot spasms for a few seconds and then settles still.

It has been so long for Delacompte. She's nearly forgotten the sublime buoyancy that comes with taking a human life—the confident rush of power. Bending forward, she lowers herself to a single knee.

"You know," she says, coolly gathering herself, "when the CPB recruiters first brought your file to my attention, Lee, I felt you were an excellent executive assistant choice for me because you were so responsive to taking orders. It's the truth. You were a perfect—oh, what is the phrase? Aide-de-camp? Never a misplaced step or ill-advised word, never a snotty reproach. Despite all outward appearances, please know I did sort of like you. But let's be honest here. You've been slacking off as of late. Perhaps that is my fault. Perhaps I should have started your junior executive penalty count sooner to snap you back in line, but oh well. Spare the rod, hmm?"

Delacompte gently seizes the sides of Lee's blood-spattered face and hauls his head up to meet her own. She makes a small circling motion with her chin as she looks for the right spot. Flexes her jaw.

How does one do this again?

Oh, that's right. She needs to set her teeth right over the supraorbital bone and use her tongue to probe and scoop, sucking at the same time. Then you have to pull back and sever the optic nerves with a crosscut sawing motion of the front teeth.

Delacompte counts to three and bites down on Lee's right eye.

Pulling back, she rips the flesh free and swallows the eye whole, letting go of Lee's head and dropping it to the floor with a flat crack.

Standing, Delacompte uses her forearm to smear the dribbling blood from her mouth.

THIS JUST IN...

Meanwhile...

...<u>newest</u> authorities verify blood and DNA re-civ
identifiers—23 losses aboard second free zone host barge class
ALAUNGPAYA, including 3 progenics, 50-plus related injuries—
confirmation pending—ALAUNGPAYA lockdown initiated
<u>newest</u> larita international partnership (WG INDEX SYMBOL—
LIP Credit PPS/56¼) acknowledges talks with worldwide
syndicate fund managers, related bond indexes inch higher
on news <u>newest</u> weather: continued deficient soy harvest
conditions in northern polar regions, 5-day high above 37.7°C
expected <u>newest</u> last month's lunar mine collapse corrected,
holding at 89%, confidence potential officially corroborated
<u>newest</u> // E-X-C-L-U-S-I-V-E! // are de-civ convict sitcom hits
MYSTRIFE4LIFE and *GUILTY, PLEASE* canceled for the next feed
cycle? know now-now! update in fifteen seconds <u>newest</u>...

UP FRONT

Entering the ship's cramped cockpit, Koko hacks a crisp half-strike into the first mate's neck and the young woman droops to the floor like a wilted flower.

Kicking her heel backward, Koko slams the cabin door shut behind them and tells Flynn to seal the locks. Flynn futzes with the hatch's keypad as Koko jumps forward and presses the barrel of her Sig deep into the wispy gray hairs of the seated captain's temple. The captain is a grizzled, brown-skinned man of possible Indian descent and he wears a red wool watch cap snugged down to cover his protruding ears. He appears well past seventy years of age.

Koko voice is ornery and frank.

"Fly."

Slackjawed, the captain starts slapping at console switches with shaking hands. He steadies an oval insect-looking yoke between his legs as a moment later the frigate's engines hum to life. The captain trembles and sing-songs his vowels.

"Me, I am no brave man."

"Better not be," Koko warns.

Koko throws a look back at Flynn to make sure the cabin's door is secure and the safety measures are online. He gives her a thumbs up to indicate they're good to go. Koko steps over the unconscious first mate's body to cover the starboard cabin window.

The automated holding chocks securing the vessel to the main deck spring free beneath them, and the frigate lurches upward into a hover. A message squeals hysterically over the ship's com.

"Waste cargo ship G-Class! What the hell are you doing? Depressurization sequence is terminal, you morons! Repeat. Depressurization sequence is terminal! Power down! I repeat, power down right now!"

Koko doesn't leave her position by the starboard window and holds tightly to a strap that dangles near her head like a noose.

"Shut that off," she says.

The captain throws a switch and terminates the inbound communications. The ship's height above the pad increases and they drift forward over dozens of similar parked vessels, skirring to and fro in the air like a bee swollen from the cold.

"Sh-sh-she won't m-make it," the captain stammers. "Look! *Alaungpaya*'s outer doors are starting to close across the protective membrane. We will crash, I am telling you. We are hauling over eight hundred tons of human waste and this old beastie moves like a cow!"

Flynn glances at Koko. He waits for a reaction but he doesn't get one.

Waste cargo? Flynn thinks. Well, that certainly explains the horrible stink in the hold: human waste recycled for methane energy pumps in industrial farming cooperatives and power-grid interests worldwide down on Earth. Boy oh boy, he sure knows how to pick them.

Flynn looks out the bow's bubbled window. Ahead of them, like a great clattering jaw mucused with cascading jets of steam, *Alaungpaya*'s heavy hangar gates yawn inward from the recessed storage wings, port and starboard. The flight deck's protective pressure membrane crackles in the narrowing gap, and rapidly shifting fluxes of air shake the vessel from side to side as they drift toward the light. Beyond the membrane, boulderish outlines of knotty, dark clouds can be seen. Flynn tries to do the math on the closing distance, taking in the ship's size, the refuse cargo weight, and the perilous opening before them. It doesn't look good, and he gives them shattering odds.

Once again Flynn is utterly flabbergasted at how calm Koko is despite all the craziness. Her gun is still trained on the captain's head and a single finger curls around the weapon's trigger.

"She may be a cow, captain," she says, "but the thing is—me and my boy here? We're both ready to die, and you're not. Make it."

The captain secures a set of flight goggles over his eyes and jams the throttle forward with the butt of his hand. The sudden accelerative force is so strong it knocks Flynn backward against the cockpit hatch, and he topples down onto the legs of the unconscious first mate, biting his tongue. The engines bawl louder and louder, and a blasting flare from one of *Alaungpaya*'s sweeping outer klieg lights pours through the cabin windows, whitening them all.

Their airspeed increases, and the flight deck below recedes faster and faster behind them. Three hundred-plus meters ahead, the light of the pressure membrane dazzles.

"Fifteen seconds to full depressurization... Thirteen—"

Flynn spits strings of blood from his mouth, and when he raises his head Koko gives him a "better hold on" look from across the cabin. Flynn wipes his mouth and reaches forward, gripping the fittings on the base of the pilot's seat as if they can steady or even save him. Swirling dust and debris reel past the windows, and from the rapidly changing pressure Flynn knows the outer hangar doors are close. Flynn's stomach sinks as Koko puckers her lips and blows him a parting kiss.

Unbelievable.

Flynn shuts his eyes, resigned for a quick, explosive end.

A sharp bang and a brassy squeal cut through the rumbling engine noise, and the ship swings hard to port.

For the ten thousandth time in his life, Flynn flashes on the prospect of his own death. From his study of history he knows that some ancient cultures believed if you died in an act of desperate evil you were destined to repeat and suffer through that same evil death over and over for all eternity. Crashing a septic freighter on takeoff? Man, that's really going to trump the karmic suck.

But they don't die. To their collective amazement, they are still alive and propelling forward, gaining more critical speed. Seconds later they punch through the pressure membrane, whisking through by mere fist-sized fractions on either side. Sudden moisture sluices over the bow window as the sky opens up, and then—

WHUMP!

A robed body slams into the cockpit bubble and tumbles away. A second later, two more screaming faces fly past the bow's view, and Flynn glimpses hands inelegantly clawing the air.

Koko cries out. "Holy shit! I thought they canceled Embrace! Look! They're jumping, Flynn! The Embrace jump is happening!"

Flynn forces himself to raise his head and look out. The horror is everywhere. Scores and scores of Depressus-afflicted citizens are leaping to their stoned-out deaths, their ceremonial robes snapping back behind them like so many broken wings. Tucked in a cannonball, one of the jumpers plunges past and actually waves. Ten more follow in free fall, locked in a brave chain and spilling end over end.

Oh God, Flynn thinks. They must have taken matters into their own hands. They must have bypassed the Embrace protocols.

The ship's air speed continues to increase, and—to all of their dismay—the captain, Koko, and Flynn realize one terrifying fact as the bodies plummet all around:

The frigate is falling too.

TAKING LUMPS

In her office, Portia Delacompte disgracefully hangs her head before the floating board member faces. The projections streaming in from Rome, Caracas, London, and elsewhere are beet-faced and beyond apoplectic. Delacompte endures it all. All the degrading condemnations, belligerence, screams, and insults.

BSGD.

Bad shit, going down.

"Have you anything to say for yourself?" the jowly director from Buenos Aires asks.

Delacompte attempts to find some placating words but fails. Across the room, CPB cleaning personnel roll up the sections of Lee's body like links of milled sausage in the ruined carpet. Delacompte can see the priggish smirks behind their transparent bio-hazard masks, and it makes her blood boil. Bunch of peons. She wants to yank the New One Roman Church of the Most Holy Liberator medallion from around her neck and flog each of them to pieces with it.

"I shamefully accept full responsibility for this matter," she says quietly.

The jowly director puffs his cigar. "Of course you do."

A flickering translucent forest of held up V-ed fingers lingers for a moment before all transmissions cease.

Reaching into her jacket, Delacompte takes out her vial of Q, shakes out a double dose, and slaps the capsules into her open mouth. One of the cleaning crew, apparently the group's supervisor, steps away from the rest and presents his data recorder for Delacompte's authorization.

"Looks like we're done here, Madam Vice President. If you'll just input your code, we'll be out of your way in a jiff."

Delacompte snatches the data recorder from the man and swallows some spit to chase her Qs. She enters her authorization as the supervisor glances around the office. Delacompte hands back the recorder.

"Um, I hate to be a stickler—" the supervisor says.

"What?"

"Did Mr. Lee have any personal relations who might want to be notified of his termination? It's standard CPB personnel procedure to notify significant relations, you understand."

Delacompte waves a hand. "I don't know. I think he lived with someone. A man. Some merchant sea hand or something."

The supervisor nods. "I see. So, I assume you'll be forwarding the termination notice to this individual? Um, hello? Excuse me, Madam Delacompte?"

Delacompte hatchets an arm through the air. "Just handle it! Somebody around here knows who Lee was better than I ever did. Just copy me on whatever you need to copy me on, all right?"

"Roger. Copy you. Got it. Absolutely."

A few minutes later the cleaning crew lift Lee's body onto a hover gurney and haul him out to a service lift down the hall. As the group waits for the lift to arrive, the supervisor opens a boilerplate notification on his service recorder.

CPB Resource Realignment Services

Date/cycle: [Insert]

To: [Name, Address]

Staff: [Insert Name/Title]

Subject: Employee Termination—[Insert Name, CPB Employee ID Code]

CC: [Insert]

To Whom It May Concern:

It is with great regret that we must advise you that, due to unforeseen circumstances and/or significant dereliction of duties, [Insert Name, CPB Employee ID Code, Office Location], has been eliminated. This notification is being given to you pursuant to the Custom Pleasure Bureau and The Sixty Islands' Worker Adjustment Contract of 2509 and as an official courtesy, and senior staff lament any hardship this action might cause you. Final balance of CPB credit pay and/or personal effects of [Insert Name, CPB Employee ID Code] will be forwarded once approved. Again, The CPB and The Sixty Islands wish you the best of luck with your grief and transition. [Insert Staff Authorization, CPB Employee ID Code]

RIGHT-RIGHT THE COURSE

Koko hikes a boot and braces her footing against the back of the empty co-pilot's seat. The ship's steep forward dive has her practically toppling forward into the bow bubble.

"Hey, captain?"

"*What?*"

"We're going to pull out of this, right?"

The captain's whole body shakes from head to toe as though he's been stuck with a cattle prod. He desperately tries to steady the oval insect-looking yoke in front of him. The sky is now a pearly wash of fast-moving clouds, and the shrieking creaks overwhelming the small cabin are too numerous to count. Through clenched teeth and acidic spittle, the captain despairs.

"Those poor souls! Oh, why? Why? Who hijacks a waste ship? Who are you people?"

The captain lets one hand leave the yoke for a split second to adjust a dial nearby, and the repercussions of this seemingly insignificant move are instantaneous. Navigation gyros whirl; the vessel banks radically and nearly barrels. The captain regains his grip and strains backward on the yoke. Like a waking monster, little by little the nose of the frigate lifts, but then suddenly it falls back.

"We'll be lucky if we don't collide with something," the captain cries. "This rate of speed, the lower heavily traveled flight paths? No-no! This vessel, she is not meant for such recklessness. Eight hundred seventy-three kilometers per hour now, mach tuck stall imminent!"

The bottom of Flynn's stomach falls out, and he hangs on.

God, how he wants it all to be over.

Koko shouts over the surrounding noise. "Do you need a hand? Hey! What's your name anyway?"

Behind the flat glass of his goggles, the captain's eyes go saucer wide.

"*Me?* I am Jot! *You know how to fly?*"

Koko doesn't answer the captain and instead crawls over and drops into the co-pilot seat. A fierce jolt flies her face down onto the controls and lacerates the thin skin on her left temple. She recovers quickly and reaches behind herself for the safety harness. Koko pulls the belt over her shoulder and thrusts the clip home. After locking in, she stuffs the Sig under one of her legs and seizes the second jiggling yoke rattling in front of her. Between Koko and the captain, iridescent green airspeed digits gleam from a three-dimensional rectangular projection.

[AS889km.h]

[AS941km.h]

[AS954km.h]

[AS960km.h]

Together, they fight the beast.

The captain blabbers, "No-no-no-no-n—"

Koko cuts him off. "Hey, Jot, do me a favor, huh? Tell me where the stupid stabilizers are on this thing."

"Power stabilizers, starboard top!"

Koko finds the controls and quickly inputs the adjustments. With a chattering rock and roll, the ship responds instantly and the nose starts to rise. Soon the tumult of sounds all around them begin to quiet and even out.

With more than a little wonder, Jot says, "I think we're pulling out of it."

Koko rolls her eyes. "Duh…"

Jot risks a hand and tenderly strokes a thumb on the small multicolored Ganesha statue taped thickly to the cockpit console. The arms and the elephant-like trunk of the statue are animated, and the statue responds to the touch with barely audible stick drums and sitars.

The nose continues to rise, and a minute later they level up to a manageable cruising altitude and airspeed. Koko lets out a self-assured laugh, and Jot looks over and scowls at her.

"This is not funny," he says. "No-no. You two people hijack my ship, you kill my co-pilot, you two are not funny people at all. You two are evil, yes-yes. Hijackers. Terrorists. Sky pirates!"

"Relax, Jot. And for the record, I didn't kill anyone." Koko throws a thumb over her shoulder. "Little Miss Flyweight back there is just taking a nap. By the way, your co-pilot sweetie got a name?"

"Helmsman First Class Hoon."

"I think you and Hoon should be grateful, seeing as how I just saved your asses from meeting whatever supernatural pachyderm you think is watching out for you. So, tell me, captain. Where were you two headed in this stinky bucket of bolts anyway?"

Jot grumbles and draws up a screened monitor on a retractable arm mount. He punches a few buttons and pulls up the ship's intended flight plan and then swivels the monitor to face Koko, shoving it in her direction with a repulsed huff. Koko pulls the screen closer and settles back in her seat, her face illuminated by the screen's yellowish glow.

"One hundred forty-seven east and forty-two south? No way."

"This was our destination had we not been hijacked by you two savages."

Flynn finally gets to his feet and sways his way across the cabin. He looks over Koko's shoulder as she pores over the arrays and motions with his finger to the leaking cut on Koko's forehead where she slammed into the console earlier. Koko smears the blood up into her blue hair like styling gel and mashes her fingertips on Flynn's sleeve.

"So what is it?" Flynn asks. "What's at one hundred forty-seven what-do-you-call-its?"

"A place you may have heard of. Ever heard of Papua New Guinea, Flynn?"

"Papua New Guinea? Yeah, sure, I've heard of it. The flooded platform settlements. Nasty place, if I remember correctly. What's the deal with Papua New Guinea?"

Koko hums happily to herself. "Oh, nothing," she says. "Just that we're a couple of lucky hijackers, that's all."

Koko unclasps the safety harness. She tilts the screen back, pulls up the navigational inputs, and gets to work. Jot starts to protest but Koko fires him a look like she plans on punching him in the face. Jot glowers straight ahead, and Koko busies herself with the recalibrations.

"New course, captain. A whole ream of extra clicks northwest toward the East Mariana Basin. Micronesia. Damn, I need to pull up the weather scans on this thing."

Flynn and the pilot both look at Koko and say simultaneously, "Micronesia?"

"No," Koko answers. "Not precisely. Just north of there and due west of the sub-ocean trenches. It's a re-stabilized Ring of Fire fault locale. Hey, I trust this ship transmits an identity beacon, right? Cool. They make contact with us, I want you to hail them and ask for an emergency forfeiture and offload."

The captain tears off his goggles. "Emergency forfeiture and offload? But-but... I will lose my job." He indicates the unconscious first mate Hoon. "We will both lose our jobs."

Koko drawls, "Yeah, well, we could just dump you and Hoon out the back and fly this thing ourselves. Horrific death that, just ask my partner in crime here. Hell, he might even join you because he kind of has a hard-on for a big screaming jump—don't you, lawman? Seeing that you missed your chance back on *Alaungpaya*."

Flynn shakes his head. Captain Jot looks confused.

"Wait," Jot says. "You? *You* have Depressus?"

Flynn droops, embarrassed. "It's kind of a long story."

Jot reaches across and draws the navigational display's screen around to his face. After a quick study of the recalibrations and the charts, he peers uneasily over the display at Koko.

"They need a lot of power down there to make the party rev hot," Koko says. "Trust me, captain. They'll pick us up and gladly take the vile stuff you got off your hands. My bet is they'll prioritize our approach on the service runways and shoot us straight to the front of their queue."

"Uh, so where exactly are we headed?" Flynn asks.

Koko looks at the captain. "Tell him, Jot."

"We are headed to The Sixty Islands."

DETAILS, DETAILS

On her feet behind her desk, Portia Delacompte leans on her knuckles and scours the reports on more than a dozen screen prompts projected in front of her.

Concentrating on the prompt displays makes her eyeballs ache. It's more than challenging to decipher so much fuzzy nonsensical chatter and bulletin analytics. It appears that none of the freelance bounty operatives Lee dispatched to take Koko out have checked in, which leads Delacompte to believe either (a) they are flat-out ignoring her and still hunting Koko down or (b) they are already dead. Instinct and experience tells Delacompte it's probably the latter. She pats the pocket on her jacket and debates whether to swallow yet another capsule of Q.

C'mon, think, Portia. Think.

From what she can discern, post-explosion on *Alaungpaya* only one vessel cleared the barge orbital before emergency depressurization was finally initiated. This in and of itself isn't that unusual. Delacompte knows that most service rig and cargo pilots play loose with procedures and ride it a bit cowboy, especially if the rules eat into their delivery deadlines. There could be a dozen different reasons why this particular vessel broke off when the alarm sounded. But it's truly odd that the vessel flew through a panicked wave of people bypassing Embrace ceremony restrictions.

That ship must have had a good reason to high-tail it out of there.

Delacompte pulls up the flight identification records and notes that the vessel last to clear was a septic G-Class cargo ship on a waste-disposal run to Papua New Guinea. With her security clearance she is able to access the flight plan databases and discovers that, not long after departure, the cargo ship altered its course. Again, a change of flight plan is not all that unusual for freighters, but *holy frigging shit* unusual is the revised destination.

The craft is on a course for The Sixty Islands.

"No, it can't be…" Delacompte whispers.

Koko.

She's coming back here? Here? The quarry coming for the hunter?

Well, Delacompte supposes she did *ask* for it.

Delacompte immediately secures a patch to ATC at The Sixty Islands' main tower. Yes, they have the G-Class vessel from *Alaungpaya* in their pattern and the ship's ETA before the outer beacons is at forty-five past the hour. She asks if the G-Class has declared an onboard emergency. No, no signs of any trouble other than they left *Alaungpaya* during a required security activation and changed their course intentions. Two crew aboard and eight hundred tons of solid human waste in the hold. Delacompte advises flight that she needs to meet the vessel upon landing, and flight tells her this won't be a problem. They have the frigate scheduled for biohazard de-rack on runway nine for offload.

"No one but me meets this inbound, understand? That's a direct order."

Flight responds. "Um, roger that. But shouldn't we advise recycle retrieval? We can have four hangar tanks on the pad out there, no problem."

"No. Extinguish all meet orders."

"They're going to squawk."

"Just do it," Delacompte says. "No one meets this inbound without my authorization. This is a disciplinary issue for CPB and SI executive management, and I am handling the matter personally."

Delacompte terminates the ATC patch transmission. She rubs her forehead and then stalks over to her office credenza.

When she presses a button recessed into the paneling at hip-level, the top of the credenza rolls back and the crystal water pitcher and glasses that sat there—flecked with Lee's blood—crash to the floor. Delacompte gently steps into the spilt water and broken glass.

Letting her fingertips graze from piece to piece, she looks down and drinks in a neat display of guns and close-quarter ammunitions. The weapons are organized from the smallest to the largest. With one hand she picks up a bandolier of pulse grenades, and with her other hand she lifts up the compact stock of an Italian prototype pulse rifle.

"Time to accessorize," she says.

Delacompte gears up.

FLIGHT TO FIGHT

The chopped down co-pilot and helmsman Hoon groggily comes to, and Flynn lifts and leads her by the elbow to the co-pilot's seat. Like a slug stretched beneath the skin, a neat purple bruise the length of Koko's hand creases the young woman's neck. She sniffles and stammers a stream of terrified whats and whys—wanting to know what has happened, why they are flying, why they appear to be off course—but Jot gives her an order to be quiet and the girl clams up. Meanwhile, in the rear of the cabin, Flynn studies Koko as she sets both the Sig and his Beretta to the guns' most powerful discharge settings.

"I don't get it," Flynn says. "I mean, the entire world and the Second Free Zone. The whole planet to choose from. Why would you go back to the one place where you know someone is looking to kill you? You could go anywhere, Koko. Anywhere."

Koko seats both guns on her belt, draws, and snugs them back home again. "I know," she replies.

"I'm serious. This is totally nuts."

"You don't get it," she says.

"You're right," Flynn answers angrily. "I don't get it. I'm just some pathetic loser who helped save your life and got a bunch of people killed."

Koko reaches out and pats his arm. "And I thank you for that. Really. Not for getting people killed, but you know what I mean. Look, Flynn, you have to understand. This is who I am. This is how I've always dealt with things, or how I used to deal with things, anyway. Me? Be hounded? What, I get to look over my shoulder every day in some far-flung piece of bankrupt supersprawl until someone sells me out and plants a knife in my neck? Uh-uh, no way. I am not signing up for that. Portia Delacompte sent those bounty agents after me up top when the Second Free Zone is supposedly off limits. Just how long do you think I'd survive on Earth with a price on my head? And Portia Delacompte? Ha. Even if she's painted her actions as some kind of CPB public-relations mop-up or me as a loony SI vendor gone rogue, she won't stop, Flynn. Not ever. Not when I know her secret and I'm still alive."

"Yeah," Flynn says, "her big secret. You weren't exactly clear on that back on *Alaungpaya*. What the hell is all this about anyway? I'm thinking it's got to be something pretty heinous for her to risk unleashing those killers. God, there must have been close to a hundred people milling about the terminal when that pulse grenade went off."

"Maybe it'll be safer for you if you didn't know."

"Safer for me? What, you want me just to move on and *forget*? Those were innocent people, Koko. Innocent civilians going about their lives. You think their lives don't matter? You know what? Fuck you, Koko. Fuck you. The last time I checked, I'm more than an accomplice here. I think I deserve to know the details of this big, bad Delacompte secret at this point. And anyway, you've said it yourself. Me, I'm a dead man. You owe me the consideration."

Koko looks down at her feet. She takes a few calming breaths before she finally looks up into Flynn's eyes. She allows another beat to pass between them before she lifts her chin and addresses Jot and Hoon.

"Hey," Koko says. "You two wingers have headsets?"

Jot and Hoon shake their heads no.

"Stick your fingers in your ears, then."

Reluctantly, Jot engages the frigate's autopilot system, and the ship quivers from side to side. Jot and Hoon push their fingers into their ears, and Koko edges closer to speak softly to Flynn.

DAMNATIO MEMORIAE (AND THEN SOME)

The years since Delacompte left the mercenary life to pursue her schooling and business aspirations hadn't exactly been a cakewalk for Koko.

One might say Koko's once unshakable commitment to anonymously mucking out the stalls on international re-civ stability efforts and buttressing syndicate bottom lines as an expendable asset had reached a critical juncture. That is, she was one more screwed-up assignment or disciplinary action away from burning out altogether.

Finishing up a tedious hitch on the Venezuela mining plateaus for the SA Mineral Corporation, Koko decided it was high time for a well-earned breather to recalibrate her bearings. After her SAMC credit transfer came through, she lit out for an available safe-house compound on the Balearic Islands of the western Mediterranean to reflect on things. True, it was not the safest of locales, but the Portuguese and Spanish bird plagues had played out a few years before, and the largest of the islands, Majorca, where the safe house stood, was a speedy hover hop to the ceaseless, rankled jaws of North Africa for work if her credits wore thin.

Days of sipping warm wine, nibbling salty cheeses, and staring out at the deep-rig, sub-core mining platforms. Loafing in a king-sized bed and recharging her depleted faculties with soft drugs and anonymous, hard sex—it helped alleviate some of her discontentment, but still, it wasn't enough. After a while, Koko thought that maybe what she really needed to refresh her depleted outlook was a heavy-handed dose of big-sister authoritarianism.

It wasn't that Koko was overly sentimental or anything. She wasn't. But she also realized that she didn't have many real friends in her life. The pressures and responsibilities of her kind of livelihood sort of put the kibosh on those types of personal sentiments. She found herself thinking more and more about Portia Delacompte and their combat bonding.

She hadn't heard from Delacompte in a while, and it dawned on Koko that perhaps Big D could infuse her with some direction. Delacompte's confidence and zeal had always seemed to do the trick before, fired her right up and fixed her center. Maybe Delacompte could light the path for her. At the very least, she was sure her old friend wouldn't spare her a good mental ass kicking.

Cue Koko the sleuth.

Sitting at a long table overlooking the Med in the safe house, she started calling in a bunch of favors with her contacts. Combed intelligence research sources for hours upon hours and stared into archival projection prompts until she felt she was losing her marbles. It seemed Delacompte had become a ghost. No matter where she looked or who she hammered with questions, no trace could be found of the woman. Koko had a sinking feeling that Delacompte had vanished from the Earth. After a week's worth of frustration, Koko was about to forget the whole deal and take an assignment down in Cameroon, but then an old associate who ran geosynchronous tactical intercepts relayed in a patch to her that Delacompte had taken a top-secret executive position at a leisure finance firm up in Finland.

Koko packed her bags and was on a transport north two hours

later. After half a day of banging around Helsinki and getting her bearings, she had a plan.

Like a wobbling hurled tomahawk, the fuselage of the hired helo sliced through the freezing sleet above Helsinki under the cover of darkness. Gull-winged micro-fusion lift engines keened a triphonic, ear-splitting chime as Koko keyed her headset mic near her mouth.

"So, you're a lousy pilot on top of being a crook?"

The pilot, a freelancer known only as Fredrikkaa, used her thick lips to work her cigarette to the other corner of her mouth and drew in some smoke. Her profile, puffy and red from drink, glowed creepily as the tip of her cigarette cherried. She mumbled something, but over the engine noise Koko couldn't make out the words. Koko was familiar with a few key phrases in Finnish, especially operational commands and such, but she found herself coming up short on the profanity front.

The pilot didn't bother using her own headset mic and shouted, "This building you want, this *pilvenpiirtäjä*? Defenses heavy!"

Koko keyed her mic again and gestured to the console. "I told you. The target is fortified on the lower levels, not on the roof. I've triple-checked the specs. Besides, this is a Eurofire Insert-40. What're you worried about? The triangulum countermeasures on these birds come standard."

The pilot swung the helo south-southeast, and they bounced across some chop.

"No-no," the pilot replied. "I fly civil only. No weapons. This now a tourist birdy!"

Koko shook her head. Great. Whatever. Just get her close. That was all Koko needed and what she paid double for.

After studying the building, Koko had memorized Delacompte's floor and unit number. Delacompte's high-rise quarters were several floors below the structural outcrop on the roof that Koko planned to drop down on. With the crummy weather, she knew doing a staged rappel and climb-down would really heighten the surprise. Yeah, Koko thought, it's going to be a hoot. Remind Big D of her good ol' days.

Out the sleet-slicked forward canopy, Koko observed the *pilvenpiirtäjä*, the target building, approaching fast. She unbuckled her safety straps and moved aft to get into position. A moment later the pilot engaged the craft's whisper drive and the engine racket softened as though the world around them had suddenly been swallowed whole. Using a single finger, the pilot pointed to the building and informed Koko via pantomime that they were one minute out.

Koko held up a clenched fist to demonstrate that she understood. She slipped on her harness, checked and clipped into the anchor hook above her head, and prepared herself. After pulling her deployment bag onto her shoulders, she gave the pilot a "go" signal and the cabin door *chik-choked* and slid wide. The cold wet wind gusted hard, and Koko saw they were directly above the roof. Koko threw out her nylon rappelling line to the rooftop below.

Koko stepped out onto the helo's slippery landing skid. The sleet slashed her face and she pivoted one hundred eighty degrees, bracing her feet shoulder-width apart, keeping herself relaxed but steady on the skid. Heart beating hard, Koko looked down and saw the end of the rappelling line light up green, indicating the rope had made contact with the gravel on the building's roof. Depth perception at their perilous height along with the weather and darkness was a mother, but having the guidance light hot on the line helped.

Out at a forty-five-degree angle, Koko gripped her brake hand on the line at the small of her back. In her head she recalled faint echoes of her trainers from years past. *Go slow, brake, then descend. Do not go hard or you will die.*

Koko slipped off into the darkness.

* * *

After releasing the line for her harness, Koko watched the Eurofire helo wheel off over the skyline and disappear. All that lay ahead for Koko now was a gymnastic scale down to Delacompte's flat. Luckily for Koko, the building's architectural design included great bulging bars on each unit's terrace, presenting her with easy consecutive leaps of eight feet in between floors. Smiling with the anticipation of her upcoming surprise, Koko took her time and reveled in the physicality of her descent. A minute and a half later and she hit the final overhanging ledge above Delacompte's unit. Slowly she lowered her feet until she was able to swing herself and softly, silently land on Delacompte's balcony.

In front of Koko, two sliding nine-foot-high window doors glowed. Thick, mushroom-brown curtains were drawn nearly tight but a sliver of light escaped. Koko combed a hand through her wet hair and freed the small deployment bag from her shoulders. Yes, she thought, this dropping in all of a sudden might seem a mite rude, but Koko was positive they'd share more than a few hearty laughs over the stunt. Then she wondered if Delacompte was alone. Whoops. What if Delacompte was entertaining or, worse yet, what if she was scandalously indisposed? This could be a new chapter in Koko's long list of embarrassing life screw-ups. Fuck it. Too late for second guesses now.

Behind the sliding glass windows, a vertical rift of light between the curtains beckoned. Koko took a tentative step and then another, but she froze when she heard a pained shriek inside.

What the hell?

Two quick steps forward and Koko cupped her hands to peer through the glass.

The scene inside hurled a pole of ice straight through her stomach. A well-appointed living room with blinding white features and furniture draped in transparent plastic tarps spread wide as if the room was set to be repainted. Delacompte, pallid-cheeked, sweaty and awkward on the floor with her legs in obstetric akimbo, a half-empty vodka bottle tipped to its side and leaking to her right, a vial of scattered pills nearby. Delacompte writhing, her face contorted in pain, hauling up something from within her, higher and higher to her wheezing breast. A deflated, smeary umbilical cord trailing.

No.

An appalling knot of expression on the infant's face—shrieking.

NO!

Delacompte's four trembling fingers and the thumb of her right hand pinching off and squeezing the baby's neck.

Koko pounded on the glass and screamed. She lunged sideways for the handle on the terrace window, yanking hard and to the left, but found the sliding window's mechanism locked. There was no time. None.

Koko launched herself shoulder-first through the glass.

Her crash ripped the curtains from the rod. Delacompte looked at her, her expression shorted out by shock, her groggy, blood-starved brain unable to assimilate the fact that Koko was actually there, rolling to her feet and moving. Koko spun sideways and kicked out with all her might, the toe of her right boot connecting with Delacompte's open jaw. The impact instantly rendered Delacompte unconscious and threw off Koko's equilibrium. Koko collapsed to the floor in a heap by Delacompte and her dead child.

The gravity of her friend's desperate act lowered onto Koko, and with it a profound sorrow so new and so disturbing it felt as though her insides were imploding. Broken glass clinking beneath her, Koko lolled her head to the right and wiped the salty sting from her eyes. She found herself reaching out for the child, inert and facedown on the plastic.

Never in her life had Koko touched the skin of an infant, let alone a newborn. Never once in the collectives or even the de-civ warzones when she guarded hopeless refugees wailing from hunger and despair. The slippery softness on her fingertips shocked her and pulled the breath from her chest.

Five tiny, pebble-sized toes. A foot now in her fingers and a lifted leg revealing the cleft of the child's sex.

Koko rolled wildly left and vomited. She puked for a full minute until it seemed nothing more would come forth and her throat felt as though it'd been flossed with frayed wire. Finally, when she stopped heaving, she rolled back and felt the grief and disbelief inside changing. The thick emotional calluses from a lifetime of warfare and capitalized catastrophe had vanished. A blizzard of symphonic confusion welled inside her, overwhelming her practiced discipline and control. Koko convulsed and sobbed and sobbed and sobbed.

"What have you done?"

MISTAKES

Flynn's face blanches.

"No…"

Koko shuts her eyes and wrestles against the surge of memories. She deflates heavily after a long intake and expulsion of air. "Yeah," she says. "I should have just gotten the hell out of there, but I didn't. I stayed."

"But why?"

"What do you mean, why? I was traumatized, you dope. I was overwhelmed and confused. I mean, I've seen and done a lot in my life, Flynn, but never, ever something as bad as that."

Flynn notices that Koko is shaking, so he reaches out and touches her shoulder.

"What did you do?"

Koko thumbs both of her eyes and blinks. "What did I do? I called out for a good, hot curry—the hell do you think I did? I found some heavy tranquilizers in her bathroom medicine cabinet and cleaned up everything."

"By cleaning up everything you mean even the—"

"Yeah. The building's thermite disposal flue. I kept Delacompte sedated and tied down in her bed for two full days until she came around. And you know what? That was the hardest part of the whole thing. Suffering her shame and the distress in her eyes. For a while she fought it, thinking I was some kind of hallucination, but I stayed with her and drew her out. When she realized I was there for real she confessed to me she couldn't go through with it and forced a premature delivery. When I asked her why she didn't terminate the pregnancy or why she waited so long, she made the worst and weakest of excuses. Stupid, horrible stuff. Work overload, procrastination, disbelief—she'd always been dutiful in her hygiene so it couldn't possibly be true.

"I couldn't accept it myself. I mean, this was a woman I'd always looked up to and measured myself against. It was all so pathetic. She said she considered it impossible. Thought she had a tumor or maybe a cancer, refusing on all fronts to accept the idea that she'd been pregnant. It made me sick. Fuck. She begged me, Flynn, begged me to understand the opportunities of her new world. She couldn't have a baby. It would destroy everything she had worked so long and so hard for."

"What about—"

"The father?" Koko sniffs and clears her throat with a couple of shallow coughs. "She didn't say, and I didn't ask or even care. I'm not saying I'm proud of what I did, but when she was through with giving me her excuses I told her I had her back. I made a promise, you know? No more questions, no judgments. I just bucked up and powered through. I put my trust in the mercenary code—thinking, hell, it was understood, right? I thought that's what friends are supposed to do for each other when they're up against a wall."

"Covering up an infanticide can't be high on anyone's list of favors."

Koko knocks his hand from her shoulder. "You bastard! You think that was easy for me?" Koko glares at Flynn before shaking her head. "I guess part of me didn't want to believe it'd happened. I didn't want to know Delacompte wasn't the person I thought she was. This screwed-up world is hard enough, but when people you look up to let you down by being weak, vain, and stupid, I don't know, you start to lose your bearings and the entire sham stares you right in the face. You fray apart. At least that's what I felt back then, and I couldn't live like that. So, I did what I had to do, got through it, and tried my best to forget the whole mess even happened. Anyway, that's what went down in Finland. So, fast-forward a couple of years. Delacompte ends up in an oversight position on The Sixty, and I'm blown completely away when she reaches out to me. She goes on and on and tells me she wants to set me up carte blanche with my own bar. At the time I was feeling pretty ragged out from all the syndicate work I'd been assigned, and I said yes even though deep down I knew something didn't feel right. Stupid, right? But a job like that on The Sixty Islands? Delacompte positioned the opportunity as a way for me to retire from the gun-for-hire lifestyle with reasonable comfort. What was I supposed to do? Hell, I'm not getting any younger and a chance like that doesn't come by every day for someone like me."

"So it was a payoff."

"Maybe initially, I guess so. I don't know."

"And now all of this is about some kind of a cover-up? But why? You've kept quiet all this time and you helped her. She's the one who hired you."

"Are you familiar with New One Roman Church of the Most Holy Liberator?"

"The fundamentalist extremists? Sure, of course, who isn't?"

"Every big-shot board executive at CPB is a member, and it's no mystery that Delacompte has set her sights on a top slot. Shit, the CPB do extensive background checks and interviews at the senior board level—"

"Meaning?"

"Meaning sooner or later they'd probably call me in because they know I was Delacompte's hire. I'm the only one who knows what she did, and if the CPB ever gets wind she killed her own baby to keep her stupid career on track, she's done for. The one thing the

Church can't turn a blind eye to is the taking of a life before it's even had a chance to corrupt itself."

"This is crazy."

"You want stone crazy? How's this for a chaser. Delacompte's had selective memory treatments."

Flynn's eyes just about double in size. "Don't tell me she doesn't even remember what happened."

"Nope. Like I said, I should have known something was screwy right then and there when she sweet-talked me with her recruitment spiel and told me she'd undergone SMTs. And she might claim she's found religion, but that's a crock too. Delacompte is about as likely to be grounded in the holy word of God as I am to go down without a fight. All this? This is about climbing the corporate ladder for her, nothing more. This is about saving her own butt."

"But the SMT therapy. Why is she after you if she can't even remember you were there?"

"Maybe she filed away an order to get rid of me at a later date. I mean, it is possible. Delacompte is a buttoned-up sort when it comes to logistics. But what really ticks me off is I was right under her thumb all this time, working on The Sixty. Whether she can remember the whats or whys of what went down back in Finland doesn't even matter. I think the woman bided her time until she could pick her shot and take me out."

"I can't believe this."

"Believe it. Holy smokes, Flynn, have you any idea what CPB board members even make?"

"I guess it's a lot."

"Think of an obscene number of credits and then cube it."

"I don't know what to say."

"Say nothing, but now you know."

Flynn holds Koko's eyes for a few seconds and then looks away. He tries to digest and shut away the information she has just shared with him, the folly and ghastly revulsion of it all, but he simply can't. The frame of the nightmare is beyond comprehension. He feels washed out and weary, hollow to the bone. Koko squeezes his arm.

"Hey, are you okay?"

Flynn shakes her off. "No! I'm not okay!"

"This isn't your problem, Flynn."

Flynn scoffs. "Don't tell me this isn't my problem. Am I not standing here? Hello! We've hijacked a septic vessel. What did Jot call us? Sky pirates? I'm supposed to be fish food right now, but no, now I'm a terrorist and I'm trapped above the Pacific with a former mercenary who has the nerve to tell me this is not my problem. This can't be happening. We've got to figure another way out of this."

Koko shakes her head. "Ever since I ran into the first bounty agent and let her live I think I've been in denial, Flynn. Yeah, at first I thought maybe, just maybe, if I went to ground I could finagle a way clear. But I know now that's not even remotely possible. Now I'm warmed up and I'm mad. There isn't any other way out of this but to take the fight straight to Delacompte. We may end up killing each other in the end, but I think I can live with that. Given my hand in cleaning up her mess back then like I did, I guess I might even deserve it."

Koko puffs out her cheeks and drags a hand over her face as though to clear her thoughts. Flynn finds her eyes again.

"But there's still time," he insists. "We could turn this frigate around. I don't know—maybe make a run for it. The Australian territories can't be that far away now."

"No thanks. Too many memories in Oz for me."

"Fine. What about New Zealand, then?"

Koko jeers bitterly, "The Kiwis? God, Flynn, the Kiwis are so depressing since the commonwealth crashed and the syndicates snapped up their natural resource rights. Auckland is like an open gangrenous wound, and the south island strip mines are overrun with insurgent Maori de-civs."

"But there has to be some other option."

"Look, I appreciate your concern. Really, I do. After all, you've done a bang-up job getting me this far."

Flynn palms his hands together, pleading. "But what if you just out Delacompte to the CPB and their church? Skip this grudge nonsense you think you're due and come clean on the whole mess? You could blow the whistle and all of this could just dry up. The CPB might even offer you clemency and consider it all extenuating circumstances."

"An accessory to an infanticide? Yeah, right. Those CPB sons of bitches are hardly going to take that lightly."

"You're not the one who started this."

"Doesn't matter. No, I've thought about it and there's no other way. Delacompte has to go, and she's going out on my terms." Koko takes a step and raises her voice. "Hey, Jot? Hoon? You guys can unplug your ears now."

The pilots lower their hands. Hoon disengages the autopilot.

"How much longer until we reach The Sixty?" Koko asks.

"Not long," Hoon says. "One hour fifteen minutes, give or take. We have pretty strong headwinds on the nose."

"Push her if you can."

Flynn trolls for a small flicker of give in Koko's eyes, but the determination cemented in them tells him there's no talking her out of her decision. Frustrated and exhausted, Flynn slides down to the cabin floor and draws his knees to his chest. He looks up.

"You're something else, you know that?"

Koko stares out the bow bubble and cracks her knuckles. Clouds rush past in a tunneling gauntlet. Her eyes fork hard into the distance. Cold.

"I'll take that as a compliment," she says.

WELCOMING PARTY

Delacompte commandeers a terra-sled from the SI transport pool and streaks toward the landing fields on the southernmost dot of The Sixty Islands chain. Pushing the throttle to maximum velocity on the access roads, she whip-steers in and out of resort and maintenance traffic like a missile hot on target, her trajectory a mere meter off the ground.

Delacompte hums past the simulated killing lagoons. Hurls past the open, burning blight of the Trauma Quadrant. Over the bridges and past adrenaline-pumped vacationers writhing in outdoor orgies of simulated butchery and lust. SI flight control in the main tower patches in on the terra-sled's com, and Delacompte demands an update on the septic ship's estimated time of arrival.

"Inbound G-Class in twenty-two minutes. Biohazard de-rack team dispatched. G-Class queued for touchdown on runway nine."

"To whom am I speaking?"

"This is Flight Administrator Bardsley. Identification number 2245—"

God, she didn't want this jerk's entire life story.

"Listen, Bardsley," Delacompte says, "I told you guys to eighty-six the biohazard de-rack."

The com clips silent.

"Come again, Vice President Delacompte. Not sure I got that."

"Did you guys kill the de-rack on runway nine or not?"

"Uh, the biohazard de-rack teams are already on the ground and setting up in the hangar for arrival and transport."

Delacompte banks the terra-sled, and the road opens up on a vacant straightaway. Hemmed in by the jungles zipping by, she flies parallel to the drainage ditches feeding into the archipelago's conservation scuppers, petals and leaves twirling in her wake. Like popcorn in a skillet, insects snap and pop against the terra-sled's triangular windscreen. Pleased not to see another vehicle on the straightaway for at least two kilometers, Delacompte redlines the controls.

"You people are worthless," Delacompte says. "I want the hangar perimeter and runway area completely vacated. If I see any of your de-rack personnel within two thousand meters of that hangar, I'm going to track you down and rip your lungs out through your balloon knot. Got it? Clear it. Clear it now. ETA is one minute plus."

"Copy that. De-rack canceled. Perimeter seal orders confirmed."

"And don't do something stupid to give me away. Procedure your hustle to the letter. If this inbound spooks because of something you do or don't do I'm personally blaming you, Bardsley."

"Understood. Have you on visual, outer bands and closing. Um, Vice President Delacompte?"

"What now?"

"You might want to slow down."

The straightaway in front of her curves abruptly to the left and the thick tropical rainforest peels away. Banking hard into the sudden turn, Delacompte adjusts her weight and barely avoids a head-on collision with a ground shuttle packed with SI tourists.

Delacompte downshifts, brakes, and nearly spins out of control, but she corrects and regains momentum. An open security gate looms ahead, outgoing transports filing up behind it, and Delacompte gusts through it at one hundred thirty-seven kilometers per hour.

From above, The Sixty Islands' aircraft landing fields resemble the front wheel of a massive pennyfarthing bicycle. Twenty kilometers in diameter, the combined runway and servicing apron is rimmed by moats of sloshing, brackish seawater. Once past the outer security gate, Delacompte punches the controls again and follows the airfield circumference around the inner runway beacons. Each of the runways on her right is marked with giant, bright orange numerals illuminated by solarized dynamos underground. When she reaches runway nine, she slows the terra-sled to a floating stop and releases the terra-sled's hatch.

The hatch lifts with a muted reptilian hiss, and Delacompte glances toward the morning sky. The rising sun is a massive fireball on the horizon, and she has to shield her eyes from the glare. Idling in the terra-sled, she estimates the air temperature to be over forty-four degrees Celsius. Twenty or thirty more degrees and you could positively poach an egg. Roars of incoming and outgoing aircraft vibrate the gelatinous, moist air.

Wiping the sweat from her brow, Delacompte recalculates the frigate's arrival time in her head. Less than eighteen minutes, give or take. Once the ship lands, the rising sun might be an advantage for Koko if they end up engaging in the open, but SOP for inbounds is to taxi to the hangar before disembarking and offload.

Delacompte knows what she needs to do. She lowers herself back into the terra-sled, seals the hatch, and burns east, streaking up the heavily skid-marked runway.

Pin Koko in the hangar and have a standoff. A warrior-on-warrior moment of principle and pride in which they agree to set their weapons aside and finish this business with some good old-fashioned hand-to-hand.

Sure, that might be fun, Delacompte thinks, but a total waste of time. As soon as Koko shows herself, Delacompte is going to make her a grubby stain on the ground. Delacompte can almost smell the stench of fried flesh, and once again she wishes she could remember.

Why is she doing this again?

INCOMING

As the frigate slopes downward, cutting their altitude, Flynn's inner ears click.

Jot and Hoon have confessed to delivering to The Sixty before, and now they are locking into the SI's pattern as flight control confirms and acknowledges their inbound approach. The exchange of technical gibberish sounds normal, and Jot and Hoon don't say anything that might give away the fact that they have been compromised. Koko hawks their movements just to be sure that everything is on the up-and-up as Flynn rises to his feet.

"How much longer?" he asks.

Hoon responds with a sniff, rubbing the bruise on her neck. "They have us locked in for runway nine," she answers. "We should see the primary navigation beacons in a few minutes. Port side, ten o'clock. Then we'll turn a bit, and when we level off they will be directly in front of us. Traffic is pretty heavy down there this time of day, but it's mostly personnel transports and private commercial crafts on lower paths. Anyway, they kind of give operators like us a wide berth."

"I can imagine," says Flynn.

Jot smirks. "No one ever wants to see or even smell revolting business such as ours. Takes away the pricey resort charm."

Beneath them, the landing gear lowers with thumps from its locked, recessed position. Koko moves forward and grips the back of Jot's seat, and Flynn does the same with Hoon's. They both dip their heads a bit to see out the bow windows. Stretching out in a dappled, corduroy azure, the semi-toxic cyan seas churn.

Hoon points. "There!"

Flynn sees it, and the grandeur of The Sixty is amazing. The landmasses look just like the advertisements he's seen on the feeds, a perfected lush hoop of manufactured tropical islands, complete with artificial stratovolcanic spines. A trick of the morning's parting clouds and the sun's light behind them, the low jungle hills glow greenish gold. While Flynn hasn't much experience with terrestrial vegetation, he thinks the light might be the kind one sees in turned tree leaves before a terrible storm. Seems fitting, Flynn thinks, in any case.

Koko: a one-woman whirlwind.

"Turning," Hoon announces, working the rudder and flap controls. "Decreasing air speed…"

"I have her now," Jot responds. "Flight level forty-two hundred meters. Prepare for landing and arrival. You two will have to hold on back there, as there are no safety harnesses or jump seats for you. Try not to get in the way, yes-yes?"

Hoon busies herself with quick fingers swiping across various screens and projections. The ship's altitude continues to decrease.

"Pretty smooth flying, Jot," Koko says. "I guess you've logged a lot of hours hauling solid waste around. I mean, what with your advanced age and all."

Jot's red wool cap is soaked dark with sweat. "Almost two hundred twenty-five thousand hours. I may be an old man, but I am a very good pilot. After our miserable takeoff from *Alaungpaya*, anything close to normal will seem smooth."

"What happened back on *Alaungpaya* anyway?" Hoon asks.

Flynn places a hand on Hoon's shoulder.

"We almost didn't make it. We flew through the Embrace jump."

"We *what*? We flew through Embrace? But I thought the whole place was in emergency sequence and they were depressurizing. They still went ahead with the ceremony?"

"Apparently the afflicted couldn't wait for the all-clear and took matters into their own hands."

"Whoa, that's really messed up."

"You're telling me."

Hoon's eyes flicker across the projections slipping and shuffling in front of her. From the change in her expression it grows apparent that something isn't quite copasetic. Her brow pleats.

"Hey, Jot? Are you seeing what I'm seeing here?"

All heads turn to Hoon.

"Look."

Jot examines the projections, but doesn't grasp what Hoon is referencing. Hoon heaves a small sigh and addresses Koko and Flynn. "Normally, this far out we get a personnel file grid listing all service marshals who'll be overseeing the biohazard de-rack. It's for our flight records. But we haven't received one."

"Meaning what exactly?" Flynn asks.

Hoon swipes a panel away and reviews a second avionic projection with a squint. "Meaning it's just odd, is all. We're in their queue, and it's possible they might have forgotten it, but that's pretty unlikely. These things are programmed directly from the main tower and dumped solid. I don't know. It's probably nothing."

Flynn squeezes her shoulder. "Hail them."

Hoon looks back.

"You think I should?"

"Just to be sure," he says. "You're right, it probably is nothing. But we should check anyway."

Hoon engages the com and speaks in terse bursts. "Sixty Islands flight? This is G-Class waste frigate incoming, runway nine, in your pattern, over. We've not received service marshal manifest on biohazard de-rack. Still being met for offload, yes-yes? Please confirm, over."

Koko looks at Flynn as flight responds.

"Affirmative, G-Class. Uh, sorry about that. We're kind of in the midst of a nav programming defrag. Bit of a mix-up, our apologies. Got you on approach. Hangar de-rack confirmed and manifest grid uploads will be ready on the ground, over."

"Roger."

Hoon shuts down the com.

Koko's lower lip overlaps her upper. Her eyes shift back and forth as she snorkels through her thoughts.

"What do you think?" Flynn asks.

Koko wrinkles her nose.

"Damn it," Flynn says. "We should pull up. This could be a trap. Delacompte could kill us all."

Jot whimpers. "*What?* Kill us *all*? No, no, no, no. Who is this Delacompte you speak of? Why would this person want to kill us?"

"Just shut up, Jot, and keep flying," Koko says.

Flynn stamps a foot. "Koko!"

"Maybe I wasn't clear with you before," Koko says, wheeling her head around. "This is personal for Delacompte. She's not going to bring in a whole squad to take us down outright. Oh, sure, I suppose she could use the SI batteries to blast us from the sky, but we're well within range now and if that were the call she probably would've taken her shot already. Plus, when you consider her colossal ego and the bad press? No way. Trust me, she'll want to meet me face-to-face and alone. Like the tower just said, this might be some kind of a programming error."

"Yeah, but you don't believe that."

"Listen, Flynn," Koko says, "Jot and Hoon. You've all been super. Really. Hijacking and knockout blows notwithstanding. And there's no reason for you to get hurt. Especially you, Flynn. So let me ask our pilots here something. Once we touch down, is there any way of dropping out of this bird while we're taxiing toward the hangar?"

Jot and Hoon ease their yokes from side to side as the ship continues its descent.

"There's a maintenance tube behind you," Jot answers. "Inside that tube is a small ladder leading down to a second series of hatches that open directly below the front landing gear. There, the yellow stripe. Lift that flap. There's a red D-ring lock under it. You twist that red D-ring lock counterclockwise to release. What is it? What are you planning to do?"

Koko eyes the yellow strip. She bends over and lifts the metal flap with the toe of her boot, exposing the red D-ring lock Jot has just described. She returns to her position behind Jot's seat and leans over.

"What's the inside of the hangar look like?"

"Why?"

"Just give me the damn details, Jot. Windows. Platforms. Exits. Hazards. Dimensions. I used to work on The Sixty but I never spent a lot of time out there, so tell me everything you can think of."

"But we can't help you," Jot protests. "They could bring us up on charges if we assist a hijacker. Oh, I am too old for the re-civ penal camps."

"Relax, Jot. No one is going to a re-civ penal camp, and nobody's ever going to know you helped me. I keep my word to the grave, and Flynn here? Well, like I said, he's planning to off himself anyway. Ain't that right, Depressus boy?"

Hoon swivels her head, dropping her jaw.

"No way. You have Depressus?"

Flynn recoils. "I was scheduled for the jump we flew through."

"Oh, wow. That really sucks. I'm so sorry."

A curious pang catches Flynn by surprise. It's strange, but in the wake of all the vivid, near-lethal stimulation he suddenly has difficulty pinpointing even a shred of his malaise. Maybe Koko was right after all. Was a cognitive shift of gusto enough to set him free? Could it be that simple? Flynn isn't sure, but still he finds himself offering a heartening, modest smile to Hoon.

"Don't be."

A heavy waft of thermal turbulence bumps the ship about, and Hoon's attention spins promptly back to her screens. Steadying their flight level, she helps Jot try to describe the insides of the hangars on The Sixty as best as they can remember. While they've never docked at hangar nine before, they are pretty sure the structures are uniform and consistent.

"Great," Koko says, slapping the top of Jot's seat. "Okay, this is what I need you guys to do."

TAKING UP POSITION

Runway nine's hangar is a hulking steel and aluminum Quonset-style vault built to accommodate three freighter-sized aircraft side by side, and the hangar doors are drawn back, leaving an opening of approximately three hundred fifty meters. Spiraled collections of gray and yellow power and fuel cables protrude from housing panels locked into micro-fusion reactors on either sides of the building, and there is enough random hardware to fully service a full house. Three triangular-shaped ladders on locking casters, assorted hover tows, and a group of corrugated cargo bins are parked at the rear of the hangar beneath a set of massive sliding wall winches. Other than that, the hangar is barren with little room to hide. Delacompte parks her terra-sled out of sight just behind the recessed hangar door on the left side of the building.

Sweeping her eyes over the space, she assesses the baking-hot structure. Above, weathered crossbeams the width of the building's curved ceiling frame off in double X-shaped steel catwalks. Delacompte considers the angles and the possibility of rappelling right on top of the craft when it eventually parks after taxi and power down, but no. The catwalks are too exposed. She could easily be spotted from the ship's cockpit as they pull in. Then Delacompte notices a rain catch bolted above the parted hangar doors. The ledge projects several meters outside into the air, curving slightly downward for tropical downpour runoff, and inside the metal creates a small ledge. The inside ledge is a sheer parallel to the ground. Basket ladders accessing the catwalks are bolted to both sides of the hangar. She might have to do some free climbing to reach the inner ledge but dropping down from there and catching Koko *in flagrante* is the call.

At the back of the hangar and scabbed and flecked with rust, a faded digitized wall display runs an arrival-time countdown. The numbers indicate she has mere minutes to get into position. Taking her pack, she sprints across the open hangar floor and then prowls up the rubberized rungs of one of the basket ladders.

Up top, the X-shaped catwalks give her a bird's-eye view of the hangar floor below, and Delacompte is struck with a passing sense of vertigo. If she slips and falls, it's easily a fatal drop. The temperature up top is roasting, and perspiration slicks Delacompte's face. Even with the solar reflectors affixed to the hangar's roof, the sun on The Sixty is brutal. Like God's own fist hammering down.

Maybe she should have waited for Koko in her quarters or perhaps the silky cool of her air-conditioned office. Koko would have eventually shown up and tried to make her play. Oh, well. Too late for showboating on familiar ground now.

Soot from blown exhaust is thick and loose on the rusty beams above Delacompte, but she manages to pull herself up and lock her arms around a padded section of pipe that tracks toward the ledge before it elbows out in opposite directions. Delacompte figures the pipe will get her close enough, so she tests it for her weight, and it seems sturdy. The padded insulation gives Delacompte a decent grip, so she loops her legs around it and inches her way along the pipe in an upside-down commando crawl.

As she nears the ledge, she lowers her legs and pumps herself in a draping, pendulum swing to clear the final distance to the ledge.

She counts to three and releases, and her feet land with a clean, loud echoing bang. But then a bolt of panic seizes her chest. Her balance wavers.

Frantically, Delacompte windmills her arms in an effort to forward the last of her momentum. It seems almost to the very last second that she has completely miscalculated her impromptu gymnastics and she'll now plummet backward to an ungracious and stupid death. However, her balance steadies and her weight shifts forward. Her hands reach out and grab hold of a coarse edge of sectioned seam in front of her eyes. Delacompte lets out a titter of relief. She wipes a hand across her face to clear some of the sweat and turns her head to look at the hangar floor.

Phew.

That was close.

Delacompte gets to work. She finds a distended rivet in front of her where she can hang her pack and slips off the nylon rucksack. She hangs the pack by a strap, unzips it, and inventories her gear. She removes a Browning 70 sub-compact and the bandolier of pulse grenades, and then assembles the close-stock Italian prototype that, on full auto, burps out an astounding one thousand pulse rounds per minute. She knows from experience that at that rate of discharge the pulse from the prototype will be a solid beam of burning blue light and will blister her skin—so she tugs on protective gloves. Delacompte gently sets the prototype down on the ledge by her feet and inspects the Browning. She adjusts the incendiary setting on the smaller weapon, releases the safety, and blasts two matching holes through the wall of the hangar in front of her.

As the molten metal drips from the two holes on either side of a perpendicular beam, Delacompte loops a holster strap over her shoulders and secures the backup Browning 70 sub-compact.

Still waiting for the metal to cool, she retrieves a climbing harness from her pack. She delicately steps into the climbing harness's loops as though trying on a twist of skimpy lingerie. The climbing harness is programmed with augmented intelligence, and its straps and fasteners adjust to her thigh and hip measurements like snakes locking off in mid-helix. After attaching an auto-feeding A.I. rappel hammer to the center hook on the harness, she threads the end of a black nylon line through the slides of the mechanism and ties off a double safety surgeon's knot on the end. The opposite end of the line she feeds through the two cooling holes she's cut into the wall, and then she ties off her base.

Delacompte carefully flakes the black line, making sure there are no kinks. Even with an A.I. rappel device, everything has to flow clean on a combat descent, and she wants a smooth slide before she brakes and opens up on Koko. It will be so perfect. Death delivered in a swoop from above.

She reaches into the pack and removes a sheathed seventeen-inch Kukri machete, which she clips to a slot on the climbing harness. Her plan, once down, is to cut the line, and if Koko is still alive, well, the machete's carbon steel edge will sing true. Sure, her marking bite will take Koko's eye and provide her with some satisfaction, but with one blow the Kukri will easily free Koko's skull from her spine. A trophy is a trophy, and taxidermy isn't a totally forgotten art.

Make a nice addition to her office.

Right over her fucking door.

Delacompte puts on the pulse grenade bandolier, tightens the straps, and crouches down to wait. The Italian prototype cradled in her arms, she evens out her breathing and orders her thoughts as she glides a single finger over and over the stock of the weapon.

As she fine-tunes her hearing to the roars of arriving and departing aircraft, one whine becomes more distinct in the surrounding airspace din. Delacompte eases up to a half-stance and presses an eye to a sliver of light escaping one of the holes where she tied off the rappelling line. Through the slivered crack she sees the septic frigate's crescent silhouette bull's-eyed in the rising sun as she grips the Italian prototype nestled in her arms.

Finally.

ON THE GROUND

As the massive rubber wheels bite the shimmering tarmac, the waste frigate's reverse thrusters roar. The ship slows to an advancing roll at two thousand-plus meters, bumbling on to its final destination like an overgrown puppy heading for a well-deserved bowl of kibble.

The shadow in front of the frigate's nose is half the length of the craft, and at four hundred fifty meters from the hangar's mouth, Koko drops from beneath and rolls quickly out of the way of the bow's secondary landing gear. A quick scramble to her feet behind the massive front wheels and Koko keeps pace behind it.

Almost two kilometers away, ensconced in the dark globe of The Sixty Islands' control tower, Flight Administrator Bardsley cranks the focus on a pair of binoculars wedged across his eyes. Even from the remote distance, Bardsley is fairly certain that the blue-haired woman who has dropped from the frigate's nose and is now running behind the landing gear has some kind of weapon in her hand.

Bardsley whispers, "A CPB discipline issue, huh? Pull my lungs out through my balloon knot? Looks like you've got a surprise on your hands, Vice President Delacompte."

A co-worker sidles up to Bardsley and peers through the tinted glass in front of them. The co-worker—stouter, slightly smaller, and balding—drinks from a plaque-stained ceramic mug of black coffee. He has a paper napkin tucked into the neck of his uniform, and the napkin is blotched orange—the result of the man's hasty breakfast of reheated pigeon wings. Bardsley can smell the curried grease and briefly considers the nauseating combination of scavenger fowl with the cheap coffee CPB provides flight control and shudders. The co-worker dabs his lips with the edge of his napkin.

"Hey, chief. There a problem out on the LZ?"

Bardsley lowers the binoculars and pauses. He then raises the binoculars to his eyes again, an amused smirk edging his lips.

"Nope," Bardsley answers. "No problem at all."

OUT FOR BLOOD

A deck of big, hairy *ifs* shuffle and reshuffle in Koko's mind as she keeps pace behind the front landing gear.

If—she were Portia Delacompte…

If—Jot and Hoon did exactly what she told them…

If—her aim is keen and her timing is perfect…

If—Flynn hadn't helped her…

If—she'd never dropped down on Delacompte's balcony back in Finland and seen her snap the neck of her own child.

If—she had just taken a big bite of the shit-pride sandwich and gone to ground.

All the ifs are too late now.

Koko slims her eyes. She takes in everything, every strategic vantage point and possibility. Even with the heat glistening off the runway and humidity pressing in, Koko feels an electric cool icing through her veins. Part trepidation, part levitation, it feels like it has always felt. Like she's floating, the rims of the world honing in with coalesced, clear-cut detail. The anticipation of combat. The steady rhythmic bump of blood thudding in her ears.

Delacompte won't wait for debark, she thinks. *No, she will come at me quick and she will come at me hard.* Someplace not entirely unexpected, but certainly from the advantage of cover.

Jot told Koko that the hangars on The Sixty are kept fairly neat. Some cargo bins. A hover lift or two. A couple of caster-based ladders with retractable boarding gantries for accessing hulls. From what Koko can discern, it looks like Jot was spot on. She counts three caster-based ladders and all three have corrugated cargo bins with bright yellow number nines painted on their foundations. Koko's eyes roll over alternate possibilities, hoping for a telltale sign, but she knows her old friend too well. Despite her new veneer of corporate proficiency, Delacompte is, at heart, a battlefield-tested warrior and way too smart to screw up that easily.

Koko can see the lower edges of the catwalks with their X-shaped, grated walkways Jot described. Could Delacompte pop her cold and distant from there like a sniper? The option is likely but, then again, if Delacompte wanted to cut Koko down from long range, she probably would have taken her shot by now.

After all, there's Delacompte's smug sense of superiority and personal satisfaction to consider. With the level of excruciating mortification the woman is no doubt suffering, Koko knows Delacompte will want Koko to see her own end coming.

Then again, I could be wrong.

Maybe she'll wait until I'm inside the hangar and then drop in hot and blasting. Hell, if roles were reversed, that's what Koko would do. Quit all this messing around and be done with the problem already.

The frigate's nose pulls closer to crossing the hangar's threshold, and the bone-shivering whine of the engines devours the air. Just over a hundred meters now. If Koko is going to roll out right or left and not be cornered beneath the ship, her time to act is closing fast. But with so much advance exposure, Koko realizes she needs to wait till the very last second. The big landing gear provides good cover, and she is reluctant to let it go.

Like the open maw of a massive oven, the giant building waits.

Above her, Jot and Hoon engage the brakes and the ship shudders and slows down. Koko raises her gun.

Now.

OH, FUCKING COME ON ALREADY

The tightened tissue of Delacompte's thighs aches. She can't huddle in this crouch much longer.

Delacompte dips the barrel of the Italian prototype and licks her lips. The sonic buzz of the engines whistles high in her ears.

Oh, fucking come on already.

Come on.

PRAYERS

"What are you mumbling?" Flynn asks.

Jot nips crabbily back at him. "I am not mumbling. I'm praying for you! I'm praying for your friend, I am praying for us all!"

"Oh."

"He does that," Hoon commiserates. Hoon increases the hydraulic pressure on the ship's brakes. "Good ol' Jot. Prays on takeoffs. Prays on landings. Prays in flight and during bad weather. Drives me bonkers."

Flynn looks out the bow window and places a hand on Jot's shoulder.

"We all might need a little prayer right now," Flynn says.

"Your blue-haired friend out there is crazy, you know," snorts Hoon.

"Just be ready when she gives the signal."

"Oh, sure," Hoon replies, rolling her eyes. "The signal. And what if she doesn't give us the signal, huh? What if she gets herself killed? What do we do then? Are you just going to shoot us too?"

Flynn flicks his eyes down at his Beretta in his right hand. Koko gave the Beretta back to him to keep Jot and Hoon in line, but the gun is useless because she removed the weapon's power chip in the off chance Flynn might have a change of heart and try to stop her or even shoot himself. The gun is now as effective as pointing a box of dried pasta at the two pilots, but Jot and Hoon are clueless.

"Like the woman said," Flynn says, "nobody needs to die here. Trust me, Koko knows what she's doing, and this should all be over in a few minutes."

But even as he assures the two pilots, Flynn's mind is taken with an awful precognitive vision. A nightmare string of scenarios, actually. What if Hoon is right? What if it all didn't go as Koko planned? What if Delacompte isn't even here? Koko might have miscalculated Delacompte's response; maybe she dispatched a whole army and they are waiting inside the building to kill them outright. What if Koko gets killed first? Flynn pictures Koko being cruelly blazed to the stubs of her boots by pulse fire and he sees himself, Jot, and Hoon being dragged off by SI security. He imagines the pilots' pleas of innocence going ignored and unanswered. With an abrupt shake of his head, Flynn snaps his concentration back in line.

On his left, Jot carries on in his soft, Hindu-laden tones.

SHOWTIME

Koko takes off from her position behind the bow wheels and charges for the right side of the hangar.

Flynn sees her clear from beneath, and he orders Jot and Hoon to swing the craft hard around and to port. The pivot is sluggish, and from the cockpit Flynn sees that Koko has successfully closed the distance. Elbow cocked and gun grip parallel to her right ear, she flattens her back flush to the hangar's outer siding and turns her head just as the heavy flow from the starboard engines pummels her chest. Then, out of the corner of his eye, Flynn sees something terrible.

A black, silver-haired spider descending from above.

Futilely Flynn cries out to warn Koko, but she has already opened up on the falling spider—her marksmanship nothing short of miraculous. Two quick rounds sever the spider's arm in a grisly pop of meat, and by some far-out marvel of physiological physics the detached arm's hand holds fast to the weapon still in its clutch. As both the arm and weapon plummet end-over-end toward the ground, the trigger trips and the gun begins to fire. Searing blue streaks slice the air—full-bore, deadly auto.

Flynn's eyes jump right as Koko dives for cover. She unloads more rapid bursts in mid-air and one of the rounds cleaves the out-of-control weapon from the severed arm before it hits the ground. On impact, the weapon clatters away, and Koko forward-rolls. When she comes up, she aims higher on the spider's line—her gun spitting rapid blue light.

Jot and Hoon duck as pulse rounds from the out-of-control weapon zoom past the cockpit windows. Jot begs Flynn to tell him this is the signal, but Flynn yells at Jot to wait. Flynn prays that Koko will be out of the way when the frigate finally labors into its final position. He can't be sure, but Flynn believes the spider has just jumped from the rope.

Jumped?

Holy sh—

The frigate completes the turn.

Damn it, Koko. Do that crazy bitch and get out of the way.

Still crammed beneath the controls, Jot bumps his head on the helm's cusp and knocks his red wool hat loose. The tight tuber of gray hair on top of his head unravels.

"Did she get her? Did she get her?"

Flynn looks at Jot incredulously and then over at Hoon.

"Get who?"

"Your girl!"

Flynn starts to answer that Koko is not his girl, but his words are eclipsed by a huge explosion.

MISSED

Even as the shattered ground lifts her off her feet and hurls her ass-over-tit backward, Koko can't help but admire Portia Delacompte's aim.

Got to hand it to the woman. A free jump from a rappelling line, one arm completely shot off, and still Delacompte manages to chuck a pulse grenade with pinpoint accuracy?

If Koko lives, she might actually applaud.

When Koko finally crunches to the ground, a whole host of skeletal bones snip clean on impact. Both her collarbones. A chipped ulna. Her right shoulder blade fissured apart in a cracked, inverted V. Bits of broken rock lash through Koko's clothes like falling daggers and she begins to skid. Her face burns, and Koko fears it may be her own cooking blood.

Her sprawl across the ground is agonizing and endless, but when she finally comes to a rest Koko quickly realizes that the pulse grenade's blast has knocked her gun free. Blindly, she slaps the ground at her sides, searching.

Given the height, Delacompte's leap from the rappelling line might have snapped one of her ankles or even knocked her out, but Koko can't see her to be certain. Even if she is hobbling and missing an arm, if Delacompte manages to roll a second pulse grenade in Koko's vicinity that will be it. Game over. Koko knows she is supposed to squeeze off a tracer round to signal Jot, Flynn, and Hoon to char-broil Delacompte with an engine hot start, but Koko figures that part of her big plan is in the shitter now.

A shout to her left.

"Koko!"

The shouting voice sounds hollow and tinny, as though it has wound its way to Koko's ears through pools of thick, ringing water. She attempts to roll her head toward the voice, but a poleaxe of unbearable pain sledgehammers her vision white. Stabbing, wracking breaths. Through the drifting smoke, Koko catches a glimpse of something. Someone running toward her.

Oh, God.

No. Not like this.

Delacompte coming to finish her off.

Eat her fucking eye.

As the figure nears, Koko finds herself questioning what she's seeing. The grayish figure, blurred against the morning sky, bends and picks up something from the ground. From the hazy outline it looks to Koko like her missing gun. The Sig 1-9Z.

Oh great, Koko thinks. *After all this, the quasi-religious, infanticidal cunt is going to execute me with my new gun? Just perfect.*

Koko closes her eyes and waits for the end.

"Koko! Talk to me! Koko! Can you hear me?"

...Flynn?

As if from a dream, the figure above her comes into focus. The beard. The sad and sleepy eyes and hangdog face. Koko blinks. It is Flynn. Flynn, staring down at her.

"Can you hear me?"

Battery-flavored slop leaks from the edges of her lips as Koko manages a spellbound smile. With a sprained arm she numbly reaches out to Flynn as he lowers his body to her side. She struggles to hear her own scream.

"*Delacompte!*"

Flynn's head jerks up in the direction of the fallen spider. Across the radiating tarmac, the broken doll of Portia Delacompte wrestles with a shoulder holster still strapped to the good side of her body. Delacompte has managed to get herself into a sitting position, and the ugly stump of her left arm pokes out at a bizarre, snapped-branch angle and pumps a ridiculous arc of blood.

Flynn sweeps Koko's gun across Koko's field of vision as his other hand rises up to cup the butt in a two-handed grip. Flynn aims, squeezing the trigger just as Delacompte clears her backup Browning 70 sub-compact from the shoulder holster.

All those years of law enforcement, never once discharging his weapon in a tactical situation… Flynn, to his astonishment, doesn't hesitate. The weapon whelps blue once—then twice. Flynn, the poor, depressed doofus, misses completely.

Flynn's third shot tags Delacompte on the edge of her squashed pelvis, spinning her backward. It's like crimson and pink streamers twirling on a maypole, a long section of guts following her around and around until she stops. Delacompte screams, drops her gun, and braces her remaining arm against her stomach.

Flynn looks behind him and up at the cockpit windows just as Hoon and Jot raise their heads. He drags a hand across his throat and shouts at them to shut down the engines, and a moment later the frigate's engines start to slow and grow quiet.

Flynn rises to his feet. As he plods forward, Delacompte's face becomes a study of chalky, gore-splattered rage. A widening puddle of blood spreads out around her, and a glistening bulb of intestinal tract gleams in her fingers. Flynn doesn't relax his aim.

"It's over, Delacompte," he says.

A range of confused looks hiccup through Delacompte's fury.

Moaning, she struggles to turn around on her ravaged axis, looking for her dropped weapon.

"This isn't your fight!" she screams. "This is… this is a CPB security matter. That woman is… she's… wanted for… f-f-failure— *Fuck! This hurts!*"

Flynn moves closer. "You're bleeding out."

Delacompte almost laughs and spits up an alarming wash of blood. "Bleeding out?" she says slushily. "I am not." She glances down at the open ruins of her stomach and briefly over at her missing limb lying on the ground like a discarded drumstick. "This is nothing," she says dismissively. "But you. You're interfering with official CPB directives—I'll have you executed, I'll have you sent to a re-civ penal camp, you-you'll—" Delacompte stops and screams at Flynn with all her might.

It takes a dozen seconds for Delacompte's tantrum to subside. Flynn hears the distant, approaching sirens of the SI emergency vehicles streaming their way across the landing fields as he inches closer.

"It's over, Delacompte. I know everything. What you've done to Koko. To those poor people up on *Alaungpaya* with your hired thugs, to your own flesh and blood back in Finland."

Delacompte's face skews. "My own flesh and *what*?" A large bubble of pink-tinged saliva pops messily on her lips. "I've no idea what you're talking about."

"Of course you don't," Flynn says. "Your selective memory treatments took care of that."

Delacompte's eyes flutter. "My what? My selective memory treatments? How do you know about my—"

Then it's as though a great light crashes through Delacompte's eyes. She shivers with a rattled breath, and her face slackens. Flynn wonders if at last the unbearable demons of her own repressed memories have savaged their way to the surface of her mind. Delacompte teeters woozily for a moment before she flops back. As she rolls her head from side to side in her own blood, an anguished wail unwinds from her throat and slowly becomes a tormented howl. Her remaining hand leaves her stomach and she frantically pats her chest.

Flynn finally sees the pulse grenades on Delacompte's bandolier. *Oh, shit.*

"Don't—" Flynn says.

Finding the outline of a grenade, Delacompte flicks the device's armament button. With her last ounce of strength, she lifts her head and bares her teeth.

Flynn squeezes the trigger. The suppressed blast from Koko's gun vaporizes Delacompte's skull in a thick red spew and throws her backward, but he's too late. The armed grenade spools out onto the ground like a top.

Flynn turns and bolts toward Koko. It feels as though he has an eternity stretched out before him, and somehow he believes he can actually beat the grenade's countdown. But, of course, he's wrong. The protracted moment peels away in an ineffable wallop of noise and heat. Flynn is raised up—up and up and up. To his continued amazement, Flynn's legs keep pumping through the air. He feels light as a feather, finally an angel in a world all afire.

Flynn wonders if he'll ever come down and imagines he's already dead. But reality comes with a terrible jolt when his feet brutally strike the ground.

His legs buckle beneath him. His ensuing tumble and spill scrapes skin from his body as he draws his hands over his head. *Oh, God... are my arms still attached?* Hair. Flynn thinks he feels hair. That's good, that means he's still—oh shit, *I'm still alive?* Broken ground strafes all around him. He can't breathe.

When the worst passes, grayish dots cloud Flynn's vision and it takes all his effort to inhale. Smoky air and a cough. No sound now except for the swooning tolls between his ears, an ache worse than any migraine he's ever experienced. Flynn's gut goes cold as images beat through his vision.

Smoke. Blackness.

Humid morning sky. The swirling red and electric blue lights from emergency craft pulling close.

More blackness.

The open hangar. Jot's and Hoon's septic ship.

Black, black, black.

Then the sour whiff of roasted human flesh, and Flynn snaps to consciousness. Strange hands fall on his chest, his shoulders. Groping.

Flynn pushes the hands away and rolls to his side. Using his elbows to fulcrum his legs, he drags his body forward. It turns out Koko is much closer than he thought. A mere meter and a half later, Flynn collapses by her side.

The strange, groping hands continue in their attempts to draw him away, but Flynn fights them. He leans his body over Koko and warm droplets roll off his face and plink on her battered, upturned cheeks. Is it his own blood? His tears? Flynn can't tell, and he doesn't care anymore because Koko is smiling up at him.

He leans in close.

Flynn kisses Koko's bloody mouth.

GIMME, GIMME... MORE AND MORE

THE SIXTY ISLANDS PROMO "HOT STUFF/PF SPOT"—0:30

CLIENT: Custom Pleasure Bureau—The Sixty Islands

PRODUCTION ENGAGEMENT: 2516 All Seasonal Hemispheric Cycles

AUDIO: GURGLING OCEANIC SOUNDS, SHIFTING SAND

[FADE IN] VISUAL FEED 1: UNDERWATER, THE ROLLING BACK OF A BREAKING REEF WAVE. AS THE WAVE TUBES, A NUDE SURFER IS SILHOUETTED IN THE WAVE'S MOVING SURFACE. THE NUDE SURFER DRAGS HER/HIS HAND ACROSS THE WAVE FACE AS A CYBERNETIC TIGER SHARK CRUISES BEHIND IN PURSUIT. CAMERA TRACKS UP, BREACHES THE WATER'S SURFACE, AND MOVES FORWARD ACROSS THE BREAKWATER TOWARD LAND. ON THE BEACH AHEAD, A SIMULATED EXECUTION IS IN PROGRESS ON THE SIXTY ISLANDS. A GUILLOTINE PLATFORM TOWERS ABOVE A THRASHING, HALF-NAKED CROWD OF SUNTANNED SPECTATORS.

AUDIO 2: AGGRESSIVE, LOUD MUSIC. DRUMS.

[CUT TO CLOSE-UP] VISUAL FEED 2: GUILLOTINE BLADE AS A HOLDING PIN IS JERKED FREE. THE BLADE FALLS.

[CUT TO CROWD SHOT] VISUAL FEED 3: CHEERING EXECUTION SPECTATORS FROM BEHIND THE SHOULDERS OF A BLACK-HOODED EXECUTIONER HOLDING UP A BEHEADED SKULL BY THE SCALP. CAMERA PANS OVER THE CROWD AS THEY HOIST SPEARS AND ROAR.

[FADE IN] VISUAL FEED 4: GORGEOUS, MONTAGED IMAGERY OF EXECUTION SPECTATORS* DANCING. THE DANCE MOVES OF THE SPECTATORS SOON MORPH INTO SOME OF THE MOST DEPRAVED, INGENIOUS SEX ACTS IMAGINABLE. QUICK-CUT MONTAGE BUILDS AND VISUALS ARE INTERSPERSED WITH RANDOM SIXTY ISLANDS DEBAUCHERY AND VIOLENCE. FACES BEYOND THE CREST OF DESIRE. EXPLOSIONS—EVERYTHING MOVING FASTER AND FASTER TO A FRENZIED, ANIMALISTIC CLIMAX. [*NOTE: Not actual SI patrons, models preferred for montage.]

[CUT TO] VISUAL FEED 5: BLACK

AUDIO 3: WHIMSICAL MUSIC—STEEL DRUMS, SLACK KEY GUITAR, ETC.

[FADE IN] VISUAL FEED 6: THE SIXTY ISLANDS logo.

VOICEOVER: What are you waiting for?

(BEAT)

VOICEOVER (CONT.) The Sixty Islands—paradise found.

LET'S HEAR IT FROM THE NEW BOYWHORE

Oh my, our Koko-sama be flying truer than true now. Yes-yes. Jump-up proper, she be on all freaky and high-happy these days. And we be new-fresh recruits for her, and all of us, we got lotsa, lotsa work to do.

Hey, big re-opening coming up a week out no less. Oh, we creamy with excitement, but we sweat plenty to get ready.

Me love my new boss, Koko-sama. Some of the other boys and girls and tranny *rae-raes* not so much. Koko-sama be big sugarhoney and take care of us all on the kind, right-right? Not that we ungrateful tummyachers 'cause we on The Sixty, man! Drong! The Sixty! Big dream come true even if we all be whoring for the credit ching-a-ching-a-ling.

Koko-sama still be limping with the great white cane like when she done come down to Melbourne to recruit me and me mates. Koko-sama say her stumpy walk and stick soon be gone with all the physical pump and jump we all do. Koko-sama, she be big bad on keeping us all fit, you bet. Customers like the lovey talent prime, she say, so all of us, we get up at first light and run forever in the beautiful island jungles. We lift fallen trees and heavy stones and even chase them syntho-piggies for bacon and barbecue. Like the last of the old fish in the big salty, we even swim every day a bunch too. Beats mining rock and dodging hook and claw back in Oz, but The Sixty chiefs also want us all healthy-planned whores now.

Master Flynn be waiting on two more shipments of good liquor before he say we got us a full bar. Me, I like Master Flynn. Good boss. He go on proper like how customers on SI need tasty options, so a full working bar is a must-y. Got us a purification still for refining cheap liquor for big parties too. Handy thing, that. Keep all the bad liquor on the yum-yum.

Master Flynn, he a funny one. Don't mess with any of Koko-sama's whores 'cause he and Koko-sama be special lovers like. Hear he used to go big boo-hoo up top, and me done seen them bodies fall from the clouds on the feeds a few times. Sad stuff, but Master Flynn, he be much high-happy now too.

Yeah-yeah. We all got lots and lots of work to do.

INTO THE GREAT, NEAR FUTURE

Koko lifts a hammer from a nylon tool belt secured around her hips. Her pink T-shirt is saturated dark with perspiration, and the muscles beneath her camouflaged shorts shine brown.

She steadies a four-inch carpenter's nail against a large, carved wooden sign on the siding above the tin porch roof and readies herself to drive the nail home. Her mirrored goggles flash with the sun as she twists her head back.

"You're sure it's even?"

In rolled khaki cargo pants and an unbuttoned white linen shirt, Flynn squints up to check the sign's alignment. Even with Flynn's own pair of sun goggles the potent light on The Sixty is so fierce it makes him feel like he's getting punched in the face over and over. Hell, the sign looks even enough, Flynn supposes. Why Koko can't wait until the much cooler dark to hang the final touch on the new building is beyond him. It's a modest, purlin structure. Eleven rooms with a bar and café area and a small winged alcove arranged with tables of chance. It looks just like one of those airy tropical places Flynn remembers seeing on the history feeds. Tall open windows with slatted hurricane shutters and lazy ceiling fans fashioned to resemble round palm fronds. The rear of the building opens up onto a large grass-plotted patio sliced down the middle by a stone-lined lap pool with a regenerative spa on the far end in the shape of a heart. Heavily scented citrus trees surround the patio area, and just beyond the area an electrified wire fence corners off the property—a measure to keep the islands' half-and-half synthetics from disturbing the guests.

"Bang away," Flynn says with a magnanimous wave.

Koko turns back and pounds the nail between her fingers. Limping sideways, she pounds a few more nails in place. Sweat flies from her skin as she swings, and she doesn't miss her mark, not once.

Koko's hair is now back to its original deep black shade and has grown out some, feral and unkempt. When she's finished, she drags her sun goggles down from her eyes and hangs them loose around her neck. After loping across the roof, she straddles her boots on either side of an aluminum ladder and drops down to join Flynn. Together they admire her handiwork as he hands Koko her white walking cane. Soon the sign's solar-powered lettering begins to flicker, and one word glows in a radiant, cobalt blue.

SALOON

"What do you think?"

Flynn slides his sun goggles up to the crown of his head.

"Simple and direct," he says. "I think it looks pretty sweet."

Koko grins. "Yeah, I think so too."

Flynn shuffles his bare feet in the sand. "I still can't believe we're doing this, though."

Koko angles back slightly and playfully slaps his arm. "Oh, don't be such a spoilsport."

"Yeah, you say that, but I don't know. I still don't trust those CPB bastards, despite their assurances…"

Koko huffs. "Oh, will you stop it? The CPB board know I'm more valuable to them alive than dead. Even with my being Delacompte's quasi-accomplice way back in Helsinki, they realize it was all her madness in the end. You were right, Flynn. I'm irrelevant. After all that went down, CPB needs a good spin on the narrative."

"Still—"

"Still what? Honestly, Flynn, I know you have a real hard time seeing the good in things, but everything is back to where it should be. Both of us have been cleared of any charges, and I got my life back. Hell, we both got our lives back. And you? C'mon, man, just look at you."

"What about me?"

"Do you need me to spell it out? Off those stupid meds, looking all tan and buff. Your so-called Depressus symptoms are all but gone. You're a whole new person. You've a brand-new life ahead of you. A life of noble purpose."

"Pimping whores and slinging booze? Hardly noble purposes."

"There are worse things."

They stand and regard the sign some more.

"Besides," Koko says, "you really make me tingle."

Flynn arches an eyebrow and laughs. He lunges lustfully for Koko's waist, and she spins into his arms.

"Really, I make you tingle? Is that what you call it? Woman, I'll have you know you have me walking cross-eyed and sore-cocked. I'm surprised I can still get out of bed in the morning and walk a straight line."

Koko giggles. "Aww… it's all part of your therapy, lawman. All part of your therapy. You're finally coming around to what living is really all about."

She pinches his cheek and hobbles off. As Flynn watches her go, he once again finds his feelings all a-twirl for Koko. Is he in love with her? Maybe. Such loopy sentiments and affections have always seemed impossible and unreachable for Flynn. All he knows now is he doesn't really care if he is or isn't in love. The woman is nothing short of amazing.

With the shamble in her caned gait, Koko pops her way up the building's short steps, crosses the broad porch, and slams the batwing doors inward. Immediately she starts giving orders to all the whores assigned to last-minute preparations inside.

Flynn looks up and reads the sign on the building once more. Shielding his eyes, Flynn gazes beyond the building and past the tree line. Thick slates of weather are brewing in the sky, and it appears an afternoon thunderstorm is on the way. A web of cloud-to-cloud lightning crackles on the horizon as miles higher and further in the distance a lone Second Free Zone barge creeps through a rising orbit. Even at that range, Flynn can see the navigational beacons on the barge's hull strobe, twinkling on and off like dying stars.

Indeed, he thinks, *there are worse things.*

Meanwhile, a mere three hundred meters south of the new building, a clump of glossy leafy vegetation rustles and parts and a small orange lizard switches out into the open road. Another one of the resort's countless synthetics, the lizard stops and raises its shiny diamond-shaped head before it darts off into the dark brush on the road's opposite side. A moment later, a second creature emerges from the parted vegetation. Standing and stretching from a long bush squat, the second creature adjusts a pair of sunglasses over her ocular imbed, draws a HK U-50 from a leg holster, and patiently waits for the bearded man to head inside.

Ultimate Sanction.

The bounty agent known as Wire walks slowly toward the bar.

ACKNOWLEDGMENTS

Foremost, the most heartfelt appreciation has to go out to Stacia J.N. Decker at the Donald Maass Literary Agency for believing Koko had the onions to go the distance. In that vein, I also wish to express my gratitude to Cath Trechman and everybody at Titan Books for their tireless dedication and can-do professionalism with this book.

No one gets a book published alone, so big, pumping thank-you handshakes with extra hand sanitizer to my ever-widening hoop of writing comrades, ass-kickers, and first readers, including Greg Bardsley, Stephen Blackmoore, David Cranmer, Steve Weddle, Chris F. Holm, Benoît Lelièvre, Cameron Ashley, Dan O'Shea, Chris Rhatigan, Jimmy Callaway, John Hornor Jacobs, Keith Rawson, Ruth and Jon Jordan, Karen E. Olson, Patti Abbott, Frank Bill, Bob Randisi, Sophie Littlefield and (of course) the big, crinkly dog—Ed McCarthy. A special tip of the hat goes out to Anthony Neil Smith for pushing back on some of my early forays into speculative fiction, and Jed Ayres deserves at least a six-pack of beer because he saw Koko's potential way back at NoirCon 2010.

Naturally, I also wish to thank my wife and family for always being there for me. To say you mean the world to me falls short.

Peace.